DARK PRINCE'S CAPTIVE

A REALM OF DRAGONS & SCROLLS 1

ANNA ZAIRES

CHARMAINE PAULS

GREY EAGLE
PUBLICATIONS

Published by Grey Eagle Publications
www.greyeaglepublications.com

Cover by Alex McLaughlin

ISBN: 978-1-64366-921-2
Print ISBN: 978-1-64366-942-7

CHAPTER 1

ELSIE

"Ms. Barnikoff... I'm terribly sorry to tell you this, but your heart is failing."

"Uh-huh." I return my attention to my laptop, on which my Greek Lit paper is taunting me with its awkwardly worded third sentence. "Go on."

Dr. Moore clears his throat. "Ms. Barnikoff—Elisa —I'm not sure if you heard me—"

"Call me Elsie, please."

I correct the sentence and look up in time to see the doctor throw a confused glance at my mom, who's quietly wiping away tears in the corner. My dad, standing next to her, is stoic as always, but even he looks paler and stiffer than usual, which is already pretty pale and stiff.

I sigh and close my laptop, giving my full attention to the doctor—a slim, youngish man who looks like he's desperately wishing he were anywhere but in this hospital room in Cleveland, delivering this news to us.

I feel bad for him. Almost as bad as I feel for my parents. Which is why I paste a smile on my face and say, "It's okay. Just give it to me straight. Am I dying?"

He nods grimly. "Unfortunately, due to your medical history, you're not a candidate for a transplant."

That's nothing I didn't already know. "How long do I have?"

He winces. "Weeks. Possibly days."

Mom lets out a sniffle, and Dad wraps an arm around her, pulling her closer.

"Gotcha," I say and open my laptop. "I'd better hurry and get this paper done then. It's due in two weeks."

Dr. Moore looks like a guppy as he opens his mouth and closes it several times. "Ms. Barnikoff—Elsie—I'm not sure if you—"

"Oh, no, I get it, really. I just have work to do, that's all." I turn my attention to the screen in front of me, ignoring the erratic rhythm of the dying organ in my chest and the fatigue threatening to fog up my brain.

There's a long minute of silence, during which I correct another sentence in my paper while Mom sniffles some more. Finally, Dr. Moore says in a strained voice, "If you don't have any questions, I'll leave you three to talk it over."

"Thank you! You were very helpful," I call after him as he exits the room, closing the door behind him.

It's important to be gentle with doctors. They suffer greatly when delivering bad news.

Mom's sniffles grow louder as she approaches my

hospital bed. She perches on the edge and reaches for my computer. "Elsie..." Her blue eyes are red-rimmed and swollen. "Darling, why don't you let me take that and—"

"No." I snap the computer closed again and stuff it under my blanket. The slender laptop weighs a pound and a half at most, yet moving it tires me out—yet another sign that Dr. Moore isn't lying. Not that I have any reason to think he is.

Between the never-ending cough, the dizziness, the nausea, the heart palpitations, and the swollen legs, I have all the symptoms of heart failure, and I've known it for a while, which is why I resisted coming to the hospital for so long.

"Darling, please..." Mom lays her hand over the blanket covering my laptop. "I know how dedicated you are to your studies, but that's not what's important right now. You should—"

"What, travel? See the world? Eat all the food that makes me vomit?" My tone is sharper than I intend, but I can't help it.

My parents have been on a mission to make me "live" ever since this all started, a.k.a. since I was in diapers. If they'd had their way, I wouldn't have attended school or done anything other than frantically grasp at experiences that are, at best, uncomfortable and, at worst, fucking agonizing for someone with my physical limitations. They can't seem to comprehend the fact that my body does not want me to have fun or enjoy life in any way, shape, or form. My best bet at a semblance of happiness is escaping into my mind, which is exactly what I do when I focus on my studies.

I may only have a few days left on this earth, but I'll be damned if I spend them moping about my fate and gazing at the sunset or whatever. I have a fucking paper to finish.

Mom must realize she's not going to win this fight, so she sniffles a bit more, kisses my forehead, and stands up. "Okay, darling, whatever you want."

"You are the strongest girl we know," Dad says gruffly, coming to stand next to Mom. "If there's anything you need—"

"I'll be fine tonight." I cough and pull out my laptop from under the blanket, doing my best not to show how much effort the movement entails. "Thank you, guys. I love you."

"We love you too," Mom says, wiping at her wet face. "So, so much. We'll see you in the morning, okay?"

"Okay," I say and blow them an air kiss. "Bye."

It's not until the door closes behind them that I drop my face into my hands and start to cry.

I cry for about an hour before I pull myself together. So what if I'm dying? Aren't we all, in a way? Granted, most of us get seventy, eighty, maybe even a hundred years on this planet, while I've just barely made it to twenty-two, but that's twenty years more than I might've had if things had gone differently, so it's really a win.

I've had a lot of practice dying. Well, almost dying.

My first bout with childhood leukemia happened when I was just thirteen months. I don't remember any of it, so that ordeal was definitely rougher on my parents than it was on me. I beat it, obviously. Then the leukemia returned when I was three. I do remember that time. Lots of needles and hospital visits and parents crying. Not fun for a child. Zero out of ten, would not recommend. But I beat it again. Yay, go me.

My third and final round with leukemia took place when I was seven. The doctors were convinced that this was it. None of the chemo drugs were helping, so I was advised to say my goodbyes. My parents withdrew me from school and signed me up for one of those Make-A-Wish things, where I got to meet a singer that I once told them I liked. In person, she was much less impressive and way too awkward about the fact that I was a little bald kid who was dying. Then my parents took me to Disney World, which I absolutely hated as I felt deathly ill the whole time. And that was supposed to be the end of me, except the day before I was due to enter hospice, I got enrolled in an immunotherapy trial and my stubborn cancer actually responded to it. Elsie —three, cancer—zero!

Of course, with my luck, the cancer wasn't the only thing that responded to the immunotherapy. My immune system did too. It decided to go into overdrive and attack whatever it could get its grubby killer cells on. My pancreas was the first to go—hello, type 1 diabetes. Then my stomach kept acting like I was still on chemo, so they discovered I also had Crohn's. Then lupus. Then rheumatoid arthritis. To control all that, they prescribed me a witch's brew of immunosuppressive drugs, and then I got diagnosed with melanoma when I was fourteen—despite the fact that I was hardly ever out in sunlight. Thanks to my practically living in hospitals, the melanoma was caught early, so I just have a nasty scar on my leg as a reminder of that fun little battle.

So yeah, when my kidneys failed shortly after my seventeenth birthday, I took it pretty much in stride. Dialysis three times a week is nothing compared to the fun that is chemo. With all my autoimmune issues, I knew I wasn't a candidate for a transplant, and I was fine with it. Then my body started to attack my heart.

More drugs, more trials, yadda, yadda, yadda, and here we are.

I'm officially dying. Again.

This time is probably for real, though. My parents have reached out to just about every medical establishment on the planet, and nobody is pulling a miracle out of a hat for me. Once the defective ticker inside me goes, that'll be it.

In the meantime, there's my Greek Lit paper to write. And Physics final to study for. The latter is in three weeks, so I might not make it, but on the off chance I do, I want to be prepared. It's bad enough I'm a college freshman at the age of twenty-two thanks to my parents pulling me out of school each time I had a health scare. If my body holds up, I *will* finish this semester. And I will do it with straight fucking As.

My vision, which is not all that great to begin with, is blurring by the time I finish editing the paper. It's come out pretty well, if I say so myself. Writing is not my forte—I'm more into math and science and all things logical—so I have to put a lot of effort into the humanities side of the core curriculum. I do enjoy the challenge, though.

It keeps my brain from ruminating on things it shouldn't.

With my last remaining strength, I save the paper and email it to my professor. That way, if I croak tomorrow, he'll have it. I doubt my parents will bother sending in my assignments while dealing with funeral arrangements. I told them I want to be cremated and have my ashes used as fertilizer on our lawn, but I'm pretty sure they're going to do the whole coffin and fancy burial bit.

I love them dearly, but they never listen to me when it matters.

Yawning, I close my laptop and rub my burning eyes.

Then I rub them again because what the fuck?

There are lights flashing.

In a circle.

In the air in front of me.

I blink. And blink again.

Still there. And getting brighter.

Blue, purple, and pink lights, all swirling together into something utterly surreal.

Shit. Did I die without realizing it? Is this the portal to the afterlife? Am I about to see my body from above, meet the angels, and all that stuff I don't believe in?

But no. I'm still in my body. Still feeling shitty to the max. Yet the lights are right there in front of me, the circle gradually widening and drawing nearer until it's... oh, fuck!

I scream as it sucks me in, and everything inside me breaks apart.

CHAPTER 2

ELSIE

The mouthwatering aroma of barbecue hits my nostrils, waking me from a bizarre dream.

Wait, why is there barbecue in the hospital? And why does the fried meat smell so appetizing when I haven't been able to smell anything edible without wanting to barf for months?

I sniff again, not yet daring to open my eyes in case the visual stimulation brings back the nausea.

Still smells like barbecue. Still smells good.

And there's something else. An earthy, loamy scent that makes me think of Costa Rica. My parents took me on a rainforest vacation there after my third and final bout with leukemia, and it was one of the few trips I didn't hate because I was feeling good for once. We saw howler monkeys, and I tasted a bunch of tropical fruits.

It's a good memory, so the wet jungle smell isn't unpleasant, but it definitely doesn't belong in my sterile hospital room. Nor do the male voices speaking in some guttural foreign language nearby. Also, I'm wet and cold, especially where my back and my bare feet touch the damp ground.

Seriously, what the fuck is going on?

I open my lids a tiny crack.

It's dark. Like pitch-black kind of dark.

The kind of dark that's all but impossible to achieve in our age of modern electronics.

The kind of dark you *never* see in a hospital.

My heart begins to hammer. Hard. Much harder than should be possible, given that said heart is on the verge of failure.

Is this it? Am I dead?

Is this what there is after death—darkness, wet earth, and barbecue?

Wait a minute...

I cautiously turn my head, sensing something in my peripheral vision.

Yep, there's a red glow from a fire to my right. And dark figures silhouetted against the flames, sitting with their huge backs toward me.

No. No fucking way.

Even if hell were real—and the future scientist in me is still convinced it's not—I haven't done anything to merit that kind of punishment in the afterlife. Wait, what am I saying? I don't believe in the afterlife. That's just a comforting myth people made up to try to come to terms with the fact that eventually, they simply cease to exist.

So… if this isn't hell, where am I? And who are the figures around the fire?

Shit. Did I get kidnapped?

No, that's ridiculous. Who would want to kidnap a dying girl?

Unless… oh, fuck. Of course.

I sit up, outraged. "Hey, you! Tell my parents to get me back home, pronto. I don't have time for this farewell nature immersion or whatever. I have fucking exams to study for!"

The figures around the fire—all five of them—stiffen, then rise to their feet and turn to face me. The firelight illuminates their faces, and I swallow as my outrage evaporates, replaced by a cold wave of fear.

I don't think my parents hired these men to take me from the hospital and show me the good life before I kick the bucket.

I'm actually not sure they're men at all.

Even if I were to ignore their linebacker builds and the skintight snakeskin clothes they're wearing, their features are unlike anything I've ever seen, in real life or on television. Their eye sockets are comically big, and their glittering, red-hued eyes sit deep within them, with no hint of eyebrows on the narrow, sloping foreheads above. Their noses are just two nostrils in the middle of their faces, and their chins recede into their necks, while their disproportionally wide cheekbones jut out sideways. And their mouths are—wait, do they have mouths?

One of them opens the horizontal slit below his

nostrils, and upon hearing the guttural speech that emerges, I realize that they *do* have mouths. Flat, lipless mouths filled with shark-like teeth.

Now I'm sweating. It's a cold, clammy sweat that gathers under my armpits and trickles down my back. Have I been wrong all my life? Is there, in fact, an afterlife, including heaven and hell? And have I somehow ended up in the latter... maybe because I didn't believe in it?

I run my tongue over my dry lips and try to think rationally.

Unlike the demonic figures before me, I do have lips, and they get dry. That's good. And my armpits sweat. That's even better. Would there even be such a thing as sweat in the afterlife? Wouldn't it all be metaphysical? Then again, how do you burn in hell if you can't experience physical sensations? You have to have nerve endings to feel the fire scorching you, right? So why not sweat glands as well?

The man—demon?—who spoke before says something again. His tone is sharper, angrier. A command. It's not directed at me, though, because one of the other demons responds to it by heading toward me.

My heart rate spikes, and adrenaline floods my body.

Maybe this isn't hell. Maybe these creatures aren't demons but football players in strange masks. Or maybe I've fallen asleep over my laptop, and this is a really vivid nightmare.

Whatever it is, I don't wait to find out.

I turn, and I run.

Or at least I try to run.

I make it exactly two steps before my bare toes catch on some root and I faceplant onto the wet ground.

A ground that hisses and bucks underneath me as stinging needles bite into every inch of my exposed skin.

"Ahhh!" I leap to my feet and back away, frantically slapping at my burning arms, face, and legs as the "ground" rears up in front of me and opens its horrific vertical maw, the dripping sideways fangs inside glinting in the distant firelight.

Oh god, oh god, oh god.

I *am* in fucking hell.

The hairy, tube-like creature—which I'd call a caterpillar if it weren't my fucking size—hisses again and lunges at me, maw open as if to swallow me whole.

I let out another scream and turn to run again, only to hit a steel wall.

Or, as I realize with the small portion of my brain that still retains some functionality, the chest of the demon coming after me. He must be wearing a metal plate underneath his snakeskin attire because I bounce off his chest, hard, and fall backward on my ass.

Right next to the giant caterpillar thing and its stinging hairs.

I scream and cover my face as it drops down onto its dozen legs and lunges at me.

Instead of its fangs biting into me, there's a whooshing sound, followed by a cold, slimy spray across my arms and face. I gag and cough-spit as the taste, bitter and acidic, seeps into my mouth.

I'm still coughing and spitting as a huge, clawed hand yanks me to my feet and a rough palm sweeps painfully across my face, wiping away most of the slime... which I'm now realizing is the caterpillar's guts or blood or whatever it had inside.

To say that I'm grossed out to the point of puking would be a major understatement.

I dry-heave as my demonic savior drags me toward the fire, where the other figures are still hanging out. As we approach, they growl something in their foreign tongue, and he replies, not looking at me. Which is good because I'm still trying to process the fact that I was just attacked by a creature straight out of an entomophobe's nightmare.

Seriously, am I in hell? Is that what the weird circle of lights was about—a portal to the underworld?

The demon dragging me shoves me in front of him, making me stumble and nearly fall into the flames.

"Excuse you," I snap and twist my arm against his grip. He must not have been expecting any resistance because I actually break out of his hold.

For a moment, that is. In the next instant, he grabs my wrist, growls, and twists my arm behind my back with such force that I scream and fall to my knees.

The fucker laughs—full-on cackles, like a movie villain—and his buddies join in.

Then he releases my wrist and backhands me.

He probably uses only a fraction of his enormous strength, but my ears ring and I taste copper in my mouth.

I've never, ever been hit, and I can't say I'm a fan.

I do, however, have a high tolerance for pain—and apparently zero common sense. Operating purely on instinct, I scoop up a handful of dirt and embers and fling the mixture at his face.

He roars in shock, and this time, the retaliatory blow across my face is less restrained. I can practically feel my brain rattle inside my skull, and my vision darkens as sounds fade in and out.

When my vision clears and the worst of the ringing in my ears stops, I spit out blood, along with something small and hard. I run my tongue over my upper and lower teeth until I find the tender, gaping socket where one of my lower canines should be.

One of the other demons barks out an order, and my assailant releases me.

I fall onto all fours, too dazed to do anything but pant weakly. If I were still in the hospital, I'm pretty sure I'd be diagnosed with a concussion. No, scratch that. If I were still in the hospital, none of this would be happening.

Why am I not still in the hospital? What the fuck is going on? Nightmares aren't supposed to be this detailed or prolonged, and despite all the weirdness surrounding me, I can't bring myself to believe that I'm in literal hell. Or that I'm dead. I smell, feel, and taste things far too acutely for some metaphysical realm. Not to mention, the empty tooth socket in my mouth and my split lip are throbbing like I'm very much alive.

Something else is going on, but I'm nowhere near figuring out what. Until I do, I should probably operate on the assumption that I *am* alive and avoid getting myself killed. So, as the demons launch into what appears to be an argument, I stay meekly on all fours and do my best not to draw any more attention to myself. Silently, I study them, taking note of the reddish-orange hue and leathery texture of their faces and the way their snakeskin outfits cover them from the neck down, fitting them like second skin. Unless... that is their skin.

I peer closer.

Yep, it's attached to them, their leathery but smooth facial skin transitioning at the neck into the snake-like scales covering the rest of their bodies.

Driven by a prurient curiosity, I sneak a peek below their waists.

Huh. I don't see any manly equipment whatsoever, though each demon does have a bulge in the groin area that suggests *something* is there. That's what made me think they were wearing skintight snakeskin pants. Their lower bodies look like those of male ballet dancers in tights, only way bulkier and more lizard-like.

Wait a sec...

Are these actual *lizard people*? The ones the

conspiracy theorists would have you believe are secretly ruling Earth?

My mind makes another, more logical leap.

Have I been kidnapped by *aliens*?

Holy shit. I can't believe I didn't think of it earlier. Aliens are at least theoretically possible. Humanoid aliens are highly, highly improbable, even lizard-like humanoid aliens, but they're more likely to exist than demons.

So… have I been abducted by aliens? Like for experiments and stuff?

Argument against: I'm not on a ship—at least I don't think I am—and these lizard dudes huddling around the fire like cavemen don't look like anyone's idea of alien scientists.

Argument for: My throbbing face and burning skin aside, I feel… fine. I ran and fought, got hit by a linebacker-sized demon and stung by a giant caterpillar, yet my heart isn't giving out. It's pumping in a strong and steady—albeit very alarmed—rhythm, and I don't feel any dizziness, weakness, nausea, muscle spasms, or any other fun sensations that come along with having various organs failing. It's as if I've been healed… or given a new body.

Fuck. Could it be?

I quickly scan myself. There's no mirror, so I can't see my face, but my hands—small and skinny—look the same to me, and what I can see of my knobby knees is familiar as well. Oh, and I'm still in the pajama shorts and T-shirt I insist on wearing in hospitals in lieu of a typical hospital gown. They wouldn't bother changing my body and then putting the same clothes on it, would they? I wish I could see my hair to check if it's still the same shade of strawberry blond, but it's not long enough.

Ever since all the chemo, I've kept it in a pixie cut, just in case.

A familiar clawed hand grips my upper arm, once again rudely cutting into my thoughts. I fight the urge to struggle as the lizard dude who hit me drags me up to my feet. This is not a battle I can win. The top of my head barely clears the middle of his chest, and he has the bulk to go with that height.

At least I'm assuming it's a "he." Could just as easily be a "she," given the lack of obvious male equipment. I'm going with "he," though, if only because of the mile-wide shoulders and the a-hole behavior. He drags me closer to the fire and forces me down into a sitting position before shoving a piece of charred meat into my hand.

"Bvcherru," he barks, staring down at me.

Huh. Does he want me to eat the meat?

He brings his hand to his face and opens his shark-like mouth to bite at the air above his empty palm.

Yeah, okay. That's definitely a command to eat.

I debate not obeying—who the hell knows what this meat is?—but I *am* hungry, weirdly enough, and presumably, humanoid aliens who kidnap earthlings should know what to feed us. There's no point in bringing someone through a swirling-lights portal if you're just going to poison them, right?

Fuck it. I'm supposed to die in a few days anyway. Or was supposed to. Whatever. I bite into the charred meat in my hand.

Holy guacamole. It's like the juiciest, most tender chicken ever. There's no salt or spices on it, but it's still freaking good—and I don't even normally like chicken.

"Can I have more?" I ask, looking up at the lizard dude and mimicking an eating motion.

He shoves another piece of maybe-chicken into my hand.

Okay, I'm starting to change my mind about his a-holeness. That is, until my tongue lands on my empty tooth socket, and my bruised jaw begins to throb harder as I chew. Yeah, no. A-hole all the way.

I eat until I'm full, and then I notice the sky—at least I presume it's the sky and not, say, a super-tall ceiling on an alien ship—starting to lighten. I squint, peering at the tree-like shapes that I can now make out around me.

My nose didn't lie. I *am* in some kind of jungle. Only it's unlike any jungle I've been in. As orange and pink rays streak through the darkness above, painting it with a warm glow, I see that we're in a sizable clearing ringed by enormous trees. Their black trunks look wider than an average single-family house, and their canopies are so high up they seem to disappear into the glowing sky. Lush green-and-red ferns of various heights cluster on the ground around them, mixed with purple, red, and pink-striped palm fronds. In a few places, brilliantly scarlet plants sprout from the ground in six-foot-tall clusters of tentacle-like tubes.

Tubes that, upon closer inspection, seem to expand and contract rhythmically, like arteries through which blood is pumped.

Toto, I've a feeling we're not in Kansas anymore.

Or in Cleveland.

Or anywhere on Earth.

Okay, yeah, now I do feel dizzy. Probably because I'm hyperventilating.

Sucking in fast, shallow breaths, I drop my gaze to the ground—just in time to see a rat-sized spider-ant thing stroll casually onto my hand. I shriek and flap my hand in the air, shaking it off. Then I spot more of the same giant insects around me.

I'm on my feet before I remember that I'm supposed to be trying not to draw any attention from my lizard-ish captors.

Thankfully, the bastards just guffaw as I hop from foot to bare foot in a futile attempt to prevent the spider-ants from crawling onto me. They're all around me, so it's not an easy task. I hop closer to the fire, and that seems to do the trick. The insects stay a respectful distance away from the hot embers, and after a minute, the swarm of them moves on, crawling on their merry way to terrorize someone else.

I blow out a relieved breath and stop hopping around. My heart is still racing, and I feel shaky from all the adrenaline, but I'm safe. For now, at least. I can't stop staring at the ground, though, and my gaze happens to fall on my feet.

They're dirty, as expected. But they're also skinny, like my hands.

I blink.

Yep, no swelling around my feet or ankles.

I bend over and touch my legs.

They're my own. I recognize their shape from before my heart started failing. But there's no swelling and, more importantly, no scar on my left calf from my melanoma surgery.

The scar is simply gone.

I straighten to stare at the lizard dudes.

Did they do this?

Did they heal me, right down to the old scars on my body?

They must have. It's the only explanation. But how? And more importantly, why? Why bring me here and heal me?

What do they want from me?

They notice my staring, and the one who fed me says something in his guttural language. His buddies cackle-laugh—I'm guessing at my expense.

That's it. I've had enough.

"What's so funny?" I demand, placing my hands on my hips. "Who and what are you, and where the fuck am I?"

They guffaw harder.

My annoyance rises. Since waking up here, I've

been stung, hit, attacked by giant spider-ants, and now they're laughing at me? Granted, I probably look funny with my muddy clothes and bare feet, but still, have some fucking respect for another sentient being.

I shoot them all a dirty look. "Fuck you all. Open the portal and let me go home. Now."

They continue laughing. Then the one who spoke originally, issuing the command to the lizard dude who grabbed me, comes up to me. His lipless shark mouth moves, but instead of his language, what comes out is guttural, heavily accented English.

"Shut up, human. You on Zerra now. You slave."

And as I stare at him, jaw slack, he reaches out a clawed hand and forces me to my knees.

CHAPTER 3

ARUAN

The whispers float in the air, wafting through the oppressive bubble of silence that surrounds me as I walk through the Great Hall of the Water Palace.

They think I can't hear them. They think they're safe in the other quarters. They don't know I've modified my ears to sharpen my hearing, just as I've modified my muscles, bones, and tendons to increase my strength. I've also enhanced my eyes to improve my vision, enabling me to see through solid matter. So I glimpse them scurrying about the various palace rooms, huddling in their little groups to whisper fearfully about the Terrible One, the Alit prince they wish had never been born.

The Alit prince who should've been killed before his power grew too strong to be contained.

Reaching the waterfall at the end of the Great Hall, I part the sheets of falling water with my mind and exit onto the ledge connecting to the Sky Bridge. I walk onto it and head for the platform at the central intersection. It's my favorite place to watch the sunrise and take in my kingdom.

This morning is particularly nice, the air cool and fragrant, the bridge ropes damp from the night's dew. The midday winds will arrive soon, but for now, the air is still and calm, the dark sky just beginning to glow with hints of orange and pink. The only sounds out here are the songs of the small winged dragons and the roar of the waterfall, though if I strain my ears, I can still hear the goings-on inside the palace—the never-ending whispers, plots, and intrigues.

There are many in that palace who regret keeping me alive.

Some of them would like to try and remedy their mistake.

I sigh and lean onto the thick woven rope ringing the platform. When I was a child, I loved to hang on this rope, my feet dangling over the edge as I swung back and forth between safety and danger, between the boring stability of the bridge and the lethal tree-height drop below it.

I never fell, but I could have.

Maybe should have.

The entire kingdom would've rejoiced.

A distant screech of a dragon reaches my ears, pulling me out of my morbid mood. I clench my teeth and step back from the rope. It's been happening more lately—the random darkening of my thoughts, the growing numbness inside me. For several seasons, nothing has brought me joy, and I know that eventually, the numbness will spread until everything ceases to matter.

The sky lightens further, and I inhale a deep breath, dragging fresh morning air into my lungs.

What the dragon?

Confused, I take another breath.

There's something in the air. Something almost… sweet. But it's not a smell. More like a vibration.

I inhale again.

What is it?

I can't pinpoint it, but the sweet vibration is stronger now. I can feel it with my entire body. It's as powerful as the eastern storms that tug at the very roots of the trees, yet nothing around me is moving.

All the movement is within me, inside me.

I'm vibrating from within.

Vibrating so fast that I'm hot.

No, not just hot. Every part in my body is on fire.

I grip the rope in front of me, the edges of my vision darkening and expanding at the same time. The sensation is surreal, all-consuming. I'm here yet elsewhere. I'm falling apart yet being made whole. The scorching vibration expands, filling me, deafening me, blinding me, hijacking all my senses, and when it dies down, I'm different.

I'm… not empty anymore.

My skin prickles all over, as if lightning shot through my veins.

No.

It can't be.

I can't have found my mate.

She's dead.

They told me so, and I knew the truth of it when I looked for her. She was nowhere to be found on this world, our connection severed, destroyed.

But like the scrolls say, the soul doesn't lie—and mine has just recognized hers.

She's here, somewhere nearby. I can feel the pull of her being. It's like a dragon's claw has hooked itself deep into my chest, but instead of pain, there's an ache, equal parts sweet and terrible, an exquisite longing that permeates everything I am.

I'm not cognizant of my body moving, of my feet taking me to the wall of water guarding the entrance to the palace, but somehow, I'm there. The water particles dissolve before me, and I pass through the waterfall and stride into the Great Hall.

"Gaia!" My shout shakes the palace walls as I turn in a circle, looking for my sister through the thick layers of wood and stone. "Gaia!"

I don't know if my sister hears me, or if someone tells her that I'm looking for her, but a swirl of purple lights appears in front of me. Regally, she steps out of the portal, flicking her dark braid over her shoulder with an impatient gesture.

"Yes, brother?" she drawls. "How may I be of help?"

I grip her slender hand. "Come with me. Now."

It won't help much, of course. The rumors are

already flying like embers on the eastern winds, but I need to maintain at least a semblance of secrecy for now. To that end, I shepherd her into my quarters and seal the entrance behind us before activating the shields.

By the time I turn to Gaia, she's tapping her foot on the floor, looking irritated. "Well?"

"I need you to find someone for me."

She blinks at me. "Who?"

"A woman. I can sense her, but I don't know where she is."

She frowns. "What woman? And what do you mean, sense her?"

I stare at her, stone faced.

She gasps. "No! Aruan, that's impossible."

"Is it?" I reach out and take her hand. "Here, feel it."

Her eyes go wide as I feed her the sensations in my mind. She gasps again and yanks her hand away, then covers her mouth with her palm as she stares at me, shock and fear battling with disbelief on her face.

"Aruan… That's—" She takes a step back. "I don't know what to say."

"Don't say anything. Just help me find her."

"I…" Her gaze darts to the sealed entrance, and I know what she's thinking.

This is too big to keep to herself. This affects not just me, but the entire royal family. The entire kingdom, in fact. Maybe even the whole of Zerra.

Too bad I don't give a dragon's ass about that.

"Father and Mother aren't to know about this," I tell

her bluntly. "Nobody except you and I is to know until she's safely in my arms. You understand why, don't you?"

Gaia opens her mouth but closes it without saying anything. Reluctantly, she nods—but not before her gaze jumps to the entrance again.

Once more, I sense her thoughts.

Should she try to make it out and warn the rest of the family? Or should she play along and not risk my anger?

"The latter," I say when her gaze returns to my face. "Don't be foolish. You can't portal out of here, and I won't let you leave until I bring her here."

She blanches. "Did Kian—"

"Just do as I ask."

I'm not admitting anything one way or another. If she thinks our powerful brother has trained me in mind reading, that can only be to my advantage.

My sister stares at me for a long moment, then nods, defeated. "Do you have any idea where I should start?"

"All I know is that she's nearby." I analyze the strength of the dragon's claw tug inside me. "Maybe a local portal's distance away."

Yes, that feels right. My mate is not so close that I can reach her on foot, but not so far that more advanced portal work would be required.

"But that could be anywhere in Lona," Gaia protests. "It'll take me forever to find her."

I bare my teeth in a humorless smile. "Better get to

work then."

Gaia sighs and sinks to the floor, crossing her legs in front of her. "Fine. But you'll owe me for this."

"I know I will." And she'll collect, I have no doubt. "Now make it happen."

She closes her eyes and goes to work, opening a small trial portal into the middle of the town center—the location she must deem most likely to harbor my mate. I don't feel the pull inside me strengthening, and I tell her so. She closes that portal and opens another, this one to the south side of the river bank. Then another in a random clearing in the forest. And so on until a hundred portals have been opened and closed, and sweat is dripping down her face.

"You can take a short break," I say after another two dozen searches. "Then we'll continue."

As impatient as I am, I can see that my sister is on the verge of collapse, and that won't benefit anyone. I, like the rest of the royal family, can generate a portal or two, but Gaia is the only one of my siblings who can do it repeatedly and systematically, bending distance with her mind over and over again.

Our mother can do even more, but I'm not asking for her help in this.

"I need water," Gaia says, licking her cracked lips. "How about we go down to—"

"I'll get it for you here, don't worry."

I pick up an empty stone bowl from a nearby table and mentally reach out to the components of water in the air. With effortless precision, I combine the gaseous particles and slow their movement, letting the resulting vapor turn to liquid and collect inside the bowl.

My sister tries not to flinch as I hand her the newly formed water. I smile sardonically. I haven't done anything particularly extraordinary—several of us royals can do the water trick—but it's a reminder to her that I can do more. Much, much more.

Giving up on any further attempts to escape my quarters, Gaia drinks the water silently and resumes her work, opening portal after portal as I check each one, determined to find the one woman who's going to complete me.

The woman they told me was dead.

The one they're afraid will bring about the destruction of our world.

CHAPTER 4

ELSIE

I'm busy spitting out blood and am thus distracted when I stumble over a protruding purple root—one that promptly stings me, causing me to yelp and jump aside. It's a motion my captors interpret as yet another escape attempt, and they promptly reward me with a harsh blow across my face.

"I wasn't trying to run. It was the root," I protest when my ears stop ringing, but they don't care.

Which isn't surprising.

After all, I'm here to be a slave.

Sour bile rises in my throat at the thought, mixing with the copper tang of blood coating my tongue. While this particular stumble wasn't an escape attempt, the previous three times I "tripped" were—and the third attempt resulted in another tooth being lost. One of my ribs may also be cracked. It's been painful to breathe and talk since they kicked me.

Their leader, the one who spoke to me, hasn't said much after informing me of my status, but I'm guessing they're taking me somewhere to be sold. It's the only logical conclusion, as my captors don't have much use for me. At least that's what it seems like because so far, all they've done is drag me through the jungle—the wonders of which I'm not even able to properly appreciate due to my head throbbing from their blows and my stomach churning either from the "chicken" I ate earlier or the whole "you slave" business.

What kind of advanced civilization that's mastered interplanetary travel has freaking slaves?

Not that I'm seeing signs of any advanced civilization around me. So far, it's been jungle and more jungle, with lots of scary—and ridiculously oversized—bugs. In addition to the giant caterpillar and the spider-ants, on this trek, we've encountered several millipedes the length of a small bus, dragonflies with bigger wingspans than eagles, and lots of mosquitoes the size of my fist. I understand neither the hugeness of these insects nor their similarities to the insects on Earth, but all the questions I've posed to my lizard captors so far have gone unanswered.

All I know is that I'm on Zerra, I'm a slave, and they're taking me somewhere.

Not a promising beginning, that's for sure.

The most puzzling thing about it all is that at least one of the lizard dudes speaks English. How? Where could he have learned it? Do Zerrans—or whatever they're called—often steal people from Earth to be their slaves? If so, for what purpose? Free labor? Pest control?

They clearly have need for the latter, but a random dying girl is hardly likely to be a giant bug eradication expert.

I'm so lost in my thoughts and in my efforts not to step on any more stinging roots or scary bugs that I only look up from the ground when the wind picks up. That's when I realize that we've exited the densest part of the jungle and are standing on a strip of black sand in front of a large body of water. A river? A lake? I'm not sure, but it's so wide I can barely see the other bank across from us, and I can't tell where it ends on either side of us.

The wind picks up further, pelting my skin with grains of black sand, and I squint to protect my eyes. It's also much brighter out here without the canopy of the super-tall trees, and as I glance at the sky above, I see that it's blue, like I'm used to on Earth. Which makes sense—I'm breathing the air here, so Zerra must have an Earth-like atmosphere.

Come to think of it, Zerra must also be roughly the size of Earth and possess a similar composition because I'm neither bouncing like an astronaut on the moon, nor do I feel like I weigh five hundred pounds, the way I would on a bigger or denser planet.

In general, this place is suspiciously Earth-like, even with all its unusual flora and fauna.

I have no explanation for that or for anything that's

happened to me thus far, so I don't even try to speculate. Instead, I sneak a look at my captors.

They're staring at the water, which is now frothing with waves from the rapidly intensifying wind. Before long, I realize what they're looking at.

A boat. Or maybe a barge, given the low sides and rectangular shape. Whatever it is, it's big and it's swiftly coming toward us, driven by the waves.

On it are more lizard people, at least a few dozen of them. And also... humans?

I almost jump in excitement—that is, until I see their postures.

Hunched over and defeated, these humans look like what they most likely are.

Slaves.

My stomach twists, and I taste bile again.

I can't believe this is happening. Any of it, but especially this part. How is it possible that I've traveled to a different planet, and it's so fucking barbaric? I mean, you figure out a way to bring aliens to your planet, and instead of using the opportunity to learn about another civilization's culture and technology, you decide to make them slaves? What kind of logic is that? True, Europeans sort of did the same thing in Africa and the Americas, but we've advanced past that. Why haven't these lizard people?

Well, whatever. I'm not going to be like those humans on the barge. I'm going to escape and take my chances in the jungle, giant insects and all. I just need to figure out a distraction, some way to—

A clawed hand grips my shoulder and propels me forward, toward the water. I stumble in surprise and cringe, anticipating another blow. It doesn't come. Instead, as the barge docks, the hand on my shoulder forces me to my knees, and I hear my captors rattle off something to the new arrivals.

Probably listing my attributes and price.

Gritting my teeth, I look up at the newcomers. I don't know if gender isn't a thing among the lizard people or if all the creatures before me are male, but I see more linebacker builds and scale-covered groin bulges. There are at least a dozen new lizard dudes surrounding me now, and two of them start conversing with my captors in their guttural tongue. The way they're throwing out short sentences back and forth reminds me of haggling at a flea market—which is probably exactly what's going on.

Well, fuck them. I'm not going to wait here meekly while they haggle over me.

The hand on my shoulder pulls away as my captor gesticulates to make his point, and I spot an opening in the sea of lizard chests—an opening that leads toward the water. This is my chance. I know how to swim, so I drop to all fours and quickly crawl toward the opening, counting on them being too distracted with their conversation to notice my move.

It works—for about a minute. Just as I'm about to dive into the waves, I'm grabbed again, dragged away from the water, and thrown onto my back. The sand softens the worst of the fall, but my breath is still knocked out of me, and by the time I recover it, another kick to the ribs leaves me wheezing. I roll into a fetal position to protect myself, but a rough, scaly hand drags me upright by the back of my shirt.

Still wheezing, I swing at whoever's got me. He retaliates with a blow to my face that nearly knocks me out. By the time my stunned brain gets back online, three newcomer lizard dudes are holding me in place while the fourth is shouting something at the leader of the group that brought me. He responds with a growled word accompanied by a dismissive wave, which makes all the others laugh uproariously.

Fuckers. This isn't funny in the least.

My vision is still blurry from the blow, but as I dazedly turn my head and my gaze falls on the humans on the boat, I think I see pity on their faces.

Cowards. There's at least a dozen of them. If they joined in the fight, I bet we could—

A violent tug on the front of my shirt rips it in half, yanking me out of a bloodthirsty fantasy in which I and my fellow humans drown all these monsters before feeding them to the giant caterpillars. I yelp, struggling with all my might, but the clawed hands holding me are far too strong. Also, my captors are definitely male, or at least the one in front of me is, because the scaly skin covering the bulge at his groin splits, revealing a red, angry-looking organ that resembles a giant, screw-shaped snake tongue, with two pointy heads branching off from the middle of the foot-long trunk. Each head is dripping some kind of greenish-yellow liquid. Lizard pre-cum?

I throw up a little in my mouth at the thought— only to freeze in horror as the snake-tongue monstrosity moves toward me while its owner rips at my shorts.

He can't possibly mean—

Oh, fuck, he does mean it.

Disregarding the fact that we're two completely different species, he's apparently decided to rape me.

I scream bloody murder and kick backward, bucking in my captors' grasp as hard as I can. My bare heel makes contact with something hard but slimy, and I nearly throw up again as I realize the lizards holding me have got their own groin snake tongues out. The one I kicked screeches something in a higher-pitched voice, and one of his buddies hits me in the face again.

And again.

And again.

By the time they let go of me, I slump to the ground, barely conscious, gagging on my own blood. I'm so dazed I can't even put up a fight as rough hands yank off the torn remnants of my clothes, leaving me kneeling buck naked in the sand, surrounded by demonic aliens and their nightmarish cocks.

This is it, I realize dimly. This is how I die—not in a comfy hospice with my parents grieving in the corner. Not even in the operating room during some experimental procedure. Oh, no, fate would never be that kind to me.

My death will come at the clawed hands and snake-tongue dicks of inhuman rapists on a distant planet.

Shark mouths parted, they reach for me—and I let out one last, hopeless scream.

And then... *they* begin to scream.

They scream like they're being torn apart.

No, not torn apart.

Dissolved.

Stunned, I watch as my lizard captors literally melt down, turning into goo starting from their scaly feet on up until only their terrified faces are left—and then those dissolve as well.

A second later, the goo absorbs into the sand, and it's like they never existed.

Horrified, I look up, squinting against the bright sunlight and the gritty wind, and in the air, right by the water's edge, I see a circle of purple lights.

Silhouetted against it is a man.

A human man.

Or... maybe more than human.

The fine hairs on my arms stand on end.

Even from a distance, I feel his power.

It's a dark hum in the air, a visceral vibration that warns of danger.

It's like standing next to a high-voltage wire, only with nothing to shield you from the lethal current inside.

He moves, coming toward me, and my breath stills in my lungs as I make out more details about him.

Tall and regal, he's wearing a long-sleeved silver

tunic over a pair of slim-fitting black pants tucked into black knee-high boots. His dark hair flows in shiny waves below his broad shoulders, and his skin is a golden shade of bronze that seems to glow in the sunlight. And his face... I swallow the blood and saliva pooling in my mouth as he stops in front of me.

I've never seen a face so starkly masculine—or so fiercely beautiful.

His features are a study in symmetry, all sharp angles and sloping planes. His high, broad forehead sits atop prominent dark eyebrows that frame thickly lashed eyes of an unusual silver-gray hue. His nose is boldly aquiline, and his high, wide cheekbones are sharply defined, as is his square jaw. Only his mouth, full and sensual, holds a hint of softness... and more than a hint of ruthlessness.

This being holds immense power and isn't afraid to wield it.

I don't know how I know that, but I'm convinced of it.

His silver eyes narrow as his gaze travels over me, and I flush, suddenly painfully aware of how pathetic I must look, kneeling in the sand all bloody and grimy. And naked.

Crap, I totally blanked on the fact that I'm naked.

Before I can do more than move my arm to cover my breasts—not that there's much there to cover—he bends down and unceremoniously scoops me up, lifting me against his chest with insulting ease. I mean, I know all the chemo during my childhood impacted my growth, leaving me smaller than average, but he could've still grunted or something to acknowledge that I'm an adult woman, not a child.

Also, the touch of his strong hands on my bare skin makes me warm in all sorts of embarrassing places. Warm and uncomfortably wet.

Ugh. What is wrong with me? What kind of bizarre trauma response is this? A minute ago, I was almost raped, and here I am, fighting the urge to squirm and rub myself against my rescuer like a cat in heat. A rescuer who's most likely not even human. That sensation of being next to a high-voltage wire is even stronger now that he's holding me. The hum of his power envelops me, cocooning me in the invisible field of vibrations that feels both like a shield and a cage, same as his embrace.

I don't understand it, any of it, but it freaks me out even more than my uncontrollable physical reaction to him.

Also, speaking of things that freak me out, he's carrying me toward the circle of purple lights.

"Are you taking me back to Earth?" I ask, my heart leaping in sudden hope.

Because that would be great. I'd even trade my newly healed—though now pretty battered—body for a chance to spend a few more weeks on Earth and see my parents... whom I badly miss, I realize with a jolt.

In general, I'm suddenly so homesick I could cry.

At my words, the being meets my gaze and says something in a language I've never heard, one that makes me think of underground rivers and dark alien forests. His voice is deep, his tone soothing, but there's an edge to it, like he's suppressing some strong emotion.

Is he angry at me?

Hoping that's not the case, I try again. "Earth?" I wave toward the portal we're quickly approaching. "Please... can you just send me home?"

He ignores my query this time, his attention trained elsewhere. I follow his gaze to the barge on which the humans are now milling about, clearly unsure what to do with the lizard dudes liquified and all.

"Hey!" I yell at them. "Do any of you speak English?"

A blond woman who looks to be in her thirties yells back in a British accent, "Who are you? How do you know one of *them*?" Her gaze jumps to my rescuer's face for a millisecond before she blanches and looks away.

Okay, so he's one of "them," not us. Not that I thought otherwise. Despite his humanoid appearance, there's something distinctly alien about the man holding me in his arms. Something aside from the power radiating from him like the UV rays from the sun. Also, judging by the blond woman's demeanor, "they" are scary—not a surprise either, given the whole melting of lizard dudes into goo.

"I'm Elsie from Cleveland," I shout back at her. "And I don't know any of—

The deep voice of my rescuer drowns out the rest of my words. This time, his tone is unmistakably sharp as he stops before the portal, facing the barge. All the humans freeze, staring at him, and he repeats whatever he's just said, his voice even harsher.

The blonde, who seems to be the bravest of the bunch, bobs her head, even as she shrinks back under his glare.

He seems to be satisfied with that.

Glancing down at me, he says something in a softer tone, and before I can blink, he walks into the portal, holding me clasped against his chest like some kind of prize.

CHAPTER 5

ELSIE

This isn't Earth.

Not even close.

For one thing, I didn't feel like I was breaking apart as we went through the portal. It felt more like a big sneeze, one where your whole body convulses and you lose sight of the world for a second, but then everything is the same except your nose is wet with snot. My nose isn't wet, thankfully, but that's the general sensation—like I winked out of existence, only to come back with nothing substantially different.

I run my tongue over my teeth.

Yep, two are missing, and my face still throbs painfully where I was hit, so I haven't been magically healed.

My surroundings are another big clue to my non-Earth location. I'm inside a cavernous chamber, the walls and ceiling of which glow with some inner light despite appearing to be made of wood and stone. In the middle of the chamber is a wide, shallow pit, lined on the inside with a soft-looking silvery padding. A bed of sorts? There are no pillows or blankets, so it could also be what passes for a couch in these parts.

I don't get to inspect the rest of the chamber because of big clue number three: the fact that I'm not alone.

In addition to my rescuer, who's still holding me in a bridal carry, there's a woman sitting in a lotus pose on the floor and staring at me with wide silver eyes.

She must be one of "them" because not only does she strongly resemble the man who came for me, but she also gives off that distinctly unearthly vibe.

Not bothering to set me down, my rescuer addresses her, rattling off what sounds like a series of commands. She jumps to her feet, nodding, and I watch in shock as the seemingly solid wall behind her dissolves, forming a curved entrance some eight feet tall. She disappears through the arch and down a dimly lit corridor, her steps driven by urgency. The entrance closes as fast as it appeared, abruptly cutting off the view of the hallway.

Now that we're alone and the initial shock of landing here is wearing off, my fear spikes. The man holding me against his chest as if I'm easily breakable—which I suppose I am to someone of his sheer size and strength—killed my captors and stole me. Why? Am I *his* slave now? Is that why he melted those lizard dudes? But then why didn't he take the other humans on the barge as well?

I clear my throat. "You can put me down now. And I wouldn't mind some clothes."

He arches a dark eyebrow as he stares at my face, his expression so intently focused it makes me uncomfortable. And... uncomfortably warm.

I fight the urge to squirm in his embrace. There's no way I'm turned on by the way he's staring at me. He's just probably staring because he doesn't speak English and he's confused by what I said.

Sure enough, he makes no moves toward putting me down. Or giving me clothes. Instead, his arms tighten around me, locking me into an inescapable cage of muscles, and the intensity of his stare impossibly heightens.

Shit.

What does he want? Why did he bring me here?

Am I going to end up as a guinea pig for some obscure alien experiment after all?

I'm about to hyperventilate from the disturbing scenarios running through my head when the wall opens again, and the woman returns with a stone bowl in her hands. She possesses the classical beauty of a Grace Kelly or Marilyn Monroe. Crisscrossing laces tie the bodice of her silver dress. A long black braid hangs down her back.

The wall closes swiftly behind her, the stones knitting together once more as if with a magic trick.

My captor barks out something in his language, at which she replies in a patient tone.

While they're conversing, I take stock of the

sparsely furnished space in the hope of identifying any weapons I can use. Against the far wall, there appears to be some kind of tall cabinet made from a black stone. A portion of the wall is polished so smoothly it shines—like a mirror, I realize. A huge wooden trunk with a stone lid stands next to it. Sadly, no knives or sharp objects are lying around.

I give a start as a part of the back wall dissolves. Behind it, there's an even bigger cavern with carved pillars and a small square pool in the center of the floor. Steam rises from the water. A sweet smell of milk and honey wafts to me.

Strangely, I'm becoming lethargic, as though I'm dozing off in a sunny spot in winter or, as is usual for me, being hooked up to an IV with morphine. I have an inexplicable urge to curl up like a cat against the hard chest that shelters me and drift off into oblivion. My head lolls to the side as it gets too heavy to hold up, dropping onto the man's shoulder. The bronze skin of his strong neck is inches away from my face.

For some bizarre reason, that strip of naked flesh draws me in with an otherworldly force. I want to press my lips on that spot and drag my tongue over it. I want to lick the thick vein straining down the side of his neck and taste the salt on his taut skin. The mere idea makes me tingly all over.

I snuggle closer. The sweet milky fragrance that fills my lungs isn't enough to mask the delicious woodsy and musky smell of the man that reaches my nostrils.

Is that some kind of cologne?

Whatever it is, I want to rub it all over my body. Or roll in it. It's like a drug to my system. I burrow deeper into his arms, uttering a contented sigh as I nuzzle his neck with my nose.

Even as the man freezes, his heart speeds up. It beats under my ear with a strong, healthy pace. No imminent heart failure here, that's for sure.

He says something, his deep voice sharp as he carries me to the pool. The woman rushes ahead of us and tips white liquid from her bowl into the water. The sweet scent in the room intensifies, a whiff of some exotic spice infusing the honeyed milk perfume. Almost immediately, my eyes start to droop.

What's happening?

At this point, I don't really care. I hardly feel the throbbing pain in my face or the burning stings on my skin. I'm starting to float now, the zapping electricity that vibrates in my rescuer-slash-captor's chest making my head spin.

The next thing I know, the man is climbing down three steps into the water—clothes, boots, and all.

Blinking up at him, I battle to focus on the crazily handsome perfection of his face. He smiles a reassuring smile that seems to warm me from the inside out, but something disturbing also shifts in his silver-gray eyes, something that makes those steely pools sharpen and darken at the same time.

I try to make sense of the unease that struggles to break through the euphoria fogging my mind, some kind of internal warning, but then he submerges me in the water up to my chin, and my brain detaches from my body. It feels a lot like drifting to the ceiling and looking down on myself.

The floating sensation only lasts a second before I drop like a stone and my stomach bottoms out.

Whoa.

What the hell?

I open my mouth to scream as I fall into a vortex that sucks me deeper, but no sound comes out.

The man cups my face, his big palm dwarfing my cheek, and says something almost tender and encouraging.

The darkness thickens while I barrel down a bottomless pit, my arms and legs flailing even as I lie as motionless as a marionette on a puppet master's lap.

He shifts his large hand from my cheek to cover my mouth and pinches my nose closed between a forefinger and a thumb. The hold effectively cuts off my air.

I can't breathe.

No!

I try to struggle, but as if in a bad dream, I'm paralyzed.

The light becomes thinner as my lungs protest.

Too late, I understand my captor's intention. I grasp desperately for something to hold on to, but I can't lift a finger. The only thing I can cling to is his unwavering stare.

My gaze pleads with him, begging him not to drown me in a bath of spiced honey milk. But my unspoken appeal is useless. My sadly unpracticed—or rather, nonexistent—charm has zero effect. As he dunks my head into the cloudy water, I realize what that expression on his face that I couldn't place was. Just before the opaque liquid washes out my vision, I see it for what it is.

The strangely compassionate look in those eyes the color of mercury is regret.

CHAPTER 6
ARUAN

The notion of finally having her here with me is still unreal yet so potent that my power flares with enough force to set the water boiling if I'm not careful.

With effort, I rein it in.

The turmoil within me, however, refuses to abate. Her suffering is torture to my soul. I regret that I had to rip her from consciousness and submit her to the darkness of a dreamless sleep, but it's better that she's not cognizant for what's to come.

Heart thudding, I study the delicate face that floats above the water on my palm. Her pale skin is black and blue in spots, her lips puffy and swollen, split in several places. Her sunset-colored hair is covered in mud and sand, and it's strangely short, at most the length of my finger.

Did the Phaelix monsters do this to her? Cut her hair before they beat her?

My blood boils at the thought, and the water around us warms uncomfortably.

Gritting my teeth, I rein in my power once more. The torrid heat within me dissipates as I manage to somewhat calm my anguish. She's safe now. I have her. Taking in a steadying breath, I position her so that her back is pressed against my chest and she's propped up between my legs, unable to slip beneath the water.

Dozens of questions swirl in my mind, but I focus on what's important right now—which is to repair the damage that's been done to this wisp of a woman who, in the wink of an eye, eradicated the numbness that was slowly but surely turning my soul to stone.

"Bring Vitai and Kian here," I instruct my sister in a clipped tone.

I don't miss the hope that flashes in her eyes before she rushes toward the hallway, but her relief vanishes quickly when I use a fraction of my power to hold the wall together, preventing her from opening the entrance.

I'm not taking any chances. She's not leaving my quarters until I say so. I have a very good reason for detaining her, and she knows it.

Her shoulders slump and then lift as she inhales deeply. A moment later, two portals open on either side of the room.

Kian steps through the one on the right, his mind already probing mine in search of answers as to why I summoned him.

"You called for me, brother?" he says as he fully

materializes, his tall frame dwarfing the pillar at his back.

When he notices me with my clothes in the water holding a woman in my arms, he freezes.

Like Gaia, he knows immediately. Like her, he can feel it.

Panic washes over his usually stoic expression. He opens his mouth, but before he can question me, Vitai appears on the other side of the room.

Despite being the youngest of my siblings, Vitai displays the empathy and wisdom that normally only comes with very advanced age. Slender and leaner than Kian, he moves closer with eloquent and lithe agility, his expression guarded but his slate-gray eyes ablaze with alarm.

"What the dragon?" Kian mumbles.

I look at my miraculous find, making sure the opalescent water still covers her up to her chin. Just the thought that one of my brothers could catch a glimpse of her pearly naked skin is enough to unleash my wrath again.

As if sensing the pending catastrophe, Vitai stops a safe distance away.

The column of his throat ripples as he swallows. "Is that…?"

"Yes," Kian says, both surprised and resigned. "It's exactly what you think."

Gaia comes forward, hovering at the far end of the bath. "How?"

How, indeed?

I'll get my answers.

First, I need to tend to the injuries I feel so viscerally they may as well be my own. The pain in her mouth where the Phaelix knocked out her teeth throbs in mine. The cracks in her ribs mirror in my perfectly healthy bones. The rest of her vitals are normal.

The command I direct at Vitai is brusque. "Fix her."

He's an expert when it comes to dismantling and reassembling living matter. For that reason, we often use him as a healer.

Moved by his inborn need to repair anything that's broken, Vitai is already inching toward the edge of the bath. The healing water has reviving as well as purifying properties, but it's more suited for soothing aching muscles and disinfecting scrapes. Its most useful feature is its anesthetic property. I'd need a much stronger dose to knock me out cold, but the woman floating in my embrace is so tiny that the miniscule amount of medicinal salts added to the bath water was enough.

As Vitai heals her injuries, starting with her surface scrapes and bruises, I study her more closely. Throughout my life, even after I thought her dead, I'd see her in my dreams like this, all grown up and beautiful. Long after I could no longer sense her, I could still see her in my mind's eye, the mysterious connection that exists between mates leading me to picture her first as a child, then as an adolescent, and then as a young woman.

And the bond proved true. Face-wise, she's almost

exactly the way my mind painted her for me, from the tip of her small, upturned nose to the long, reddish-brown lashes fanning over her pale cheeks. Her delicate chin is sharp and stubborn, her pouty lips pink and infinitely kissable. Her eyes are closed now, but their unique color, that of the tropical sea shimmering in the summer sun, is imprinted on my vision, as it has been for so many years.

What's different is that she's small and frail. Much smaller than she'd appeared in my dreams. More like a child than the fully grown adult she should be.

A blazing wave of protectiveness rolls through me, followed by a rush of uncontrollable tenderness. I'll have to be careful with her. I can easily hurt her by forgetting my own strength.

Sweat runs down Vitai's temples as he concentrates. Healing takes a lot of mental as well as physical energy. His body trembles by the time he's done. He doesn't have to tell me he's succeeded. I can feel it. The throbbing pain and brokenness are gone. In their place, vitality and a healthy appetite beat in my chest.

A smile pulls at my mouth. The automatic gesture is foreign and stiff on my unpracticed lips. I can't remember the last time I smiled spontaneously. My grin widens as I sense her hunger for food. Even unconscious, she's demanding. I'll take great joy in feeding her. Soon.

When I look up, Gaia and Vitai are staring at me with slack jaws.

I guess a smile on my face frightens them as much

as a grimace or growl. Maybe more. And for good reason.

Only Kian observes me with a bland expression that gives nothing away.

"What do you need from me?" he asks, carefully studying me.

I don't let him see much, only what I want him to see. My brother is powerful, but I can block him from sifting through my mind with his sharp, claw-like scrutiny.

Using my own power, I prevent him from digging around in my mate's thoughts too. That would be as invasive as seeing her naked.

"She doesn't speak our language," I say.

He stares at me with a pinched brow.

I stare back at him coolly. I don't have to dig through his mind to know what he's thinking.

How is this possible?

How is any of this possible?

There's only one guess I can venture.

"I believe she was brought here from Earth," I say, my voice steady despite the rage flaring back to life inside me. "She was being held by slavers when I found her. There were other Earthlings there. She spoke to them in their language as I was carrying her away."

Gaia gasps, and Vitai and Kian exchange a look.

They're thinking what I'm thinking. My mate being on Earth would explain why I couldn't sense her all these years, until I suddenly could. And like me, they know that at the time my mate vanished, only one person was powerful enough to create a portal to Earth, the forbidden world—and the realization, as well as its consequences, leaves them shaking in their boots.

"Do it," I tell Kian grimly. "Make her understand."

Vitai winces, but Kian doesn't argue. He knows what's at stake.

He steps closer and trains his eerily observant eyes that resemble the deep gray of cooling lava on the woman's face. A long rush of air escapes his lips as he exercises the manipulation that will facilitate communication.

When that's done, my brothers observe me quietly, waiting for my next instruction with the calmness of convicted men who've already accepted their sentence.

"You can go," I say. "She needs to rest."

"Me too?" Gaia asks, perking up.

I'll confront my family soon enough. There's no point in keeping my sister here any longer. Besides, I trust no one in a room alone with the woman who's destined to be mine.

I wave toward the far wall. "Go."

I release my hold on the stone particles, and the entrance opens.

The moment my siblings are gone, I make quick work of climbing from the bath with my mate in my arms. The purifying water has cleaned her body and hair. Not a mark or trace of dirt is left on her pale skin.

The sight of her does things to me, things I shouldn't feel when she's passed out. The heat starts deep in the pit of my stomach and travels to every extremity of my body. Flames scorch me from the inside out, erupting with a crackling of sparks over my skin.

I carry her to my bed and lay her down with the utmost care before using a small fraction of my power to evaporate the drops of water that cling to her body. I don't want her to be cold. Seeing that I'm standing in a puddle of water and dripping over the bed and floor, I repeat the same exercise to dry my boots and clothes. Then I cover her with a sheet and leave her to sleep. Resting is vital for her full recovery.

After sealing the room so no one else can open it, I make my way to the royal quarters in the west wing to get my answers.

CHAPTER 7

ARUAN

The floor quakes under my feet as my boots hit the polished flagstones. My mother is already in the sunroom where she receives her visitors, standing tall and regal in front of the arched window that overlooks the lakes and valleys on the hilly side of the kingdom.

As predicted, Gaia is with her. They're whispering in an urgent tone. I don't need my enhanced hearing to know what they're talking about.

When I enter with angry steps that shake the walls, my petrified sister shoots me an apologetic look before making herself scarce.

My mother pulls her back straight as I advance on her. I stop a few paces away. The urge to reach out and strangle the woman who gave birth to me, a woman I should honor, is too strong.

"Aruan," she says, her melodic voice sweet and filled with love. "I'm glad you've come."

Gaia got here a good few minutes before I did. My mother had enough time to summon my father to support—or rather, to protect—her, yet she didn't.

Because she's guilty.

Because she did it.

I take in her youthful complexion and soft, dove-gray eyes. Her jet-black hair doesn't sport a single white streak. She looks the same age as my sister, yet she's decades older than I am. For that reason alone, I owe her respect, but I can't respect the woman who birthed me only to doom me to an unthinkable fate.

"I know why you're here," she says, her long silver skirt, embroidered with pearls, swishing as she walks so gracefully toward me it seems as if she's floating.

I don't bother softening my tone. "You lied to me."

"My son." She reaches out to cup my cheek, but I pull away, making her flinch at the rejection.

"You told me she was dead."

"My son," she says again, this time in protest. "I don't know what happened. All I can tell you is that I had nothing to do with it."

I clench my fingers so hard my knuckles crack. Whatever my mother sees on my face makes her backtrack a few steps. The fury rises until it's pulsing in every corner of my being and my whole body is one big vibrating mass. The slavers had her. They beat her. They were about to—

The thousand-year-old pink-stained window at my mother's back explodes, colorful shards flying outward. The sharp tinkling of breaking fragments lingers in the room with a disconcerting echo. An unsuspecting bijou dragon that hunts on this side of the palace utters an ear-splitting screech and dives through the air, flapping its wings to escape the torrent of broken glass.

The eastern wind grabs the opportunity to rush inside like a greedy, invisible spirit, knocking priceless figurines off the stone slab of my mother's table beneath the window.

The freshness of the morning is gone. The midday heat and the musky, intoxicating smell of the poisonous lilies that bloom on the balcony.

My mother and I face each other from opposite sides as my anger pulses around us. She stands perfectly still, unmoved by the violence and destruction, but her rosy cheeks have lost their color.

I'm a bit disturbed as well. I haven't allowed my power to get out of hand like this since the Incident.

It must be my mate, the effect she has on me. The self-control I've developed over the years seems to be slipping.

I push my discomfort aside and smile at my mother. It's a cold, mocking gesture, reflecting the bitter betrayal and disillusionment that smolder in my gut like red-hot coals. "Shall I summon Kian to shed light on the truth?"

My mother stares at me, aghast but not surprised. I'll do what I must, even if it means using her own offspring against her.

She raises a slender, graceful hand. "You're making a mistake."

My smile turns vicious. "It's not I who made the mistake, Mother."

I still as something stirs in my chest. Awareness surfaces from unconsciousness, and it's scared.

She's awake.

The pull on my heart is immediate and undeniable. Her fear is worse than being pierced by a blade.

I turn on my heel instantly, just in time to see my cousins, aunts, and uncles scurry like insects behind the protection of the thick walls where they were listening. Their fear is palpable, following me like an offensive smell to the doorway.

"Aruan," my mother says to my back with a plea in her voice. "At least let me meet her."

I pause to flash her a sardonic grin. "Oh, you will, sooner than you think. Order preparations for a banquet. The court will meet my mate." I add in a menacing tone, "Tonight."

Worry lines crease her smooth face. "It's too soon. This is a mistake, my son. Give her time to settle in."

"I've waited my whole life," I bite out.

As my rage materializes again, a fissure appears in the roof of the cavern, and a crystal goblet explodes on the ornate stone table where exotic fruit and honey wine are conveniently set out for the queen's unending queue of morning guests.

My mother, no longer able to contain herself, lets out a terrified cry.

"I'm done waiting," I say.

With that, I leave my traitorous parent and hurry

back to my quarters. I stop outside the sealed entrance, using my enhanced vision to look through the wall. By now, Elsie should be awake. Some may call it spying, but I'm curious about what she's been up to in my absence.

My small, exquisite mate is standing in front of the sealed archway with the bed sheet twisted around her body. My own body reacts in an instant, heating at the sight of her, knowing there's nothing beneath that sheet but soft, silky skin.

The feeling is powerful. It's like nothing I've experienced. It's sweet and thick like melted honey—pure, unadulterated lust. Under the hem of my tunic, my cock stirs in my pants. It takes great effort to ignore it and even more to will it down.

I watch for a few seconds while she feels with nimble fingers along the crevices of the stone wall, no doubt searching for an exit.

When I let the wall dissolve, revealing the entrance, she stumbles backward, staring at me with wide eyes. Her short hair stands in all directions on her head, the messy style making her look peculiarly adorable.

She glances at the opening, no doubt speculating if she'd get past me if she made a run for it. Before she can act on such a futile idea, I step inside and seal the wall.

"Where the hell am I?" she demands. "What did you do to—"

She bites off the words mid-sentence, her eyes growing even rounder. "Wait." She backtracks, clutching the sheet between her breasts. "I speak your language."

"Yes," I say, giving her a patient smile. "You do indeed, my sweet."

Her pretty lips part. "But how?"

It's difficult to keep my distance. Everything inside me screams for me to take her in my arms and claim her. I can do it right now, here in my bed. But I feel her fear, so I hold back, tamping down the fierce need that fires through my veins and boils my blood.

Instead, I offer her an explanation. "My brother, Kian, has the power of reading and manipulating minds. One of the advantages of that manipulation is that he can grant someone the ability to understand and speak a language."

"Wait, what?" She holds up a hand. "Back up there for a second. Did you just say *power*?" She stares at me as if I were a dragon. "What *are* you?"

"My name is Aruan. I'm an Alit," I say, daring another step closer. "The same as you, Laliss."

"Laliss? The same as me?" She utters a laugh. "You're hallucinating." Clasping her forehead, she starts pacing. "Maybe *I'm* hallucinating."

"You're not hallucinating. Vitai, my youngest brother, healed you fully, including all the head injuries you sustained."

She looks down at her body as if realizing my words for the first time. Her tongue peeks out from the corner of her mouth. I watch with mesmerized fascination as she drags the pink tip over her teeth.

By dragon, if she keeps that up, I'm going to lose control. I want nothing more than to taste those lips and get drunk on her flavor.

A pretty flush turns her cheeks pink, and I know she feels the all-consuming heat and magnetic pull too.

"Yes," I say as she continues to draw her tongue over her small, white teeth. "He fixed your teeth too."

"Those fucking lizards," she mumbles, more to herself than to me.

"Phaelix," I say, crossing my hands behind my back to prevent myself from touching her.

"What?"

"They're called the Phaelix. They're another intelligent species on Zerra."

"It's true, then." She buries the fingers of one hand in her hair. "I'm really on a different planet."

The complexity of the situation dawns on me. There's much she doesn't understand and has to learn. If she's been on Earth all this time, the existence of our world must be a shock to her.

For all the wonders they have on Earth, the humans there are weak and powerless, and utterly unaware of Zerra.

Then again, there's much for me to learn as well. I know next to nothing about my mate. I have no idea what she likes or favors. It's going to take time to get to know each other, something I'm already looking forward to greatly—once I've secured our bond.

I'm not taking any risks now that I've found her.

I'll claim her as soon as possible.

Tonight. As soon as I've explained the situation.

Yes, that sits just about right with me.

Taking my time, I cross the floor. She stares at me, clearly scared yet standing her ground. Still, when I stop in front of her, she flattens her body against the wall, creating as much space between us as possible.

I reach for the sheet that covers her body, but before I can pull at the ends that are folded in over her breasts, she slaps my hand away, her cheeks darkening to a deeper shade of red.

Clutching the sheet in both hands with a death grip, she asks in a choked voice, "What do you think you're doing?"

Her enticing smell fills my nostrils. That strange, urgent, and sweetly painful tug in my chest rises to a new crescendo. It demands that I ease the ache. My edginess won't be put to rest until I take what's mine.

She's so close, within my reach.

Yet I don't raise my hand to caress the delicate lines of her face or to test the texture of her spiky hair because I sense her confusion and resistance. Instead, I inhale deeply, contenting myself for now with her scent, one that reminds me of the rare dragon shrub blossoms that flower only once a century under the full moon. Their aroma is subtle and delicate but the most powerful aphrodisiac.

She stares at me with round, unblinking eyes, a vein fluttering like the wings of a water dragon in her neck.

This scrap of a woman is mine.

She's destined for me.

She feels it too. Her body temperature increases marginally as her pulse kicks up. With my enhanced hearing, I can hear her heart beating in her chest. It speeds up at my nearness, pumping blood through her veins with more urgency.

"I want to inspect your body to make sure that my brother healed you properly," I say, infusing calmness into my voice to soothe her.

"I'm fine, thank you very much," she says with a defiant tilt of her chin. "I'm totally capable of checking my own body. Just because you saw me naked once doesn't mean you have the right to look at me on demand."

An uncharacteristic smile plucks at my lips. Again.

Vitai is never negligent, and I'd sense it if his work was incomplete. All I pick up now is her need to be nourished.

"You're hungry," I say, devouring her features with my gaze even though they're already imprinted in my mind. "I'll order you food and something to drink."

I'm looking forward to serving her the best Zerran dishes so I can learn her tastes and how to please her.

"Wait," she says when I tear myself away and head for the exit.

"We'll talk after you've eaten." With concern, I take in her slim frame beneath the sheet. "You need to recover your strength."

She shoots forward, grabbing hold of my arm. Heat dances over my skin where she touches me. I look at where her fingers are locked around my bicep, not even covering half of the muscle. The urge to take her in my arms is so powerful that I almost give up the fight. But then she pulls her hand away as if my clothes are on fire and draws back a few paces.

Facing her, I give her the full attention she deserves. "Is there anything else you need?"

She clears her throat. "Clothes, to start."

"That will be arranged."

"And answers," she adds swiftly. "For instance, you still haven't told me why you brought me here."

I love the sound of my mother tongue on her lips. She has an accent. It's so slight one could easily miss it, but I'm attuned to every nuance of her voice and expression. I could listen to her talk all day, but she needs to eat.

"Am I your slave?" she continues with apprehension.

"No," I say, amused. "You're not my slave, Laliss."

Her brows pull together. "Who the hell is Laliss?"

I frown too. "Don't you know your own name?"

"I do, and I assure you, it's not Laliss." I'm still considering that when she asks, "If I'm not your slave, why am I here?" The questions tumble from her lips so fast that her tongue trips over the words. "Why didn't you take me back to Earth? What are you going to do with me? Why did you save me from those lizar— Phaelix?"

She has no idea. Yes, she may feel the pull, and her body may answer to the call of mine, but she clearly doesn't know she's my future and fated destiny.

There's a right way of doing things, a correct order, but nothing about this miraculous day is orderly or normal.

Holding her turquoise gaze, I give her the truth that will change our world even before I've asked for her Earth name. "You're here, my sweet, because you're my mate."

CHAPTER 8

ELSIE

His *what?*

"Excuse me?" I say, my jaw almost unhinging as I stare at the savagely attractive man facing me.

"My mate," he repeats while crossing his massive arms over the bulging muscles of his broad chest.

I search for a hint of humor in his steely gray eyes or a quirk of his annoyingly sensual lips, but nope. He continues to study me with unwavering seriousness and perfect calm.

Yet behind that serene facade churns a ravenous restlessness. I sense the dangerous desire that lurks beneath the surface. He keeps a tight leash on it. Instinctively, I know this takes immense willpower, and the magnitude of his strength, be that physical or mental, only makes me more nervous. I may not know him from Adam, but anyone with a few brain cells can see that he's a man of unequalled power and force.

That force both terrifies and pulls at me like a dark magic spell. I should back away. Instead, I find myself stepping closer. He smells so good. Once again, I have an urge to nestle against his chest and kiss the strong column of his neck. The skin of my nape prickles with an unsettling awareness, the fine hairs standing on end.

His eyes narrow in the corners, crinkling with something like predatory satisfaction, almost as if he's happy with my response.

Wait. What am I doing? Instead of sniffing the air for a whiff of that intoxicating scent, I should be arguing my case.

I blink, trying to clear my head. "You've got this all wrong. Whoever you think I am, I'm not your mate."

He tilts his head, challenging me with the disconcerting silence of a man who's unshakable in his convictions.

"I'm not even an Alit," I exclaim, grasping for a logical explanation that I hope will appeal to his reason. "You're mistaking me for someone else. I'm Elsie, Elisa Barnikoff from Cleveland." I blow out a sigh of relief as recognition flickers across his face. "See? It's just a misunderstanding."

"Elsie," he says, trying out the sound on his tongue. "Is that what they called you there?"

"Look, I appreciate that you saved me and gave me back all my teeth. I'd love to stay and chat, but my parents must be worried sick about me. I need to get going, so if you could just lend me something to wear and show me to the nearest circle of lights, I'll be on my way."

At that, his expression darkens so much that my stomach twists with more nerves. I glance at the exit he's left open behind him. Maybe if I'm fast, I can scoot around him.

My hope plummets as two men dressed in the same fashion as the one in front of me enter. With black hair and gray eyes, they bear a strong resemblance to my captor. They must be related, if not close family.

"Aruan," the tallest of the two says, eyeing me curiously. "We came to fetch you. Father has called a meeting."

Aruan speaks without taking his gaze off me. "And you had to convey that invitation in person? Is your curiosity satisfied?"

"Can you blame us?" the other one asks in a lighter tone.

"Elsie," Aruan drawls, saying my name as if it's a rare delight. "Meet my brothers, Kian and Vitai." He gestures accordingly to each of them.

"Oh." These are the dudes who healed me and gave me the ability to understand and speak their language. The manners my parents drilled into me dictate that I thank them for their effort even though, technically, I'm still their prisoner. "Thanks for helping me."

"You're welcome," they say in unison.

The sincerity in their voices compels me to try my luck with them.

"Aruan," I say, pronouncing the foreign name

carefully, "seems to be confused. He thinks I'm his mate."

I laugh to stress my point, but when no one joins in, my laughter quickly dries up.

Holding the sheet up with one hand, I wave toward the two newcomers. "You're both Alit, right?"

They look at each other before nodding.

"You have special powers, like Aruan," I continue as an argument takes shape in my head. "Do all Alit have powers?"

"To a lesser or greater extent," Kian says.

"See?" I give them a friendly, peace-offering smile. "I don't have a power." Voila. Point proven. "I'm not an Alit."

I glance between the trio, anxious for them to connect the dots.

Kian and Vitai shoot Aruan baffled looks.

Their brother stares back, stone faced.

"It's rare for a royal Alit not to have a power, even a feeble one," Kian says. "And it's unheard of for a powerful Alit to be fated to a mate with a weak power, let alone to a mate with no power. Yet I don't sense anything inside her."

Aruan turns on him with flashing eyes. "That doesn't mean anything. Are you suggesting I don't recognize my own mate?"

"Not at all," Kian says quickly. "I'm merely saying that it's strange."

"Maybe her power was destroyed when she was sent to Earth," Vitai offers.

My gaze bounces between them like a ping-pong ball while they discuss me as if I'm not in the room.

"That could be," Kian muses. "Which would be unfortunate. She may be too weak to rule at your side, Aruan."

The silver of Aruan's eyes darkens to a deep graphite. A tremor shakes the room, the floor wobbling beneath my feet.

I slam a palm on the wall to keep my balance.

What the hell is going on? Is this an earthquake?

"Accuse my mate of being weak again, and you'll face me in the clearing," Aruan says in an icy tone.

Okay, enough is enough.

"Hey, dudes." I utter another uncomfortable laugh. "While I categorically state that I'm not an Alit, that doesn't mean you can insult me." I hurry to tell Aruan, "Although I'm not ungrateful for your intervention when the Phaelix kidnapped me."

Aruan fixes his piercing gaze on me, possession sparking in the depths of those mercurial eyes.

Kian's manner is placating. "Father is waiting, and you know how he gets when we waste his time."

This seems to bring Aruan to his senses. Bowing his head stiffly in my direction, he says, "I will see to it that clothes and food are sent."

With that, the three of them are gone, and the stone wall materializes back in place.

I rush to it and knock a fist on it to test if any part of the wall is hollow.

No luck.

I move in a circle around the room, but the walls are solid. I even press on a few stones, hoping to find a secret button that unlocks a concealed passageway, like in one of those spooky Gothic movies.

Nope.

Whatever technique Aruan uses to disintegrate the wall, he's not doing it with hidden mechanisms. He must be managing it with his mind, which is insane and terrifying.

Fuck.

I'm trapped in here.

Seeing that I've spent half my life in the narrow tunnel of an MRI machine, I'm not exactly claustrophobic, but a sense of suffocation descends on me as I spin around my cavernous prison.

No sooner does the sensation hit me than an archway opens miraculously on the other side of the room.

I dash across the floor, almost tripping over the sheet in my haste. Contrary to what I fear, the archway doesn't close when I reach it. It opens up into a spacious, rectangular cavern framed by ornate pillars. A polished, squarish stone that serves as a table and two circular, hollow stones with silver padding, which I imagine to be chairs, stand on one end. A few more of those "chairs" are scattered around, some placed next to smaller stone tables. On the other side, two carved statues of reclining men with weird bird heads and padded stomachs form daybeds. They face a huge, arched window that reaches all the way to the floor. It's one of those that you can step through, like French doors.

I rush over and peer out.

A gasp catches in my throat.

The drop is so sheer that it gives me vertigo. I inch back a step, stretching my neck for a better view.

Below, a slate-blue cliff plummets for miles before plunging into the black water of a foaming sea.

Damn.

Just my luck.

Scratch jumping out of the window.

The view is inarguably impressive, though. Curious, I test the latch on the window. To my surprise, it lifts. The window opens onto a narrow ledge with a rail carved from smooth, pinkish stone. A dinosaur sculpted from that same stone winds around the rail and between the balusters, creating an intricate trellis of claws and wings that acts as a safety barrier. Small children or pets wouldn't be able to slip through the bars.

I step out onto the ledge cautiously, gripping the rail with both hands.

A warm wind ruffles my hair. Smells of moss and forest undergrowth reach my nostrils, again reminding me of that trip to Costa Rica. But this time, it also stirs memories of the camping outing Mom and Dad organized to cheer me up after a particularly long spell of chemotherapy. In the end, what should've been an adventure turned into a vacation from hell. I puked my guts out the entire time. It didn't help that I woke up on the first morning with my face, arms, and legs covered in itchy insect bites, only to develop an allergic reaction to the repellent my well-meaning mom drenched me with.

I inhale the freshness of the air, appreciating it like I wish I could've on my one and only adventure that involved roasting marshmallows—which I was too sick to eat. Immediately, I start to feel better. It's like being hooked up to an oxygen tank. My lungs expand with the sweet air, infusing me with an unfamiliar vitality.

Wow, this is great.

For the first time in my recollection, I have so much energy that I feel capable of running a marathon.

I lean over the rail a little so I can survey the surroundings on the sides of the balcony.

Wow! I'm in a cave of sorts. Several more caves with narrow-ledged balconies are stacked like rooms in the rockface. They stretch to both ends of the cliff, forming an impressive collection of different-sized caverns. A waterfall that tumbles from the top of the cliff covers the biggest cavern that gapes in the center of the mountain, which is below me to my left.

A bridge runs from the waterfall to a cliff on the other side. A platform ringed with ropes acting as rails is suspended in the center. Steps carved into the cliff lead down to the sea. They blend in so perfectly with the rocky cliff that it's easy to miss them.

Where the cliff ends, ferns in vibrant greens grow along the water's edge. Trumpet-shaped red and purple flowers stick out from clusters of grass that cover the ground.

I lift my face, enjoying the warm wind on my cheeks. Shading my face with a hand against my forehead, I squint at the brightness of the pale blue heavens sprinkled with puffs of snowy clouds.

A black dot appears in the distance. I fix my gaze on the point that slowly grows bigger.

Amazing.

My sight is incredible. I can see so far and so clearly. I never truly realized how bad my eyesight was until now.

As the object gets closer, I make out wings that slice through the air.

That's one giant bird.

And then the bird comes into full view, and I almost tumble over the rail in shock.

A hair-raising cry splits the sky. The screeching creature flaps its wings and soars past the ledge, diving down toward the water before rising straight up again.

I pinch my eyes shut and open them slowly, but no, it's not an apparition.

It's a real-life quetzalcoatlus.

I watch, enraptured, as the most aggressive of all flying carnivores in history and the largest animal to ever fly makes another turn past the balcony.

Unbelievable.

I'm staring at a dinosaur that's long extinct back on Earth.

Well, technically, it's not a dinosaur but a flying reptile that's part of the pterosaur species.

I bet the guys at the Jurassic Park set in LA would give an arm and a leg to see this. If only I had my phone to take a video. I have to say, the movie makers' imitation of the warm-blooded reptile wasn't far off the mark.

The quetzalcoatlus moves in for another round. This time, it gets so close that the swooshing beat of its wings stirs a breeze through my hair, and I can make out a small nick on the tip of its left wing, likely a remnant of some fight.

A layer of downy, light-gray hair covers its body and leathery wings. The small crest on the back of its head is blue, while its wings are black and salmon pink. The tuft of black filaments adorning the crest quivers when the pterosaur goes into a tailspin.

For a reptile that's sixteen feet tall and weighs around five hundred pounds, it's astonishingly graceful in flight. With a wingspan of over fifty feet, it's the size of a Cessna airplane.

It stretches its giraffe-like neck as it makes another lunge through the air with its toothless jaw proudly thrust forward. I've never seen anything more awe-inspiring or riveting.

I'm bouncing on the balls of my feet, laughing with excitement as the big reptile circles a few inches from where I'm standing. Since childhood, I've been obsessed with dinosaurs and pterosaurs. Posters of every recorded species tiled my bedroom walls, and my bed was buried beneath a mountain of soft dinosaur toys. I named each of them. My favorite was Betty, the quetzalcoatlus that looked like a mutated stork.

Therefore, it's no surprise that I'm drawn to the prehistoric scavenger doing this strange dance in front of the balcony. It almost seems as if she's performing especially for me, like some kind of welcoming. What's odd is that I'm not scared in the least, even though I should be.

Clapping my hands in delight, I praise the quetzalcoatlus for the magnificent show.

"Good dragons," someone exclaims in a fearful voice behind me.

A woman grabs my arm and pulls me with a forceful tug back into the room. I stumble, grabbing the back of the nearest daybed to keep my balance.

When I've righted myself, I come face to face with the woman I saw earlier, the one who was sitting in a lotus position on the floor when Aruan brought me here and the same one who poured the milky liquid into the pool.

She lets me go and shuts the window with a firm click of the latch.

"Good, frightful dragons," she says again, turning on me with round, bewildered eyes. "You should never go near the window when the dragons are on the hunt. They'll pick you right off the balcony."

"Dragons? Are you kidding me?" I throw a thumb over my shoulder. "That's a quetzalcoatlus."

I know my stuff when it comes to dinosaurs.

Her forehead crumples into a frown. "A what?"

"On Earth, they lived between a hundred-and-forty-four and sixty-six million years ago," I continue with enthusiasm. "They're now extinct."

She cocks her head. "Our dragons are very much present. Although, the big ones like that don't come near the palace often. They prefer to stay away from the bustle of activity around the nearby village. It's rare for one to fly by that close, but there are incidents of people being snatched off the balconies. Seeing you there, nose to nose with the dragon, almost stopped my heart."

"Sorry," I say, feeling bad for scaring her.

At the same time, I'm elated. I can't get over what happened.

I sneak a peek at the window longingly, but beyond the pink-tinted glass panes, the sky is clear and quiet.

"Never mind." She makes a brave attempt at smiling. "We won't speak about this to my brother. He'll only get angry. Just don't do that again."

I have no intention of missing out on the experience if a freaking dinosaur flies past the window again.

My heart starts pumping as a thought hits me. "Are there other, um, dragons on land?"

"They're everywhere," she says vaguely, not seeming keen on the discussion. She blows out a shaky breath. "I'm Gaia, Aruan's sister." She adds with a smile, "We weren't properly introduced when you arrived."

"Elsie," I say, holding out my hand to shake hers

while making sure the sheet around my body stays in place.

She stares at my outstretched hand in amusement, not making a move to take it.

Maybe that's not how people greet each other on Zerra.

"Come," she says with an eloquent flick of her fingers.

At first, I think she's addressing me, but then a small army of men carrying loaded trays marches through the bedroom archway that has reappeared again.

While they offload dishes onto the big square stone, I use the opportunity to speak with Gaia. She seems more approachable than her brothers.

"There's been a mistake," I start carefully. "This is all wrong."

"Don't mind them," she says, waving a hand toward the men. "My brother insisted. They're here for your protection." She props a hand on her hip. "He obviously doesn't trust me, or anyone, with you—not that I blame him. We'll put up a screen so you don't have to see them. You won't even know they're here."

"Oh." I glance at the men. "I didn't mean them. There's been a huge misunderstanding." Smiling awkwardly, I continue, "Aruan seems to think I'm his mate."

Her expression remains serious. "You *are* his mate." Scrutinizing me, she asks, "Can't you feel it?"

"Feel what?"

"No matter." She takes my hand. "It'll come. Give it

time. Considering what you've been through, I suppose it's not surprising."

"He thinks I'm an Alit, but I'm from Earth." I pull my hand from hers. "Why doesn't anyone believe me?"

"Oh, you poor thing." Compassion softens her silver eyes. "Of course we believe you. The fact that you ended up on Earth is most unfortunate. But what was done can't be undone." Sadness infuses her tone. "For many years, Aruan believed you were dead. Most of us only feel the bond with our mates at adolescence, but your bond was so strong that Aruan felt it the day you were born." Tears glimmer in her eyes. "He was only five years old." Her voice turns bright again. "Look at me, getting all emotional." She blinks several times and swipes at the wetness on her cheek. "That was a long time ago. Now you're back, and that's what we must focus on."

I'm not untouched by her display of emotion, but her statement befuddles me. "Wait, what do you mean I'm back?"

She brushes my windblown hair from my forehead. "Everything must seem so confusing to you."

Yeah, no kidding. I have a million questions about this world and how it all works, but now isn't the time to indulge my curiosity. "I'm from Earth," I say insistently. "My parents are there. Don't you see? I have to go back to them."

She abandons trying to manipulate my hair into some kind of style and cups my cheek instead. "Your parents were Alit. They were from Marikanea, the kingdom in the east known for its endless oceans and cerulean skies. You were only a baby when you disappeared."

"No." I back away. "My parents are Irene and Jonas Barnikoff."

Her manner is strangely sympathetic. "They're not your biological parents, are they?"

"No, but—"

Holy shit.

This bizarre situation is starting to really freak me out.

Okay. So what if I was adopted? That doesn't mean she's right.

I lift my chin. "Where are these so-called parents? I demand a DNA test."

That should settle the argument once and for all. Unless... do they not have those here?

Gaia scrunches up her face. "A what?" She blows out another sigh. "Never mind. My dear Laliss—" She catches herself and corrects quickly, "Elsie, I'm so sorry to be the bearer of such tragic news, but your parents died in a volcano eruption that wiped out half of their capital. It happened not long after your... um, supposed fatal accident."

Ha.

Very convenient.

"I suppose you won't grieve them because you didn't know them," she says. "Still, I know it hurts."

Honestly, I'm not sure what the fuck to feel.

Gripping my shoulders, she ushers me toward the

table where dishes, goblets, and a carafe are set out. "Let's feed you, shall we? You'll feel better once you've eaten. Aruan went to great pains to locate the ingredients so that only the best of Zerran dishes could be prepared for you."

She nods at the men who stand at attention around the table. They're wearing the same white tunics and tall boots over charcoal-gray pants. Each man has a dagger strapped to his belt. It must be some kind of uniform.

At Gaia's signal, they go into the bedroom and disappear behind wooden dividers painted with flowers and scenery I recognize from outside. Someone must've placed the dividers there while Gaia and I were talking.

"Don't worry." Gaia moves behind me and pushes me down onto one of the padded chairs with her hands on my shoulders. "You can enjoy your meal in peace. They won't invade your privacy by watching you eat. They know if they do, Aruan will dissolve their eyeballs."

Ew. I hope she doesn't mean that literally.

She removes the woven basket covers from the stone platters one by one, releasing delicious aromas that waft into the space with ribbons of steam.

On cue, my stomach growls.

Now that I'm no longer permanently nauseated, my appetite is back with a vengeance. Those lizards—the Phaelix—fed me not so long ago. Or maybe it was days ago. I have no idea how long I've been out.

"How long have I been unconscious?" I ask.

"Just a few hours. It was necessary for you to recover." Gaia drops her gaze to the sheet that I tug awkwardly around myself. "My brother has already sent for clothes. We'll get you out of that bedsheet soon. But first, you must eat. Aruan was most adamant about that." Sitting down opposite me, she motions at the spread on the table. "You can try a bit of everything and tell me which dishes you prefer. Aruan will order those in the future and avoid the ones you don't like." She reaches over the table, picks up a small, forked spike, and hands it to me. "Use this. You don't want to burn your fingers."

I study the weird utensil before spearing a bright pink, juicy cube that looks like the meat of a fruit or vegetable. Chewing slowly, I enjoy the crunchy texture and sweetness that explodes on my tongue.

Yum.

It tastes like a cross between a strawberry and lychee.

The second cube I try, which is bright yellow, tastes like salty licorice.

I pull a face, at which Gaia giggles.

"That's *sagi*," she says. "It's a rare fruit that grows in the salty moors of the northern kingdom. By the look on your face, this one is definitely off the list." Pushing a dish with green, spongy stew toward me, she says, "Try this one. It's a local specialty."

I'm doubtful as I take a bite. The color and

consistency aren't promising, but I'm pleasantly surprised by the rich, meaty flavor.

"It's a stew made with the flowers and succulent leaves of water lilies." Gaia leans her elbow on the table and rests her chin on her palm. "They grow wild on the lakes, but it's difficult to harvest them because the dragons lay their eggs in that area. Men will risk their lives for a bag of pond lilies. That's why the flowers are worth their weight in black opal, the most precious stone on Zerra."

I eat a few more bites of the stew to show my gratitude for the expensive meal before trying a little of everything. My favorite dish is the paper-thin, butter-yellow flowers deep-fried in a thin batter, which Gaia tells me are *yitaki*.

When I assure her that I can't eat another bite, she pulls the carafe closer and pours a goblet full of golden liquid.

"It's honey wine." She hands it to me. "It will refresh you."

Feeling thirsty, I down the whole goblet in one go. The wine is quite sugary, so I refill my goblet with water from a terracotta jar and drink that too.

"Now for the important part," she says, clapping her hands as she stands.

"Wait." When she pauses to look at me, I continue quickly, "I was hoping you could tell me more about this place."

"About Zerra?"

"Yes." I nod vigorously. "And about how your

powers work. For example, how did your brother manage to heal me? Oh, hold on. You must have a power too, right? What's your power?"

"My specialty is creating portals."

I sit up straighter. That may be my ticket out of here. "Portals to Earth?"

"You're out of luck," she says, crushing my hope with a rueful smile. "That requires a much stronger power than mine. I can open and close portals repeatedly but not across worlds. That's how Aruan found you. The minute he sensed your presence on Zerra, he made me open portals until we discovered the right one."

"Oh." I sink back in my seat. "Who *can* open a portal to Earth?" Or is it done via a technology of some kind?

"I'm afraid your questions will have to wait. We'd better get started, or we'll be late."

"Late for what?"

Our exchange is interrupted when four women enter the bedroom with decorative boxes in their arms. The hems of their long gauzy dresses sweep their flat sandals. The one in the back of the line carries a shimmery gown that she lays out on the trunk while the others put the boxes on a rectangular slab of shiny black stone next to the part of the wall that shines like a mirror.

"Come." Gaia takes my hand and pulls me to my feet. "Let's make you pretty."

"For what?" I ask again, starting to feel a bit drowsy from all the food.

She guides me toward the boxes from which the women are retrieving decanters of oils, pots of creams, and gemstone-encrusted brushes. "For the banquet."

I hang back. I've just eaten enough food to last a whole winter's hibernation, and I want to go home, not to a banquet where more food will no doubt be served.

"What banquet?" I ask.

A smile lights up her face. "The one where Aruan will present you to the court before you take your vows."

"Vows?" I stammer. I'm wide awake now. "What vows?"

Continuing as if it's the most natural thing in the world, she says, "The vows you say before Aruan consummates the mating, of course."

CHAPTER 9
ELSIE

Despite my numerous protests, I'm massaged with nice-smelling oils and lathered with creams. Gaia shows me a primitive kind of toilet in the corner of the room with the pool, which she calls the cleansing room. The toilet is basically just a hole in a stone seat, but she explains that it magically empties itself once it's been used. When I ask her how that works, she tells me it's due to the properties of the stones.

The vague explanation only makes me more curious. Do the stones absorb the waste? Are there some microorganisms living in that hole that feed on the waste and thus dissolve it? When I ask, Gaia doesn't seem to know. Instead, she shows me how to clean up afterward using a small water fountain that seems to be perpetually running inside another stone seat—a bidet of sorts that they apparently use in lieu of toilet paper.

After the tour, she gives me privacy. Once I've taken care of my needs, I wash my hands in a bowl filled with water from a jug. The soap is a gel capsule that dissolves on my palm and smells like heaven. The minute I've dried my hands on a cloth from a stack on the shelf, two women enter with brushes and start to scrub everything clean. Then the pampering continues.

With so many women buzzing around me, I'm dressed in a long, flowing gown with my hair and make-up done in no time at all.

Gaia positions me in front of the mirror.

"You look beautiful," she exclaims in a breathless whisper, clasping her hands together.

The woman staring back at me in the shadowy reflection of the mirror is a far cry from the old me back on Earth. The permanent dark circles around my eyes are gone. My skin has a healthy glow, and my short hair shines with a brilliance that accentuates the natural platinum highlights in my strawberry-blond strands. Even my eyes, which I've always considered to be a dull blue-green, sparkle with a new luminosity.

It's so bizarre. I don't understand why I look so healthy and why my heart is beating so strongly. Did Vitai heal all my autoimmune issues? But no. Even back in the jungle with the Phaelix, I looked and felt different.

Not sick.

Not weak.

Not dying for once in my life.

What *is* this place? How do these people have these powers?

And why the fuck did they decide I'm Aruan's mate?

"What do you think?" Gaia asks, sounding pleased with herself.

I push aside my speculations for now and refocus on my appearance. The dress is made of a soft material with a pearly glimmer. It fastens at my nape and drapes with soft folds over my breasts and hips before flaring out from my thighs. The hem stops just above my ankles. The back is open, not allowing for any sort of bra—if they even wear them here. Fortunately, with my small breasts, I don't need one. The skirt is embroidered with shiny white stones, which may or may not be diamonds. Begrudgingly, I have to admit that the gown is gorgeous. I've never looked prettier.

"Shoes," Gaia announces with a clap of her hands.

One of the women rushes forward with a pair of satiny slippers. The crystal beads decorating them match the stones on the dress. She kneels in front of me while another woman takes my arm to steady me and a third carefully lifts my skirt.

I shove my feet into the flat-heeled, pointy shoes. To my surprise, they're very comfortable, not pinching my toes as I expected.

Gaia takes a small flacon from the dresser and sprays a fine mist of perfume over my hair. It smells powdery soft, almost like roses, with something exotic like ylang-ylang in the mix.

"It's a very precious and rare perfume made from

the petals of dragon flower blossoms," Gaia says as she points the atomizer at my barely-there cleavage. "They only bloom once a century under a full moon."

Puff.

"A drop is worth a hundred opal stones."

Puff, puff.

She winks before giving my neck the same treatment. "Aruan loves the smell."

I suppress a protest. Objecting to the dollying-up isn't going to help. I argued until my throat was hoarse, and it got me nowhere.

To them, it may seem as if I've accepted my fate, which is to take vows I don't mean and *consummate* some bizarre mating.

Ha.

That's not going to happen.

I'm just biding my time. My docility is all for show. Sooner rather than later, an opportunity to escape will present itself. If I'm going to a banquet, they have to take me out of this room. I'll grab my chance then. I have no idea where I'm going to go in this strange place, but I'll escape first and figure it out later.

Someone around here has to know how to open a portal back to Earth, right?

The flurry of activity comes to an abrupt halt. The women freeze.

I lift my head to see what's going on, and then an uninvited and very unwelcome shiver runs through me.

Aruan stands in the doorway, his large frame

blocking out the light that reflects from the walls in the hallway. With all those muscles packed onto his body, he looks imposing and lethal. He's changed into a black jacket with silver and red embroidery around the collar and cuffs. Knee-high boots polished to a shine are fitted over his pants. His long dark hair is tied back, exposing his angular face and drawing attention to the masculine lines of his square jaw, aristocratic nose, and broad forehead. There's no arguing that he's strikingly handsome. He stands there like a king, rendering people silent with his mere presence.

Our gazes lock in the reflection of the mirror. His piercing stare is too intense for my liking.

My heartbeat picks up, and heat rushes through my veins. It's like stepping from a snowy winter's day into a cozy sauna. I can't control it.

Gaia says something, but her words are white noise in my ears. I'm vaguely aware of the guards and women leaving the room. The air is trapped in my lungs as Aruan and I continue our stare off, yet it's impossible to look away from his foreboding gaze.

Gaia slips a tiara with sparkling stones into my hair. "Everything will be all right. You'll see." She mouths, "Good luck," and then she's gone.

Silence stretches as Aruan and I are locked in an invisible vise. What I read in his eyes frightens me. They're filled with the carnal hunger of a starving predator—and the determination to satiate that hunger.

It's more than a little unsettling that I can read his

intentions so well. Even more concerning are the responding zaps of awareness that sizzle under my skin, which I do my best to ignore. Although it's difficult to do so when, under the dress, my naked lady parts are wet, and my nipples are so hard they poke through the thin fabric. It really doesn't help that underwear was apparently never invented here.

A knowing smile plucks at Aruan's lips as he studies me. I swear he knows exactly what's going through my mind. He can't be blind to the effect he has on me. We have a weird capacity to communicate without words.

Finally, he breaks the spell by stepping deeper into the room. The archway closes behind him.

I gulp.

I don't like being locked in here with him alone.

My breathing grows shallow. He's like a huge, all-consuming vacuum that sucks up all the oxygen in the room.

He advances slowly and stops so close to me that the buttons of his jacket sweep my lower back. I resist the urge to step away. I hate being a coward.

"You look beautiful, Elsie," he says in a voice so deep that goosebumps ripple over my skin.

However light the contact, it's disturbing as hell.

Forget about acting brave and saving face. I turn around, creating a measure of distance between us, and crane my neck to look up at him. "Gaia said something about vows. Please tell me it's a joke."

"Alas," he says with a sharp, disapproving smile. "Saying one's vows is never a joke."

"What does that even mean?" The proverbial noose around my neck tightens. "Is it like marriage or something?"

"Marriage?" He tilts his head, his eyes narrowing with perceptive curiosity. "I'm not familiar with that custom."

"It's when two people decide to live together and have a family. They give each other rings and promise to be faithful. They sign a contract that's legally binding. Often, things go wrong, and then they divorce." When he frowns, I elaborate, "They leave each other. In fact, it happens to one out of two couples, and it can get really messy. If that's what you're planning with this whole saying-our-vows-thing, I can assure you that we'll end up as the one-out-of-two statistic. Surely, that's not what you want." I add uncertainly, "Right?"

He watches me solemnly. "On Zerra, each person has one mate only. When we mate, it's for life."

"For life?" I shriek. "Like penguins and seahorses?"

"I don't know your seahorses and penguins, but here, even our dragons mate for life."

Okay, I admit a world with failproof relationships sounds kind of amazing, but not if the relationship is unwanted or forced. He can't mean that's what he wants. For life. With me. Can he?

He only continues to stare at me with an unfaltering silver gaze.

Shit.

He does mean it.

I break out in a cold sweat. Through dry lips, I ask, "Are you for real?"

"Claiming one's mate is an occasion of great joy. Without a mate, a person is incomplete."

If that's what he believes, I'm truly fucked.

Literally. Maybe.

"What does this whole consummation ritual entail?" I ask with my heart beating in my throat.

The color of his eyes darkens to quicksilver. I swear he could melt metal with that flaming-hot stare.

"We'll bond physically," he announces in an even tone.

"We have to sleep together?" I croak out.

"Eventually, yes." No longer limiting his exploration to my face, he takes full advantage of sizing up my body. "After we've fucked."

Oh, crap.

I sway a little, suddenly dizzy.

I think I may swoon—in a bad way.

Double crap.

In a good way too.

The swooning has a distinct note of anticipation.

I've always wanted to know what sex was like, but a roll between the sheets wasn't in the cards for me. My medical conditions required every bit of my energy just to survive. I hardly had an appetite for food, let alone for sexcapades.

In my wildest fantasies, I dreamed about doing it backstage with the bad boy drummer of a rock band. He had a floppy fringe that fell over blue, tormented eyes and a self-assured smile with a slight hint of a smirk that said he could kiss—*really* kiss—and he knew it.

Losing my V-card to a dangerous man with superpowers who claims to be my mate has never entered my sex fantasies.

Now *that* is scary.

And annoyingly hot.

But no.

Getting jumped against a wall in the smoky shadows of a stage with no strings attached is one thing. Being bound to a man who demands vows on the first date is a whole different ballgame.

"And then?" I ask in my best bartering voice. "If I agree to fuck you, will you let me go?"

Ferocious anger flashes across his features. It doesn't replace the scorching hunger of earlier but rather adds to it, making a dangerous cocktail of simmering emotions.

With a gruff edge to his voice, he delivers the verdict. "Never."

Oookay. See? That's what I was worried about.

I retreat, forgetting about the mirror behind me until my back collides with the smooth, cool surface. "I'm flattered that you believe that's what you want, but that's not what I want."

"What we want is inconsequential. The physical call of a mate's bond is impossible to resist."

"Then it's lucky for me that we're not mates."

"The longer we wait, the harder it'll be on both of us."

"I don't even know how I got here or what I'm doing here," I say in exasperation. "One minute, I saw a circle of lights, and the next, I was in a jungle with the lizard dudes—I mean, the Phaelix."

At the mention of the Phaelix, Aruan's eyes gleam with undisguised violence. "They brought you here via a portal and then tried to hurt you. They got what they deserved."

Being melted alive? Yeah, okay. I guess empathy and remorse aren't high on my so-called mate's list of traits. Though I don't exactly disagree with him after what those monsters almost did to me by the river.

"Why did they bring me here?" I ask, shaking off the awful memory. "Was it really to sell me as a slave?"

It seems so primitive and unnecessary for beings that can open portals between worlds. Then again, the Phaelix seem to live in the jungle amid giant caterpillars, so they don't come across as all that advanced. Neither do my current humanoid captors, come to think of it. I'm getting distinct Middle Ages vibes here… crazy powers excluded.

The brutality in Aruan's gaze grows to epic proportions. "Probably. There've been rumors of Earth slaves among the Phaelix."

How lovely. "The people on the barge… What's going to happen to them?"

"I told them they were free to go."

"Go where? If they're from Earth…" I trail off, staring at him expectantly.

Maybe there's a station or something where a portal to Earth is always open. Or where someone is available to open one.

If so, that's where I'm hoofing it as soon as I get out of here.

He shrugs, like he doesn't know or care.

I grit my teeth. "Could *you* have sent them back?" Does *he* have the technology?

He shakes his head. "Not just anyone can create a portal to Earth. It requires a particular, very strong power."

A power, not a technology then. "And that's not your power," I say, making a calculated guess.

"No," he says, looking grim for some reason.

"Do you know someone with that power?" I persist. "So those people can be sent back to Earth?"

And so I can go with them, far away from all this craziness.

He shrugs again, infuriatingly. "Once we're mated, we can talk more. Now, let's go." He takes my hand. "We have a banquet to attend."

A banquet where we'll be tied together for life? No, thanks. Hanging back, I say, "Gaia said my biological parents were from a different kingdom in Zerra. You have to admit it sounds farfetched. There's no way I'm an Alit and your mate. I mean—"

"Gaia is right," he says without missing a beat. "I was told you died in an accident." His expression darkens. He doesn't even try to hide the savage anger that burns in his gaze. "As it turns out, someone sent you to Earth when you were just a baby, so you're indeed an Alit and my mate. It's all very logical, my sweet." His voice drops an octave. "When I have proof of who sent you there, the guilty party will pay."

Uh-huh. I picture the Phaelix melting away and suppress a shudder. Also, his so-called logic has zero evidence behind it. Either way... "Let's say what you say is true and I was sent to Earth as a baby. We still don't know each other. This isn't my world. Don't you see? I don't belong here."

"Your place is at my side, Laliss," he says in a measured tone, gripping my hand in a firm hold. "And in my bed."

I yank my hand from his. "You're not listening to me. I'm Elsie, not Laliss, and I'm *not* sleeping with you, tonight or ever."

The line of his jaw hardens. "It's going to happen. It's inevitable."

"Don't you get it?" I glare at him. "I'm sure you're used to having women at your feet with a flick of your fingers, but *I don't want you.*"

As I speak, a deep unease twists inside me, just like when I lie to deceive my parents into thinking that I'm fine.

An unfriendly smile curves his lips. "Careful. My patience has limits, even with my mate." Something that seems a lot like retribution gleams with a dark promise in his eyes. "When the time comes, your body will overrule your mind. You will succumb to my advances whether you want to or not." His look is calculated. "But don't worry, my sweet, I'll make sure you enjoy every moment."

I feel like hitting him over the head with one of the heavy boxes the women left behind. My dark fantasy hasn't reached its conclusion yet—where he lies unconscious on the floor—before he encircles my arm with his strong fingers and gently but firmly pulls me toward the exit.

"Come," he says. "Our guests are already gathered in the banquet hall, and I've waited a very long time for this."

I stumble next to him, struggling to keep up with his long strides as he guides me through a broad hallway and down a spiral staircase. At the bottom, we walk through a narrower hallway lit by those strange lights that seem to come from within the stones. The light flares up around us and dies down again as we advance, not only effectively lighting our way but also making it seem as if the walls are pulsing with an inner life.

At a double wooden door, we stop. Aruan pushes it open with one hand while grasping my arm securely in the other.

The thick doors swing outward to reveal a large, vaulted hall brimming with people. Long tables and benches run along the length of the room. There's not an empty place at the tables. Women in long, gorgeous gowns and men in tunics are squeezed in so tightly that their elbows are touching.

The chatter dies down. All eyes turn toward us.

In the silence that follows, Aruan leads me into the room. The men who guarded me in his quarters are stationed on either side of the steps leading down into the hall. A few more filter in behind us while four men line up in front us. We're surrounded by guards on all sides. Aruan must be a prominent figure if he takes security this seriously.

I swallow hard as he ushers me down the stairs. The people in the hall follow our every move with their gazes.

At the end of the hall, a table set with silver and crystalware stands on a raised platform. The man at the head of the table watches us with hawk-like scrutiny as we make our way down the aisle that separates the crammed benches. Like Kian, Vitai, and Gaia, he has hair the color of molasses and eyes like the silver water of a frosty lake. The resemblance between him and Aruan is uncanny, but his face is rougher and more angular. The harsh lines of his features are carved deeply on his face. His expression is mostly neutral but not enough to hide the hint of hostility shining through the stern intensity of the stare he directs at me. His black coat is embroidered in red and silver like Aruan's. Judging by the silver wreath in the shape of a dragon with polished black stones for eyes that rests like a crown on his head, he's the leader of this clan.

On the other end of the table sits a beautiful woman

with hair so black it shines blue in the light of the myriad stones glowing on the tables. Her eyes are a light shade of gray, a striking contrast to her dark hair. Unlike the rest of the party at the table, who all sport deep golden skin tones, hers is pale. She wears a white dress with lace cuffs. The crown on her head is almost an exact replica of the man's, except that hers is more delicate.

Gaia, Kian, and Vitai are seated between them. They're twisted in their seats, watching our slow march across the hall. Two men, one blond and the other with mousy brown hair, sit opposite them.

If Vitai is a kind of a healer, maybe he knows what was done to my body that makes me no longer feel like I'm dying. I'll ask him as soon as I get a chance.

A murmur breaks out in the crowd. Whispers run like a spark catching fire through the people. Their words don't reach my ears, but shock and anguish are clear in the low hiss of voices.

Ignoring the attention, Aruan brings me to the platform and guides me up the steps. We round the table under the curious stares of the spectators and stop behind two empty chairs facing the masses. Like the chairs in his room, these are circular stones too, resembling hollow nests padded with soft, silver cushions.

"Praise to the King of Lona," Aruan says. "Peace to the Queen of the Nation."

The people at the long tables stomp their feet once, making me jump.

"Loyal royals and citizens of Lona," Aruan continues, "I present to you…" Turning to me, he says with fierceness and pride burning in his eyes, "My mate."

A roar rises from below.

"May her name be uttered with reverence and devotion for all eternity." He wraps his big hand around mine where he clasps it on his arm and lifts it into the air. "Laliss!"

"Laliss!" the crowd shouts as one.

I blame my brain's inability to form words on the stupefying experience of being dumped into a hall full of people who are staring at me as if I'm the most frightful creature they've seen. Yet even as their fearful faces are turned toward me, they chant that unfamiliar name like a horde of groupies at a rock concert.

I'm the one who should be petrified.

Hell, I *am* petrified.

It's a little unnerving to be the source of so much terror. Also, I'd be lying if I say it doesn't stroke my ego a little. It's like turning up at a Halloween party in the best costume. All my life, I've mostly been pitied. Being feared isn't my number one choice of an elicited reaction, but I'll take scary Elsie over pitied Elsie any day, even though they're not calling me Elsie.

When we finally sit down, I lean toward Aruan and whisper, "Why do they look so frightened? Have they never seen someone from Earth?"

He looks at me as if he'd like to eat me. Alive. "They

fear you because you're my mate, but for the same reason, they'll love you."

Here we go again. "Aruan, what must I do to convince—"

Abruptly, he pulls me to my feet again.

A line of servers enters with steaming platters that they place on the tables. Some carry big terracotta jugs and goblets. Others present trays of strangely shaped, brightly colored fruit.

Dragging me with him, Aruan makes his way to the head of the table.

"Father," he says with a bow of his head. "It's my honor to present Laliss, my mate."

"Elsie," I say. "And I'm not his mate."

Both ignore my protest. I size up the man, who, in turn, is studying me from his thronelike chair. If he's a king, that makes Aruan a prince.

Holy macaroni.

I've always wanted to meet a royal family, but I was thinking more along the lines of scones and tea at Windsor Castle or champagne and oysters on a yacht in Monaco. Something straight from a medieval fairy tale in a different world has never entered my mind.

The king studies me with the same keen interest as before. He hardly makes a secret of his quiet disdain.

"Welcome to Lona, *Elsie*," he says with a slight narrowing of his gaze. "I hope that everything is to your liking."

Before I can answer, Aruan pulls me to the other

end of the table. When he stops in front of the queen, a palpable tension falls over the royal family.

The queen rises from her chair in a graceful movement. Her face is unlined, her skin as smooth as porcelain. She doesn't look a day older than Gaia. Like Aruan, there's a certain quality about her that demands attention. Everyone's focus is fixed on her. It's almost as if the guests are holding their breath while waiting for her next move.

Her smile is serene. "Welcome to your new home." She reaches for my hand, but Aruan yanks me away, startling both his mother and me as he places himself like a wall between us.

She lowers her arm to her side with a sad little smile. "If you need anything—"

"Her needs are my concern," Aruan says in a harsh voice.

From the center of the table, Gaia lowers her eyes. Vitai looks sympathetic, and Kian is difficult to read. Their father observes us, perched like a falcon on the edge of his seat.

The queen sits down with a wounded air, but her back remains stiff and proud.

Aruan takes my elbow and guides me back to my chair. Once he's seated me, servers approach with platters that they set down in the center of the table. One of the dishes resembles a roasted bird, but the rest is anyone's guess.

Gaia must see the apprehension on my face because she leans forward and whispers, "You only have to pick at your food and pretend to eat. Aruan knew you'd probably be too nervous to enjoy the meal. That's why he made sure you ate well earlier."

I offer her a weak smile. How the fuck am I going to get myself out of here? The guards have formed a circle around our table. Worse, more guards entered during the introductions and are now standing at attention along the walls.

Can I leave the hall with the excuse of needing a bathroom break? Will they let me go alone? Probably not, but I have to try.

Aruan seats himself on my left. There's enough space at the main table. We're not crowded like the people below, but when he spreads out his powerful legs, his thigh brushes against mine.

A jolt of electricity runs up my leg. My stomach clenches, and a feverish heat warms my skin. I slam my knees together, breaking the unsettling contact.

A flash of knowledge passes through his eyes as he turns his face toward me, but then the blond man on my right says, "Hello, Elsie. I'm Suno, Aruan's cousin."

I look at him. He has green, friendly eyes and a lively smile.

"Pleased to meet you," I say automatically.

"I hear you're from Earth," he says through the side of his mouth.

The words are obviously meant for my ears only.

"How extraordinary." His eyes sparkle. "Someday, I'd like to hear about your life in that world." He's quick to add, "If you'll indulge me, of course."

"Um, sure," I say even though I have no intention of staying on this weird planet that long.

A pretty girl with a blond ponytail comes forward, carrying a crystal carafe with translucent purple liquid. She's walking as if on a tightrope, careful not to spill a drop.

When she reaches Aruan's side, he says something I can't hear over the loud chatter that has taken over the room. Now that the food has been served, everyone is helping themselves to the dishes while staring at our table with perverse curiosity.

"Hello," the man sitting next to Suno says.

I turn my face his way. It's the man with the mousy hair. He has homely features with bushy eyebrows and brown eyes. Of everyone at the main table, he's the least striking in appearance.

He leans over Suno and holds out his wrist. "I'm Tarix, Aruan's cousin on the queen's side."

I look at his wrist, expecting a tribal tattoo or something that depicts his heritage, but only pale skin shows from under his sleeve.

Tarix frowns. "It's polite to return a greeting, unless you consider the person an enemy."

Huh?

I glance at Aruan, but he's preoccupied with pouring the purple liquid from the carafe into my goblet.

Gaia comes to my rescue. "Here in Lona, the formal greeting is done like this." She stretches her arm over the table and presses her wrist against Tarix's. "It's a sign of amiability and hospitality."

"Oh." Following her example, I do the same. Now I understand why she reacted so strangely when I wanted to shake her hand. "On Earth, we do it like this." I hold out my hand to show them.

Gaia's eyes grow round. She gives a quick shake of her head while glancing around the table. "We don't talk about Earth here. It's a forbidden subject."

"But Suno just said—"

Suno shoves a plate toward me full of greenish balls covered in a yellow sauce with blue speckles. "You should try the *egox*. The roots were dug out only this morning. They're still fresh."

Right. He doesn't want Gaia to know he proposed discussing a forbidden subject with me.

My stomach roils as I take in the rubbery balls drifting in the gel-like liquid. "I'm not hungry, but thanks anyway."

He opens his mouth as if to argue, but just at that moment, a dark shadow flies through the hall.

Startled, I turn my attention that way, expecting a bird or a bat, and then my jaw drops.

An anurognathus dives low over a table before grabbing a bite of food from a man's plate. The man swats at the tiny pterosaur, which is only three and a half inches long, but it's already landing on a beam in the high ceiling to rip its prize apart.

I can't believe my eyes.

First a quetzalcoatlus and now an anurognathus.

How many types of dinosaurs exist on Zerra?

I watch, mesmerized, as the anurognathus swallows its loot. Looking like a cross between a bat and a mouse with cat-like whiskers, it's the cutest creature I've seen. Pip is the perfect name for it.

The anurognathus looks this way and that, no doubt identifying its next steal. For a moment, as it turns its beady black eyes my way, I'm convinced it's staring right at me.

An ecstatic gasp escapes my lips. I don't know how I know it, but I'm certain it's a male. All I want to do is cuddle him, which is probably a very bad idea. I bet he'd find my fingers tasty.

"Don't mind the pixie dragons," Tarix says, waving at the anurognathus. "They're a nuisance, but they don't do harm. They fly through the open archways into the kitchen and dining hall to nick tidbits of meat. We allow them in the palace because they hunt the pesky sand snakes that like to crawl into beds or beneath piles of linen in search of heat."

I shudder. If I spend the night here, I'll need to check the sheets before getting into bed. And it won't be Aruan's bed, no matter what he says or how irresistible he is.

The thought of Aruan's bed alone sends another quiver down my spine, and the sensation isn't completely unpleasant.

The subject of my thoughts pushes to his feet, towering over the table and the hall with his goblet in his hand.

The people grow quiet. Only the screech of the anurognathus cuts through the space as he spreads his wings, pushes off the beam, and makes another circle through the air.

Next, the king and queen stand, each with a goblet in their hands. While the content of Aruan's and my goblets is purple, the liquid in theirs is the golden color of the honey wine Gaia made me drink earlier.

"A toast to Aruan and Elsie," the king says, his voice carrying across the room. "May their mating be rich with offspring and stretch across many prosperous decades. Let it be known that the royals and citizens of Lona bore witness to their vows."

The people stomp their feet once.

The king and queen take a sip of their drinks while Aruan downs everything in his goblet in one go. When Aruan and his parents have taken their seats again, he puts his empty goblet aside and picks up mine.

I look around in distress. "Is this the part where we say the vows?"

"It's been done," Aruan says.

"When?" I exclaim. "Did I miss something?"

"The king has spoken. I drank." He gives me a dark smile. "Now it's your turn."

"That's it?" I ask, my mouth suddenly dry. "I drink, and then I've taken my vows?"

"When you drink the toast, you vow to be a worthy and loyal mate."

I purse my lips. "I will do nothing of the kind."

Gaia drags in a sharp breath. "Elsie." She reaches

over and touches my hand. "The infusion is made from the petals of moon flowers. It's very precious and rare. Only future kings and queens get to taste it on the occasion of declaring their intention to mate. To drink this nectar is an honor and an unparalleled privilege. It's a powerful aphrodisiac, so it will make your first night all the more memorable. You should drink the infusion. It will make you see everything differently."

An aphrodisiac. And Aruan just downed a whole goblet full of the juice.

Oh, shit.

My heartbeat quickens for all kinds of reasons. First and foremost, there's fear, and then there's indignation.

I did *not* agree to this.

But I can't deny the insistent ache that pulses between my thighs as a mental image of a naked and aroused Aruan jumps into my mind.

"Rejecting the toast will be a terrible humiliation for Aruan," Gaia whispers with worry.

I don't want to humiliate a prince in front of his people... per se, but he forced me into this situation when I repeatedly told him I don't belong here. Being bullied into something I don't want to do really makes me mad.

Facing Aruan squarely, I offer him nothing but stubborn silence.

His gaze narrows a fraction. I give a start when he cups the back of my head in his big paw and drags me closer, so close, in fact, that I can smell the spicy, maddeningly swoony scent of his skin.

My throat closes up at his nearness. Compared to his strong, tall frame, I'm an elf. He could squash me like a bug, and it wouldn't take him much effort.

"You will drink, my sweet," he says in a measured tone. "We will make this toast even if I have to drink on your behalf and feed you from my mouth."

My pulse jumps at the threat. The idea of drinking from his mouth has me simultaneously fuming and excited. The excitement is unwanted but nevertheless undeniably present.

I definitely don't want that.

I don't want him to kiss me.

Especially not in front of a hall full of people.

Especially not when my hormones are going haywire at the thought of his lips on mine.

What I need to do is work on an escape plan—say, that bathroom break—and not submit to the crazy impulse to climb onto his lap and lick the juice from his lips.

"It's going to happen," he says, reminding me of his earlier promise. "It'll be easier if you don't fight it."

Holding me firmly in place, he lifts the goblet to my lips.

Crap.

If I'm this horny now, how am I going to behave after downing an alien aphrodisiac?

"Wait." I strain in his hold. "What's going to happen, you know…" I clear my throat. "If I drink this?"

Heat dances in his silver eyes. "Nothing that won't happen anyway. The drink will just help to relax you."

"I don't want to relax," I say, but my words fall on deaf ears.

Balancing the goblet in his hand, he pulls my bottom lip down with his thumb while watching the action with a ravenous, calculated expression. "Are you going to open for me, my sweet, or do you prefer that I open your lips for you? Rest assured, it's a task I'll enjoy very much." He lowers his voice, making sure no one else hears what he says. "Just know this, once I have my tongue in your mouth, you'll beg me to bring the consummation to completion."

Shit.

My heartbeat is all over the place now. I'm furious, frustrated, and turned on. It looks as if I don't have a choice. I'd rather swallow those green balls—which is what I imagine Phaelix testicles look like—than kiss Aruan. Because kissing him is going to fuck with my hormones. I know it.

"Aruan," I start with a plea in my voice, hoping to tap into his compassion.

He presses the goblet against my lips. "Drink, Laliss, so that we can get this over and done with."

"How many times must I tell you I'm not Laliss?" I whisper-exclaim in unsuppressed anger.

"Fine. Drink, *Elsie*. The sooner you drink, the sooner we can move on to the more pleasurable part of the evening."

I look around the room in search of an ally, but everyone is staring at us with fascinated expectation. From the way Gaia's chest isn't moving, I can tell she's holding her breath. The queen clasps her goblet in a bloodless grip. The king is watching me with morbid interest.

"Drink, little one," Tarix urges in a low voice. "It won't be so bad."

I don't know if by "it," he means sex with Aruan or being mated for life to a man from a different world whom I only met a few hours ago. I don't even have answers about this place or these people yet.

Aruan's command holds a challenge. "Do *not* defy me in front of my people. I'm warning you, mate. I will have my way. The only difference is that you still have a chance to accept my offering with grace. Do you really want all the royals and our most esteemed citizens to watch me force-feed you?"

Resentment beats with a wild rhythm in my chest. Underneath the table, I clench my hands into fists.

Okay. Aruan wins this round. Not the sex part. Just the drinking bit. But the fight is far from over.

Ever so slowly, I part my lips. Apprehension is a stone in my stomach. Approval washes over Aruan's stunning features. His smile is encouraging but also a little victorious as he tilts the goblet to feed me the first sip.

Just as the liquid is about to touch my lips, Pip the anurognathus plunges through the air and knocks the goblet from Aruan's hand.

Tepid, fizzling liquid spills down the front of my dress. The goblet falls to the floor with the unmistakable sound of glass breaking.

I look down in shocked surprise as a bright purple stain blooms over the fabric that covers my breasts.

Aruan is on his feet in a second, his furious gaze trained on Pip, who escapes through an open archway that acts as a window.

"Oh, dear," the queen says, jumping up.

Aruan grabs a napkin from the table. "Here."

Taking my hand, he helps me to stand before dabbing at the spillage on my dress.

"It's nothing," I say, both elated and scared.

As relieved as I am not to have to drink this, I don't want Pip to be in trouble.

"I'll kill that pixie," Aruan says through clenched teeth.

My heartbeat spikes. "Please don't! It was just an accident."

A scurrying noise on the floor draws my gaze.

A lizard with spikes on its back—a tuatara, if I'm not mistaken—is greedily lapping up the puddle of nectar that lies at my feet.

I can't help but smile at the prehistoric cuteness. "Aww."

Aruan pushes it away with the toe of his boot. "These pets don't belong under the table."

"Sorry," Gaia says, appearing guilty. "But in my defense, everyone lets them lick up crumbs."

The king gives her a stern look. "You mean you like to feed it treats from your plate when you think we're not looking."

"Aruan," the queen says, her voice calm despite the

concern painted over her face. "Allow me to take your mate to my quarters and help her get changed."

"You?" he says with scorn.

The table starts shaking, jostling the cutlery and crockery.

Everyone leaps from their seats.

Kian rounds the table and places himself in front of the queen. "It's better if Gaia assists Laliss—if Gaia assists *Elsie*, Mother. You're needed here. You're the only one who can order another carafe for the toast."

"But it will take hours to infuse," the queen says. "The batch the pixie spilled had brewed since this morning."

"I told you to have those insolent pixies chased out of the palace," the king grumbles. "I'd rather chase off a snake than one of those sly little vultures."

"Oh, Elsie," Gaia says, coming toward me. "I'm so sorry this happened."

"I'm fine." I rub at the stain on my dress. "It's just a little wetness."

"No, it's not," Vitai says, pointing at the floor.

We all look in that direction. The tuatara lies on its back, keeled over, its long tongue hanging from its mouth to the floor.

I bend down. "Oh, no." What's the matter with it?

I reach out to touch it, not sure what I can do to help, but Aruan locks his fingers around my bicep and jerks me away so viciously I almost get whiplash.

"Poison," Kian announces gravely.

The look of rage that comes over Aruan's face is

scary, but it's nothing compared to the crack that appears in the thick stone wall at the front, running from the top right down to the bottom.

Screams and exclamations of terror rise from the audience.

Before I have time to process what's happening, Aruan scoops me up into his arms and carries me swiftly to the exit.

Shocked whispers reach my ears as he makes his way with long strides along the aisle, and there's one sentence I make out:

"Someone tried to poison Aruan's mate."

CHAPTER 10
ARUAN

My only thought is to protect my mate.

Someone tried to kill her.

Fury wells up inside me, but I push it down because her dress is drenched in the poison. I need to get that off her skin.

I growl an instruction to the guards who stand on either side of the doors to the Great Hall as I fly across the threshold with Elsie in my arms. "Keep the guests locked inside."

Every person will be questioned. I will find the bastard who tried to assassinate her. Poison has been used to eliminate rivals for as long as Zerra has existed. It's the weapon of cowards and corrupt people who lack honor and pride.

"Aruan," Elsie says, pushing on my chest. Her blue-green eyes are wide with alarm. "You drank it. You drank a whole goblet full of it."

Her concern for my welfare warms my chest. If

urgent measures weren't required, I'd bask in her care, but I have to make sure she's safe.

"Aruan," she repeats, sounding close to hysterical. "Are you listening to me? You need to put me down. Call Vitai. He can fix this, right?"

Not even Vitai can fully reverse the effect of a powerful poison. Once it's been ingested, it quickly devours flesh and blood, too fast for a healer to intervene before the onset of death.

I don't have time to explain, but the need to reassure my mate demands that I set her worry at ease.

My reply is gruff. "If there'd been poison in my goblet, I'd be dead already."

A gasp falls from her lips, and a dragon can maul to me a pulp if I don't feel her fear as if it were my own.

The minute I'm outside the hall, I lower Elsie to her feet. I don't pause to think. I act fast, gripping the neckline of her dress and ripping the garment down the middle. I'm deaf to her shriek as the fabric pools around her ankles and she stands there naked.

My body reacts to hers naturally. Even in such dire circumstances, I get hard at the sight of her pale skin and small, perky breasts. The aphrodisiac rushes through my blood, amplifying everything until I'm about to combust, but those are only physical needs. They won't dictate my actions or influence my decisions as long as Elsie's life is in danger.

Locking my hands around her tiny waist, I drag her closer. She utters a yelp and tries to push me away, but she's no match for my strength.

I study her breasts. They're not wet from the juice. To be sure, I lean in and sniff her skin.

"Hey," she cries out. "What are you doing?"

The only smell that clings to her is the intoxicating fragrance of dragon flower blossoms. There's no trace of the cloyingly sweet scent of poison.

Beating her fists on my shoulders, she shouts, "Let go!"

"Keep still," I say with warning.

Whatever she hears in my voice, which sounds more animalistic than human, makes her obey.

Good girl.

I keep my hands fastened around her middle in case she gets it into her head to defy me again. My mate is obstinate. It's a characteristic I'm quickly getting to know.

Lifting her by the hips, I set her aside so that no part of her body touches the dress.

"Do not move," I repeat. "Disobey me, and there will be consequences."

Her throat ripples as she swallows.

I kneel down and pick up the dress between a forefinger and thumb. The inner layer is dry. The thin cloth that lines the dress is impermeable. We use it for protective clothing but also to soften the roughness of the shiny outer fabric that includes hair-thin threads of spun silver.

I'm grateful for the meticulous specifications I gave when ordering the dress. At least none of the toxic substance came into contact with her skin. If that cursed pixie dragon had knocked the goblet out of my hand a second later, things would've worked out very differently.

A shudder runs through me at the thought.

That vulturous little dragon saved her. As for me, I almost forced her to drink. I nearly sent my own mate to her death.

The rage rises again, and with it the uncontrollable power that shakes the very walls. The light inside the reflective stones goes out. Darkness bleeds through the hallway. My eyes adjust quickly, their enhanced ability allowing me to see through the inky shadows that swallow us.

"Aruan," Elsie says, my name sounding like a question on her lips.

I look at her.

She's folded her arms around her breasts, hiding her nakedness from me, but the curly triangle of copper hair between her legs is exposed, and the sight does things to me, things that are highly inappropriate given where we are and what just happened.

I almost lost her.

Again.

A snarl curls my lips.

There's only one thought left now, one ruling instinct, and for once, my mind and my body are aligned.

Claim her.

I'm on her in a wink, cupping her head in my hands and crushing my mouth to hers in a bruising kiss.

The tiara slides down her hair and falls somewhere on the floor. She utters something that's lost in the clash of our teeth. Her lips on mine are like homecoming. The vibration I first felt at her presence intensifies ten moon cycles over. When I taste the sweetness of her tongue, my mind finally fails me. My body takes over, and what it demands is to sink deep inside her hidden heat.

Her resistance is a vague notion like the fine winter mist over the lake. The scent of her skin doesn't help. It cloaks my senses and drives me mad. The man has fled, and only the beast is left. He's ruled by instinct alone. He needs to claim what's his.

A puff of air from her lips steals into our kiss.

I've backed her up to the wall. The surface behind her is rough, but it serves the purpose of keeping her up as I part her legs with my knee and slide a thigh between her naked limbs. I can feel her wetness through the fabric of my pants. I can smell her arousal and her readiness. I can sense her submission as her resistance crumbles.

The kiss turns less violent as she gives in. I don't waste time. I take what she offers by plundering her mouth. Her moans spur me on. The poison that could've killed her has manifested as the venom in my blood that makes me lose all rationality and control. The dress on the floor is forgotten, and so is the reason why she's naked. All I can focus on is that she's here, ready and willing, her naked body accessible and her mouth already mine.

My promise to make this enjoyable for her and therefore ignore my own needs is forgotten too, not by choice but because I've lost the ability to think. All that remains is the need, the terrible urge, the insatiable desire.

No longer commanded by a primal exigency to prevent her from getting away, I release my hold on her head so I can explore the smoothness of her shoulders. Her skin is like silk beneath my palms. The small mounds of her breasts were made for my hands. Those pretty nipples are going to taste so good in the gentle vise of my teeth when I've rolled them into hard little points between my fingers.

Everything I'm going to do to her flashes through my mind, tormenting me with unbearable desire. I'm going to savor the sweet honey between her legs, and then I'm going to bury myself so deep in her tight heat that she'll never forget I was inside her. I'm going to bring her to the edge, giving her so much pleasure it will border on pain. I'm going to drive her to madness, and then I'll give her the remedy. I'm going to teach her that the only remedy is me.

Elsie is kissing me right back. I'm not sure she's conscious of her actions when she hooks her leg around the back of my thighs in search of more friction. Like me, she's ruled by lust. Her body has taken over her mind. But if she carries on like this, I'm going to lose the last shred of humanity left inside me. I'm going to take her hard, and her body is too small and fragile to withstand an Alit male's strength, especially the blind, fervor-stricken strength of a mate in heat.

The thought sobers me somewhat.

"Elsie," I say into the kiss, her name a plea to pull me back from the animal to the man. "Slow down, my sweet, or I'll take you right here against this wall."

Her reply is to arch her back and flatten her breasts against my chest.

Dragons.

The little self-control I salvaged goes up in flames. I slide a palm over her flat stomach and wedge my hand between our bodies until my fingers find the wetness hidden beneath copper curls.

So hot.

She's going to spill a lot more of that honey for me before I'm done with her. I'm going to drench her in her own arousal before lapping it all up. I want to dip my fingers into her tightness and stretch her until she can take me. Then I want to watch her face as I claim every inch of her. I will look into her eyes when she screams my name as she comes.

I cup her jaw, holding her in place for a deeper kiss as I feverishly work my cock free.

"Aruan," she moans when I brush the lips of her sex apart.

"Yes." I stroke the button hidden beneath those plump folds. "Say it. Say my name again."

"Aruan."

Only, the voice that has spoken doesn't belong to Elsie.

It's like diving into an icy sea. The heat coursing through me is doused in a beat.

Cluster of cursed dragons.

That voice belongs to Kian.

Elsie gasps and lowers her leg. A flush grows over her cheeks. The haziness disappears from her stunning blue-green eyes, and as they clear, shame sets in.

I clench the hand in which I cup her sex into a fist, my fingertips burrowing in the soft flesh of feminine parts.

I won't allow her to hide behind shame.

A snarl tears from my chest. My words are directed at my brother. "If you don't want to end up as a heap of ashes, I suggest you walk away."

Most people, including my own family, would run at the threat.

Kian's tone doesn't give away fear. "It's Mother."

From the way he says it, I know it's serious.

"Don't move," I bark out.

The order was meant for Kian, but Elsie flinches.

She flattens her back against the wall, putting the distance she tries so hard to always keep between us, and turns her face sideways.

I was a second away from sinking balls-deep into her. I didn't even take the time to walk us to my quarters. The whole hall would've heard her screams. And I wouldn't have given a dragon. I would've delighted in letting the whole of Lona know I've claimed my mate.

Gritting my teeth, I tuck my cock back into my

pants. My movements are jerky as I take off my jacket and help Elsie pull it on. The garment is so big on her tiny frame that the hem falls below her knees. I try to ignore the painful hard-on raging in my pants as I slip the buttons through the holes to make sure she's covered.

I only turn to my brother when I've fastened the last button.

Kian watches me with a level stare. "You'd better come."

"Gaia!" I call, holding Kian's gaze.

My sister comes running from the hall with tears still wet on her cheeks.

Her unhappiness unsettles me, but more important issues are at stake. Crying will have to wait.

"Take Elsie back to my quarters," I say. "My guards will go with you. No one but me is allowed to enter. Understand?"

My sister bobs her head. Taking Elsie's hand, she leads her to the stairs.

Kian tips his head toward the doors.

I go ahead.

When I re-enter the hall, the guests are huddled in groups in the four corners. My father could've easily ordered the guards to let the royal family out. They answer to both him and me, but as the king, he holds the highest power. Yet my immediate family, including my two close cousins, are still gathered around the king and queen's table. My mother doesn't sit up straight in her chair. She's stretched out in it, her arms hanging limply at her sides. My father kneels in front of her, clutching one of her hands in both of his.

Kian, who follows behind me, says in a voice that doesn't carry farther than my ears, "You'd better clear the hall. Father isn't in a state of rational thinking, and the guests shouldn't see this."

One look at my mother is enough to tell me he's right. As far as the people and even the nobles are concerned, the royals are powerful and invincible. Showing weakness wouldn't only hurt the pride of the person in question. It would undermine our authority.

A nod at a guard communicates my instruction. Quickly, he organizes a team to line the people up before escorting them out. The waterfall that gives access to the palace will remain in place. For now, I'm not allowing anyone to leave.

The hall starts emptying while I walk to the main table.

Vitai studies my mother with a concerned look.

"Aruan," my mother exclaims when I stop next to her chair. "You're alive." She sags in her seat. "Thank the dragons."

My tone is chilly. "What did you do, Mother?"

"I don't know what happened." She coughs. "I swear it on your life, my son."

I raise a brow. "Is that why I'm alive but Elsie was almost killed?"

"Mind your tongue, Aruan," my father says with all the venomousness of a red jungle toad. "You will not disrespect your mother." Turning back to his wife, he says in a gentler manner, "Rest now, my love. You mustn't exert yourself. Let Vitai finish his evaluation."

Suno and Tarix stand at the edge of the table, looking on with big eyes. The only reason my father isn't sending them away is because, as the son of a favorite sister, Tarix is my mother's private secretary and protégé. Suno acts as my father's advisor. He's learned in every scroll and law that hold legal power in Zerra.

Vitai takes a terracotta bowl from the table and holds it to my mother's lips. Under my father's wakeful watch, she manages to take a few sips of water.

"What happened?" I ask.

"She's showing mild signs of poisoning," Kian replies.

I barely manage to hide my shock. "What are the symptoms?"

Vitai glances at me. "She's having trouble breathing."

It could be acting. I wouldn't put it past her.

Kian, always quick to read my thoughts, says, "Look at her tongue. It's purple."

I go cold. That can't be faked. Unless she used the petals of cardon flowers. They're dried and crushed to die fabrics. But if she didn't…

"Can you fix it, Vitai?" I ask as evenly as I can.

"Fortunately, this case is mild enough, so I'll do my best," he says. "She shouldn't have more than a fever and chills for a few days. Judging by her symptoms, she must've had light topical contact only. She's lucky she didn't ingest any."

"How could this have happened?" Tarix asks, his voice close to breaking.

"That's what I'd like to know." My father's expression darkens. "And I will find out."

So will I.

I turn to Kian. "Read the mind of every person who entered the palace today."

He nods grimly. "I was planning on it. It'll take time, though. There must've been over five moon cycles of people at the banquet alone."

My father gently arranges my mother's hands in her lap before getting to his feet. "Go. Now."

Kian leaves without another word.

"Do you have any idea how this could've happened?" I ask my mother.

She's my main suspect, but would she truly have poisoned herself intentionally to appear like a victim to hide her guilt? It's unlikely. The chances of living after exposure are too uncertain.

"I made the infusion myself," she says, turning her face toward me with effort. "Tarix can vouch for that."

"That's true," Tarix says. "No one was allowed in the kitchen while your mother prepared the precious potion."

"Obviously, the poison wasn't in the potion," Vitai says. "Or else you'd be dead, Aruan."

"Then how did your mother come in contact with it?" my father asks, his face a thunderous mask.

"It must've happened when I straightened the place settings," my mother says weakly. "I was annoyed with the maids for not setting the table properly. Elsie's goblet was slightly out of line with the others, so I put it back in place."

"Where did you touch the goblet?" Vitai asks.

"I picked it up by the stem. It was slippery, as if someone with fatty hands had touched it. I almost dropped it but managed to catch it before it hit the table. I polished the stem with a cloth and put the goblet back in the right place."

"Could you have touched the inside of the goblet when you caught it or maybe while you polished it?" Vitai asks thoughtfully.

My mother blows out a tired sigh. "I suppose that's possible. Yes, I most likely did."

"That's enough." My father bends down and picks my mother up in his arms. "I'm taking her to her quarters. She needs to rest."

"An assassin is on the loose," I point out. "One who nearly succeeded in killing my mate."

My father gives me a cold stare. "We'll get to the bottom of this but not at the expense of your mother's health."

"Someone must've painted the inside of the goblet with a poison that's not only translucent but also tasteless and odorless." Vitai looks at Gaia's dead pet on the floor. "Spiked dragons are notoriously good at smelling harmful toxins."

"Night lilies," Tarix muses.

My exact thought.

"Four moon cycles of people had access to the hall before the banquet," Suno says. "It could've been anyone."

"Precisely." I cross my arms. "And it will never happen again. From now on, no one cooks or touches Elsie's food but me."

"Don't worry," Suno says, coming closer to warily pat my shoulder. "Whoever did this, Kian will find him."

"Or her," I say, still not completely convinced about my mother's innocence in all this.

However unlikely it is that she would've touched poison on purpose, I can't ignore how convenient it is that she fell ill right before I intended to confront her about the "death" of my infant mate. I still want answers as to how Elsie ended up on Earth.

My father exits the hall with my mother in his arms, leaving us to stew over the question of who could've attempted such a terrible deed, a crime punishable by the cruelest of executions.

The truth is that it could've been anyone. Both the royals and the nobles are well versed in the scrolls. They're terrified of the prophecy about the Alit prince with a dark, uncontrollable power... and the role his mate—*my* mate—is supposed to play in bringing about the end of our world.

Personally, I'm not a believer. But I can see why they are.

Not even I know exactly what I'm capable of, and if

anything had happened to her today... Gritting my teeth, I tamp down on the thought and the rage that accompanies it, which manifests as a crack in the ceiling.

Tarix and Suno jump.

Tarix leaves quickly with an excuse to go check on the queen. Suno offers to get rid of the dead pet and to get a new one from the breeder for Gaia.

I take a deep breath to calm myself, mend the ceiling with my mind, and then go back to my quarters, unsure as to what I want to do as far as my mate is concerned. We got carried away in the heat of the mating call, but I doubt she's in the mood for another round considering someone has just tried to kill her.

As it turns out, I find Elsie fast asleep in my bed, still dressed in my jacket. Another wave of that earlier tenderness washes over me. I don't have the heart to wake her.

In the corner, Gaia is quietly crying.

I dismiss the guards with a wave of my hand. They leave quickly.

Sighing, I walk to my sister. "Mother will be fine. She'll feel like she's been mauled by a dragon for a few days, but with proper rest and care, she'll pull through."

Gaia wipes her nose on the back of her hand. "I know she'll be all right."

"What did you give Elsie?"

No one sleeps that soundly after a death scare.

Gaia sniffs. "Just a few drops of dranlaud to relax her."

That will take a few hours to work out of her system.

"Go get some rest," I tell Gaia. "It's been a traumatic evening for everyone."

Gaia catches my sleeve when I start to turn. "It's not just Mother I'm concerned about. I'm worried about all of us. No good can come of this. Where's this going to leave us?"

I fix her with a narrow-eyed stare. "Do not say you wish my mate away. Don't you dare even imply it."

She blanches. "I'd never."

"Good." I continue in a gentler tone, "Suno offered to get you a new pet."

"I don't want a new one," she says, her voice wobbling again.

My heart softens. I pull her in for a hug, but she pushes away to look at me.

"Tell me everything is going to be fine, Aruan."

I don't reply because I never make promises I can't keep.

CHAPTER II

ARUAN

When I enter the Great Hall at sunrise, Kian sits in a chair at our family table, staring dispassionately at the man who stands in front of him. The man shifts his weight while wringing a hat in his hands. The poor wretch's shoulders sag in relief when Kian waves him away and motions for the next victim to take the man's place at my brother's feet.

A woman comes closer, pinching her eyes shut even before she reaches Kian. A guard takes her arm and positions her close to Kian's chair. It's only then that she peels her eyelids open to turn red-rimmed, bloodshot eyes on my brother. Her hair has come loose from its braid, the flaxen tresses sticking out like straw around her head.

The other people don't look any better. The guests waiting their turn to be interrogated by Kian are slumped over the tables, some asleep on their arms and others conversing in tired, strained voices.

The only person in the palace who has gotten any sleep is Elsie, thanks to the sleeping potion Gaia gave her. I haven't even taken the time to change. I'm still wearing the ceremonial pants and shirt of yesterday. Between interrogating the kitchen staff and guards, I frequently checked in on Elsie and my mother. The queen, who was tormented by painful cramps for the duration of the night, appears wilted and weak. Her usually glowing skin has turned gray and damp with perspiration. My father keeps watch at her side. Gaia escaped to her room. Knowing how much she loved that pet, I let her have some space.

Kian lifts his head when I approach. The echo of my heavy steps on the flagstone floor would've been enough warning of my presence, but the gentle, almost unnoticeable prodding of my mind tells me he was aware of me the minute I crossed the threshold.

I make sure my barriers are in place, effectively blocking him from gaining access to my thoughts.

He watches me quietly as I stop next to him, not a sliver of emotion playing in his silver irises that are so eerily pale they're almost as translucent as water. They always adopt that shade when he taps into his power for an extended period of time.

"How much longer?" I ask.

The color of his eyes returns more or less to normal as he focuses on me. "Not much."

The woman scrambles away the moment Kian

releases the hold of his power over her. Having one's mind read is nothing short of a harrowing experience, or so I'm told. Kian has a way of worming invisible tentacles into every cranny of his subject's mind, hooking into a person's deepest and darkest thoughts. The unlucky interrogees always walk away with the feeling that their soul has been flayed open for all their sins and weaknesses to pour out. They may not say it, but they think it. Kian may read their unspoken thoughts, but I hear the whispers the walls can't contain.

I curl and flex my fingers at my sides. "Anything?"

Kian doesn't show the slightest sign of tiredness, which demonstrates just how strong he is. It takes a powerful mind to be immersed in the most sinful desires of Alitkind without drowning in the ravenous envy and ugly deceit. On the contrary, the blackest corners of a psyche are Kian's playground. I wonder if that's why he displays emotions so sparingly. Maybe he's seen too much of it, or what he's seen has made him lose his appetite or aptitude for sentimentality.

"Nothing," he says in an even voice that carries neither dejection nor hope.

Tarix enters from the kitchen with a goblet in his hand that he carries to Kian. "I thought you might be thirsty. I made you an infusion that will keep both your mind and body alert."

When Kian doesn't thank him or take the goblet, Tarix leaves it on the table and shuffles his feet.

The silence stretches.

Adopting a wounded expression, Tarix mumbles something about fetching food and hurries away.

"Why don't you like him?" I ask, following Tarix's rushed exit with my gaze.

"It's not that I don't like him," Kian says thoughtfully. "It's that I can't get an accurate read on him, and I don't trust people I can't read."

My lips peel back into a humorless grin. "You can't read me."

"That's different. You block me. Tarix is simply vague. It's almost as if there's nothing to read, as if his mind is empty."

"Tarix isn't an idiot. He's adept at taking care of the queen's affairs. His diplomatic skills are commendable."

"Maybe I'm just weary," Kian says, fixing a bland gaze on me. "It's been a strange night."

And a long one.

A stirring awakens in my chest, soft like a downy cloud at first, then sharp with panic.

Elsie is awake and unhappy.

I was on my way to prepare a tray with breakfast, but I turn on my heel and go back to my quarters.

The thuds of her fists on the sealed archway reach my ears from beyond the thick walls.

"Let me out!"

I let the entrance dissolve and step into the room, almost bumping into Elsie, who scoots a few steps back. I stop, not to avoid crashing into her but to trail my gaze over the tantalizing shape of her body that's still clad in my jacket.

"I need to get out of here," she says, trying to slip past me.

I cut her off with a sidestep. "It's not safe."

"You can't lock me up in here like a prisoner," she hisses. "I didn't do anything wrong."

The sensation of being trapped constricts my ribcage, and suffocation settles like a thick, wet blanket around me. The need to breathe is like claws scratching at my throat, but I'm lucid enough to realize the feeling isn't my own. Whatever Elsie experiences mirrors inside me.

I grip her shoulders and give her a gentle shake. "You're panicking, not suffocating. There's nothing wrong with your airway. Breathe, Elsie."

"I want—" She sucks in a breath. "I need to get out."

"I'll take you out," I say against my better judgment, willing to promise anything to get rid of the pressure that squeezes like a band around my chest. "But you have to calm down first."

That does the trick. She inhales deeply.

"That's it," I croon, rubbing her arms in a soothing caress.

"Really?" she asks, searching my face. "You won't lock me up in here again?"

That's not a promise I can keep, so I change the subject. "You can't go out wearing nothing but my jacket. I had the trunk filled with clothes that'll fit you. While you get ready, I'll fetch breakfast. We can eat it outside." I slide my palm up to the soft curve of her shoulder. "How does that sound?"

"What happened last night? Why did someone try to poison me?"

Fury rises inside me at the mere thought, shaking the window in its frame. I tamp down the rage with much effort. "I'll find out who's guilty."

"That's called deflection," she says, narrowing her pretty eyes. "You're not answering my question."

I grit my teeth, not because I don't want to tell her but because I shouldn't dare it until I have a handle on my anger. The wall of the banquet hall is cracked in two because I couldn't control my anger, and I've yet to fix it. I've lost control a lot since Elsie's arrival, and it's not helping the rumors.

"I see." She bobs her head. "I'm clearly on a need-to-know basis. But if that poisoning stunt proves anything, it's that I shouldn't be here."

"Don't mention the assassination attempt again," I say in a measured tone. "Not now. Not unless you're prepared for the consequences."

She glances at the rattling pink-stained panes in the window frame and quickly clamps her lips together.

My order is brusque. "Get dressed."

The sight of her wearing my jacket stokes a possessive part of me, and that part wants to continue right where we left off last night.

"I need a bath." Her cheeks flush. "And other bathroom ablutions."

I let the wall obscuring the archway to the cleansing room dissolve, reminding myself to leave the entrance open in the future. I shouldn't forget that Elsie is unfamiliar with the abilities and functions every Alit takes for granted. "You'll find everything you need in there." I motion at the ledge built into the wall. "I left a new comb and tooth-cleaning brush on the shelf."

She gives the empty pool a speculative glance. "There are no faucets."

"Faucets?"

"For water."

Ah. Of course. Even a child knows how to run a bath. But this is another example of why it's important to remain conscious of Elsie's limitations.

It's easy enough to open a small hole in the pool's stone bottom. Water bubbles through the hole.

She stares at the pool that's quickly filling up. "How does that work?"

I seal the hole when the pool is full. "The palace is fed by arteries of water that run beneath the surface. Thanks to the volcano that heats it, the water is warm."

"Is that why it has healing powers—because the water absorbs minerals from the soil?"

If my explanation is curt, it's because I'm suppressing a very enticing mental image of my naked mate in the water. "It has healing powers because we add special salts to the water." I continue in a clipped tone, "Don't linger too long. I'll be back soon."

Before it's too late to salvage the little that remains of my willpower, I leave the rooms, seal the exit, and stomp down the hallway.

The cooks and bakers gape when I walk into the kitchen where breakfast is being prepared. Last night, we fed small chunks of all the reserves in the pantry to the flock of spiked lizards that roam the palace, and none of them dropped dead. To be on the safe side, I had fresh produce brought from the village this morning and locked it in a cooling room that only I can open.

Under the astonished stares of the kitchen staff, I make quick work of preparing a basket.

Elsie is pacing in front of the window when I return. She's wearing one of the dresses I left for her. The fabric is the color of dusk and ashes, which brings out the sunset glow of her hair and the vibrant blue-green of her eyes. She's paired it with simple satin slippers that peek out from under the long skirt. The bodice hangs loose on her slender frame, the back unlaced.

Of course.

Women require maids to help them string and tie the laces.

Elsie spins around when the archway closes behind me.

I leave the basket on the dresser and advance slowly. "Turn around."

"I…" She remains glued to the spot. "Why?"

I can't help but notice her small curves under the fabric. The memory of her shape, from when I held her between my palms in the hallway last night, rushes back to me, and for a moment, it drowns out all other thoughts. The aphrodisiac has long since worked itself out of my system, but desire pulses back to life in my body, hardening me painfully.

My voice is gruff. "Turn around if you want me to fasten that dress."

I could do it without touching her, but she doesn't need to know that.

She steps closer and turns around, offering me the milky expanse of her naked back. The urge to touch her there—and in other places—is unbearable, almost uncontrollable. It's only with many cycles of practiced willpower that I grip the laces and pull the edges of the dress together, lingering longer than necessary when my knuckles accidentally brush over her skin.

The goosebumps that run down her arms gladden me.

She's not unaffected. My touch arouses her. I can smell it. I can hear it in the quickening of her heartbeat and see it in the soft fluttering of the vein that throbs in the side of her neck.

She pulls away and twirls around to stare at me with a confused expression. She's wondering about this effect I have on her. She's asking herself why her body comes alive beneath my palms. But she's also denying it, fighting hard to ignore the truth.

"I haven't finished," I say, letting my gaze play over her lovely features.

She swallows audibly as she moves her hands behind her back and says, "I can manage the rest," while deftly tying the laces.

I wait patiently, allowing her to finish.

When she drops her arms at her sides, I grab the basket on my way to the door.

"Come, Elsie."

I don't wait to see if she follows. If I linger another moment, I'm going to trap her beneath my weight, spread her legs, and spill my seed inside her in the very bed where she'll conceive my children.

The thought is so tempting that I walk faster lest I act on the alluring idea.

Elsie falls into step beside me, running to keep up. "Where are you taking me?"

I slow my stride, mindful of her shorter legs. "To one of my favorite places."

We pass through the Great Hall and, when I've parted the waterfall, onto the bridge. I take the stairs leading to the hill, holding her elbow in a firm grip to make sure she doesn't slip.

When we reach the bottom, she turns to take in the palace, and her jaw drops. I understand her amazement. The sight can be overwhelming. The palace is built into a cone-shaped mountain that stands alone, the cliff walls reaching into the sky. Open archways and paned windows with balconies run down the sides, creating an illusion of gaping mouths and blinking eyes. We've turned the existing caverns into rooms and, with time, added new ones by dissolving the rock.

At the top, the rockface is green with luscious ferns and moss. Water that pushes up from an underground tunnel running through the center of the mountain erupts from the top and rushes in a powerful waterfall over the side and in front of the Great Hall.

"That's pretty impressive." She points at the windows. "Are those all the bedrooms?"

"Mostly. Some of the rooms are the royals' quarters. Others serve as meeting rooms. The banquet hall and the kitchen, as well as the staff rooms, are at the back."

Taking her hand, I lead her down the hill on the other side of the sea toward the lake. Her palm is warm and small in mine. The touch is a practicality, ensuring she doesn't trip or fall, but the contact warms my chest in a way I've never felt. It's like a soothing balm on a cut.

Little by little, I relax until the brutal emotions that tore through me mere moments ago are safely tucked away. I point out the shrubs and flowers as we go, telling her their names. It's enjoyable. Peaceful.

The realization startles me. From the day my awareness of her stopped beating in my chest, from the dreadful day I believed she was dead, I'd never been at peace.

"Wow," she says when the flat surface of the lake comes into view. "This is so pretty."

Red, yellow, and purple cone ears grow in clusters between the succulent grass, each sticky petal curled like a tongue ready to catch any insects flying by. It does make a striking picture with the blue backdrop of the water. The air is clean here, free from the smell of cooking fires and grilling meat. Instead, it's warm and humid, perfumed with the salty scent of the grass and the sweet odor of the carnivorous flowers. For once, the whispers are quiet, and the only sound is the soft crackling of the grass as the fat blades reach for the sun.

Giggling, Elsie prods one of the succulents with the tip of her shoe. She utters a delighted laugh when the blade curls around her slipper before unfurling into the air again.

"Can I touch it?" she asks.

"The grass is safe."

She lets go of my hand to run her fingers through the blades. They twist around her fingertips, and sensing that it's not their usual food, they return to their erect state.

She laughs. "That tickles."

I take the blanket from the basket and spread it out near the shore. When I've set out our breakfast, I ask, "Are you hungry?"

She pads over and plops down next to me, sitting with her legs crossed. "Aruan, we have to talk."

Yes, but… "Food first."

She huffs.

I halve a small *thoska* cake and heap a generous helping of hardboiled, minced *yehuyk* on top. Lifting it to her mouth, I say, "Open."

She takes the savory cake from my hand. "You don't have to feed me."

I can't help the teasing smile that stretches my lips. "What if I like to?"

That earns me another huff. She shoves the entire cake into her mouth and chews enthusiastically.

"Oh, wow," she says around the food. "This is delicious."

The warm sensation in my chest increases, knowing I've pleased her with a treat I prepared for her. "It's baked with flour we grind from the bark of *thoska* trees, which is very nutritious. If the bark is steeped in water, the infusion can be used for digestive problems."

"What's the topping?" she asks, licking her fingers clean. "That was so yummy and creamy."

My gaze homes in on her action, my body tightening in response. "Snake eggs."

Her eyes grow round. She spits on the ground and wipes her mouth with the back of her hand. "Ew. Seriously? That's gross."

"It's a delicacy and a rare one at that."

Shooting me a cutting look, she says, "You could've warned me."

"Here." I pour a little juice from the flask into a bowl and hand it to her. "Drink this."

She takes a big swallow and asks belatedly, "That wasn't anything gross like frog pee, was it?"

"Frog? I don't know that animal."

"It's a cold-blooded, slimy amphibian—" At my frown, she adds, "Sort of like a reptile that leaps and croaks."

I chuckle. "It's just a sweet wine made of fruit and herbs."

"What about you?" She leaves the bowl on the blanket. "Aren't you eating?"

I'll eat when I've taken care of her needs. "Would you like to try some *scrivka*? It's a porridge made with seven grains and eaten cold with honey." I take the dish out and, after removing the cloth that covers it, place it in front of her with a spoon. "This has to be cooked overnight. Otherwise, the grains are indigestible."

She dips the spoon in the porridge, takes a tentative lick, and then finishes everything in a few big bites. When I offer her a second helping, she tells me she's had enough.

I'm preparing the sweet part of the meal, which are cubed pieces of fruit fried in fat and caramelized with honey, when she gets to her feet and kicks off her shoes.

"Elsie."

I drop the sticky *jimkia* and reach for her ankle, but she jumps out of my reach.

"I want to feel the grass under my bare feet," she calls with a mischievous grin over her shoulder as she runs to the edge of the lake.

Dragons! This woman will be the end of me.

"Elsie, no!"

My warning is not yet cold when her scream pierces the air.

Her pain is so acute it's like a blade peeling off my skin. I sprint after her and, in a few long strides, reach her where she's hopping on one leg.

My tone is calm, collected, but the hurt etched on

her features unleashes a torrent of rage like a volcano spewing fire inside me. "Where does it hurt?" I take her arm to help her keep her balance.

"My foot." She sucks air through her teeth. "Damn, that fucking burns."

"Show me," I say through thin lips.

She bends her knee and lifts her foot with the sole facing up, revealing an angry red, swollen heel. "Something in the grass must've stung me."

Our forests are full of venomous plants and creatures. I should've warned her, but how was I supposed to know Elsie liked digging her toes into lumps of clayish mud and slippery grass?

With my heart thumping in my chest, I search the succulents with a practiced eye. A horned ground crawler creeps out from under a blade, edging toward her like a parasite that has smelled blood.

My fury is so great I'm incapable of thinking rationally. One moment, the bloodsucking little leech is worming its way through the mud, and the next, it explodes in a spray of grayish white glob before dissolving into a sizzling mess of dirty-white mush and black paste.

Elsie jumps back, pulling free from my hold so violently she lands on her ass in a tuft of spongy grass.

I waste no time in scooping her up into my arms and carrying her back to the blanket.

Once I've laid her down, I take her foot into my hand. "We'd better put a poultice on your heel to pull out the sting."

Looking around, I find a few succulents within reach and break the fat blades in half. Then I cup the narrow bridge of Elsie's foot in my palm and rub copious amounts of the sap from the blades over the inflamed skin. It's an old remedy our cook taught me after I got stung by insects as a child.

Within seconds, the swelling goes down.

"How does it feel now, my sweet?"

"Unbelievable." She gapes at me. "It doesn't hurt anymore."

"Don't ever take off your shoes outside again. Some larvae that live in the soil are venomous."

"You melted that caterpillar just like those lizards." She pulls her foot from my hand, leaning on her elbows while watching me with an unsettled expression. "How does your power work? How can you dissolve something by simply looking at it? Do you have laser eyes or something?"

Caterpillar, laser... I don't know her terminology, but I'm no longer in the mood for a language lesson.

I keep my tone bland, not wanting to frighten her more. "I broke the bonds holding its living particles together."

"You... broke the bonds?" She swallows, staring at me. "Like, between its cells?"

I think I know what she means. "Between *asha*, the little self-sufficient units that make up all living beings, and then between the particles that make up asha, the ones that make up everything."

"The molecules?" she whispers, looking awed. "You can break bonds between molecules?"

"If 'molecules' are what all matter, animate or inanimate, is made of, then yes."

She sucks in a breath. "Is that how you dissolve stone to create the entrance to your quarters? By breaking the bonds between stone particles?"

"Yes."

"And then you remake the bonds?"

"Exactly."

It's so strange that I have to explain to her something every Alit toddler knows.

She swallows again. "And you do it all with your mind."

"How else?"

She lets out an incredulous laugh. "Um… with heat, radiation, electrical energy, mechanical forces, chemical reactions? Utilizing actual laws of physics?" At my blank stare, she says, "Never mind. So how do the others' powers work? Like Vitai's? How did he heal me?"

"It's the same principle," I say. "We all manipulate matter to some extent. He's good at recreating the bonds within and between *asha*."

"Whereas you're good at dissolving them," she says, and the way she's looking at me—the way everyone has looked at me all my life—leaves a bitter taste in my mouth.

I can actually heal a bit too, though I'm nowhere near as good as Vitai, which is why I prefer to rely on potions and such. Not that it would matter to her. My own mate is afraid of me. Of my power. Like they all are.

And she doesn't even know the extent of it.

Instead of sounding soothing as I intend, my declaration comes out angry. "I'd never harm you, Elsie."

"Only other living beings?"

"It harmed you," I bite out.

"It was just a sting. I'll admit that stung a hell of a lot more than a wasp, but it wasn't necessary to melt the worm into a puddle. It wasn't his fault. It was mine for stepping on it."

"It hurt you," I say a tad louder, a tad more angrily, because it's my duty to protect her.

A wry laugh tumbles from her mouth. "That was nothing compared to what I'm used to. Believe me, I've been through much worse. You just destroyed a poor, innocent worm for the misfortune of having crossed my path."

My mind is hooked on the first part, on her declaration of having been in pain before, "much worse" pain.

"Worse such as?" I ask with deceptive indifference.

Maybe if I pretend not to care, she won't be scared to tell me, and then I can hunt down the people who hurt her and give them a slow, torturous death.

"It's…" She frowns. "It *was* nothing."

My senses go on high alert. She's hiding something from me, something serious. I feel it. I know it.

"Tell me," I coax in an amiable tone, suppressing the violence that churns in my stomach before she catches a hint of my vicious intentions in my voice.

A speculative look comes over her features. "If I tell you, will you tell me why someone tried to kill me last night?"

I was going to tell her anyway—after I fed her—because it's vital that she understands the dangers of our life. However, it's not beneath me to let her think otherwise if it serves my purpose.

"Deal." Let her think she's won this round. "But you'd better tell me everything."

Her laugh is uncomfortable. "*Everything* may take a while."

My gut tightens with a nasty foreboding. "I've got time."

"Let's just say there's no life-threatening condition I haven't had. I was dying from the day I was born."

The words hammer in my skull.

Life-threatening.

Dying.

I clench my teeth to suppress the rage that rolls through me like a freak wave on a full moon tide. "What did you say?"

She shrugs, making light of it. "Autoimmune diseases, cancer, you name it." She bites her lip before continuing. "In fact, I should be dying as we speak. Only, I feel great."

Dying.

That word again. I don't know what "autoimmune

diseases" or "cancer" are, but the context is clear enough.

My reply is harsh. "You're *not* dying."

I'd feel it. I would know, as I knew when she was plucked away from me. Yet all I feel is vitality and a zest for life. A bit of a temper and a lot of impatience. But not death. Not that.

Nevertheless, the notion alone makes blackness drift into my vision. "Start at the beginning."

She shrugs again. "What's the point?"

I get the feeling she doesn't like to talk about it, but I *need* to know. "We have a deal, or have you forgotten?"

She relents with a sigh, telling me about her childhood and adolescent years that were spent either in hospitals or in convalescence. I can sense she's glossing over the worst of it, and as she speaks, I feel the horror of the diseases that sucked her life essence dry. I taste the acrid flavor of the certain death that lurked in the shadows, biding its time.

My rage is so great at the injustice of it all, at what would've happened to Elsie had the Phaelix not decided in their idiotic stupidity to kidnap her, that the big old conifer at the edge of the water ignites with a stroke of lightning before bursting into flames.

Elsie jumps to her feet, favoring her uninjured leg. Her shocked gaze is trained on the sparks shooting into the sky with sharp whistles as the gum inside the trunk explodes.

I only manage to get control of myself again after

the tree has been crisped to a stark black silhouette that smolders against the cloudless blue of the sky.

The stink of smoke, charred resin, and wood turned to coal taints the air, burning my nostrils and lungs.

"What the hell just happened?" she stutters.

"Lightning," I mumble, which isn't a lie.

I can bring down a lightning bolt from the sky by merely focusing my attention there. Like fabricating water from the air, it's a simple trick.

"You did that," she says accusingly.

I don't confirm the obvious. I'm contemplating a more important matter. What do I do with the information she's shared? I need to talk to Vitai. He may have an idea of what could've happened to her to make her so sickly when she arrived on Earth. And then I'll confront my mother.

Carefully pushing down the turbulent feelings boiling inside me, I point at the spot in front of me on the blanket. "Sit down."

Elsie obeys with a wary look on her face. "You're angry."

I try to soften my tone. "Not at you." Motioning at her injured foot, I say, "Let me see that again."

She leans back on her arms and offers her foot reluctantly.

"How does it feel now?" I ask.

"Still fine."

"Good." I set her foot down gently, avoiding her eyes while I slip on her shoes. I'm too afraid that if I look into those blue-green pools and see her suffering reflected there, I'll lose it again. "We'd better go back so Vitai can have a look at it."

After getting to my feet, I offer her a hand to help her up. "Can you put weight on your foot?"

She takes a hesitant step. "Yes."

I test her balance before letting her go. If I'm quiet while I pack up the remains of our breakfast, it's because I'm already compiling a mental list of questions to confront my mother with, and with each one I add, my fury grows.

"Aruan," Elsie says, tugging on my sleeve. "You haven't eaten anything."

Once more, her concern warms and calms me. "It can wait. I ate small meals throughout the night."

Her eyebrows snap together. "You didn't sleep at all?"

Needing the reassurance of her touch, I take her hand again. "We were interrogating the guests. It took time."

She glances sideways at me. "You owe me an answer." Using my own words against me, she says, "We had a deal, remember?"

I lead her down the slope toward the palace. My plan was to show her the majestic cliffs and the vast crops bordering the village so she'd be reassured of the abundant nature and wealth of her new home. A part of me was hoping she'd be keener to stay if she fell in love with the beauty of Zerra and got to know the richness of our resources and history. But that's an excursion best saved for another day.

A small group of people appear at the bottom of the path that runs from the village. The women are holding children by the hand, and the men are carrying bundles of firewood.

Next to me, Elsie perks up. I sense her curiosity more than see it because she's careful to school her features. I know what's going through my mate's head. What she sees is an opportunity to escape, to ask someone to help her get away.

She'll be disappointed. No one is stupid enough to risk my wrath. She'll learn soon enough that there's no escaping her fate. Or her mate.

The people fall quiet when they spot us. Their fear is palpable, but it's too late to turn back without being disrespectful or rude. Instead, they fix big, frightened eyes on Elsie and continue with obvious hesitancy toward us.

At the acceptable distance, they bow their heads and mumble, "Praise to the prince, peace to the future queen," and then, walking a wide circle around us, they scramble away.

Elsie twists her neck to stare after them. "Those people…"

"They're from the nearby village."

"Those people," she says again.

"What about them?"

"They looked… scared of me."

There's no point in hiding or sweetening the truth. She's going to find out at some point, and it's better that she hears it from me. "They're terrified of you."

She stops and tugs on my hand to hold me back. "Why? Why is everyone frightened of me? Is that why someone tried to kill me?"

I clench my fingers around the handle of the basket. "They're scared because of a prophecy."

"A prophecy?" she asks, shading her face with her free hand to meet my gaze.

"There's a prophecy in the scrolls that predicts a powerful prince, the most powerful Zerra has seen, will bring enormous wealth and prosperity to the people of his kingdom. During his reign, the kingdom will know peace and abundance. But there's always a price that comes with great power. According to the scrolls, the prince's unequalled power will also be his downfall... and the downfall of the entire world. For he'll be cursed with a loss of control around his mate, so much so that one day, his inability to control his power will bring on the destruction of the whole of Zerra."

She blinks. "That prince is... you."

My smile is wry. "That's what people think."

"And they think I'm the mate who's going to trigger your loss of control that will destroy your world," she says in a voice that's thin with shock.

"Correct again."

"What are these so-called scrolls?" She pulls her hand from mine. "Who wrote them? Where do they come from?"

"If you'd like, one day, I'll take you to visit the sacred site, and you can view them for yourself."

"Do you…?" Her chest rises and falls with a deep breath. "Do you believe the scrolls?"

If my reply is severe, it's because of the threat the prophecy poses to the woman fate gave to me. "No."

I don't need to know Elsie very well to understand how her mind works. I know exactly what she's thinking as she stares at me with ashen cheeks. She's thinking about the incidents that have occurred every time her life has been threatened—the shaking of the floors and the cracking of the wall. She's thinking about the Phaelix and the bloodsucking leech I melted to liquid. She's thinking about the tree that's still smoking on the horizon.

Not liking the direction her thoughts are taking, I make my voice hard. "There's no evidence to suggest the prophecy will come true and no facts to prove the predictions are accurate."

She backs up a step, moving away from me. The act tells me what she doesn't say in words—that she doesn't want to be near me.

My anger rises anew, mixing with uncontrollable possessiveness.

I need her near me.

By dragon, I'll hunt her if I have to.

In a blink, I eliminate the distance she put between us and wrap a proprietorial hand around her nape, dragging her to me as I drop the basket. Her lips part as our bodies collide, and I grow hard at the ambrosia-like softness of her small, pointy breasts flattened against my torso.

Unable to stop myself, I claim her lips in a fierce kiss, stealing inside her mouth with my tongue.

The depth of her mouth is like honey, the taste of her driving me wild. She resists even as her pulse speeds up to echo with hammering heartbeats against my ribs, the blood gushing through her veins sounding loud in my ears.

My own blood pounds in my temples as I mold her lips into submission until they grow soft under the pressure of my kiss, and she allows me to shape them with mine as I please. A part of me knows that we're out in the open, but I can't find it in me to give a dragon. I should've kissed her on the blanket under the veil of leaves that forms a curtain around the trees. I could've taken her there, could've driven my bursting hard cock into the soft, wet heat of her delicate pussy, and she would've welcomed me. Even now, despite her initial resistance, her arms come around my neck, holding on as I plunder her mouth with abandon. The mating call will override her thoughts until she's capable of thinking only with her body. The bonding will be completed, and it will be too late to do anything about it. She may resent me once it's over, but no matter.

I'll make her submit to me now and win her heart later.

We have time.

With that goal in mind, I give in to the urges driving me, letting them dictate my actions, which are to bunch her skirt in a fist and dip my hand beneath the fabric to brush my fingertips up the inside of her leg. The skin of her thigh is like the silky threads of the rarest spun textile. The heat between her legs is an unbearable torment to my senses.

Having left the trunk in my room empty of undergarments, I find her bare by conscious design. Yet nothing will ever prepare me for the way she feels when I touch the most secret, most intimate part of her body. Nor can I get used to the burning need that fires through my veins at the simple sweep of my knuckles over the petal-like folds hidden beneath soft coppery curls.

Her gasp slips into our kiss, encouraging me to take my exploration deeper. I curl a finger and part her gently, only to find her soaking wet for me. I nearly combust when I bridge her narrow opening and sink the tip of my finger into her tightness.

Dragons.

A drop of sweat rolls down my temple, the effort of holding back taking its toll.

So tight. Almost too tight.

Warning bells go off in my mind. Elsie is small, especially for an Alit. I have to take care not to hurt her.

I part her a bit more, push a little deeper, and by dragon, my self-control almost snaps.

"Aruan," Elsie exclaims with a breathless gasp, tearing her mouth from mine.

I seal my lips over hers again, swallowing her

sounds for fear she may utter them in protest as I tease her with shallow pumps.

Her breathing turns more labored. She's going to make me lose my head.

I'm about to sink my finger knuckle-deep inside her when the air starts to ripple with subtle waves.

For the everlasting dragons.

A growl tears from my chest. I loathe to stop what I've started. However, I don't have a choice but to pull my hand from its warm, seductive nest and set her lips free as a portal opens in front of us.

Elsie clings to my shoulders, her gaze dazed and her eyes hazy. I barely have time to offer her an apologetic smile for leaving her hanging so cruelly when Gaia steps through the portal.

The look of terror on my sister's face washes away the intoxicating heat coursing through me in an instant. Alarm takes its place.

Wrapping my hand around Elsie's firmly, I pull her under the safety of my arm. "What's the matter, Gaia?"

"Come quickly!" My sister grabs my wrist and pulls me toward the open portal. "The palace is under attack."

CHAPTER 12

ELSIE

L ike another big sneeze, we're sucked through the portal and spat out in the Great Hall of the palace. Aruan's family is gathered in front of the waterfall that acts as a barrier for the main entrance.

I hear the trouble long before I can see it. War cries rise over the roar of the waterfall, enemies gathering beyond it.

My pulse spikes. I've had plenty of near-death experiences but none of them due to being attacked—at least not by threatening forces other than diseases or my own body. And I have to say, when danger comes in the form of a weapon, it's fucking scary. If Gaia hadn't warned us, whoever is ambushing Aruan's people would've cut the two of us off before we reached the palace. We would've been trapped and exposed like sitting ducks. Unless Aruan can create a portal?

"What's going on?" I ask with my heart beating in my throat.

"Phaelix," Aruan says through gritted teeth, clasping my hand in an iron grip.

He's positioned himself in front of me like a massive boulder of muscles and is scouting our surroundings with fierce silver eyes. I catch sight of those steely pools, now narrowed to angry slits, as he turns his head from one side of the hall to the other.

I follow his gaze. All I see are stone walls and statues on both sides. The big arched window is at the front. "What are you looking at?"

"The Phaelix who are stupid enough to think they can creep up on us."

"But they're outside."

"I can see through the walls."

He makes the statement matter-of-factly, but it takes the wind out of my sails. Not that anything about Aruan should surprise me.

He's focused and collected, the quietness overtaking him the dangerous kind. This is the Aruan who's ready to kill. It's his single-minded goal, his only objective. It's an awesome and terrifying sight.

The king faces the waterfall, his palms stretched out as if he's holding the liquid particles together. Kian stands next to him with a sword in one hand and a stoic expression on his face. Vitai flanks his mother in the center of the hall.

The sickly queen is creating portal after portal with a flick of her wrist. The purple circles that light up the ground below are visible through the window. She's leaning on Vitai for support, who has his sword poised in the air. The pose says he's ready to cut down anyone who dares come near his mother.

Guards armed with daggers and swords sprint through the portals on the ground. The moment their feet touch the grass, they take up defensive positions. Gaia is working just as fast as her mother in opening portals, but hers are smaller and only letting in two or three men at a time whereas the queen is pushing through groups of up to ten.

"They waited until most of our guards had left to escort the caravan of trading supplies," the king says tensely. "Someone must've leaked the information. Can our men get back here any faster?"

"Not on their own," Aruan says. "They've covered too much distance. We need Mother to get them here now."

"Blasted reptiles," the king spits out.

"They're going to storm the bridge," Kian shouts above the noise. "They've surrounded the palace as well as the village!"

"Portal guards to the village to protect the people," the king calls out without turning his attention away from the waterfall. Contempt is thick in his voice that carries across the space. "I can hold the water, but those creatures aren't afraid of it. They might've mutated from their finned ancestors, but they haven't lost their affinity for swimming. They'll break through." He adds darkly, "Even if it means losing a few who'd be washed away and crushed on the rocks."

"And they're going to do so in exactly five beats," Kian announces evenly.

Everything happens so fast I don't have time to process it. The thumping of my heart is a mere afterthought, a natural response I barely register in the danger we face as the hooting on the other side of the water turns louder and the seconds tick on to three, four—

"They're on the bridge," Aruan shouts.

The king and Kian fall back just as a horde of Phaelix, clutching axe-sized knives with half-moon shaped blades, jump through the water. Some of them are swept away by the force of the foaming cascade, their screams piercing the air. I imagine their bodies flying over the sides of the bridge and bouncing off the sharp rocks at the bottom. But others make it through. They land on their clawed feet, their eyes narrowed menacingly and their lips peeled back over their shark-like teeth.

Aruan tightens his hold on my hand, squeezing my fingers to the point of pain as he addresses Gaia in a strained voice. "Portal Elsie out of here. She'll be safe in my quarters."

Gaia, who's got her hands full with pulling up portals to bring in more guards, doesn't have a chance to do as her brother commands. The reason for ignoring him is obvious. The queen can't keep up the work. It looks as if she may collapse at any moment.

Sweat drips from her pallid face. If the concerned glances the king steals at her are anything to go by, she's not going to last much longer.

Kian says something in the guttural language of the Phaelix. From the hand gestures he's using, waving at the space behind them and pulling a line with his finger across his throat, he's telling them to either retreat or to be prepared for the consequences.

"Let the idiots get closer," Aruan says. "Let them see what happens if they try."

The Phaelix measure our small group. Drops of water roll off their shiny scales and splatter on the bridge. They hesitate, appearing to be waiting for something.

Fuck.

In my wildest dreams, I never thought I'd be caught in a fight, at least not the kind that involves swords, daggers, and lizards.

"Go, Nia," the king yells, not breaking eye contact with the tallest of the Phaelix at the head of the party. "Enough!"

"Just a few more," the queen croaks out, nearly crumbling to her knees.

"Vitai," the king says, his voice as sharp as a whip. "Get your mother inside."

"Now, Gaia," Aruan growls. "I can't leave the hall undefended to portal Elsie myself. Get her out of here. I've got this."

Which answers my earlier question. Aruan can indeed create a portal.

The Phaelix leading the group looks toward the window. Below, an army of lizards advances up the trail toward the waterfall, marching like one man. Grinning, he lifts his face. That's what he was waiting for.

Oh, shit.

A scream catches in my throat as the Phaelix storm us, but they don't make it two steps before, with harrowing shrieks, the lot of them melt into goo.

In the meantime, the guards are fighting the Phaelix on the ground. The lizards force their way forward with vicious swipes of their knives. When a Phaelix hooks his blade around a guard's arm and chops it off clean above the elbow, I understand why their knives are so strangely shaped. I pinch my eyes shut, willing myself to unsee the gruesome scene.

A weight slams into my chest, nearly stealing my breath. My eyes fly open with a gasp. Aruan, who's still protecting me with his body, has stepped back and crashed into me. With my eyes tightly shut, I wasn't following his lead. He's slowly but surely walking me backward toward the hallway.

Caught off guard by the chilling screams of their disintegrating compatriots, the Phaelix on the ground have paused uncertainly, their bulging eyes trained on the palace. A few brave ones lift their sickle-like knives and charge the guards again, but in a second, the whole army of lizards is fizzling and bubbling.

Holy cow.

They've all been vaporized. The smell is disgusting.

It stinks like rotten fish. I swallow hard, almost retching at the stench.

The guards are splattered with green glob. The ground is covered in the sticky mess. And just when I think it's over, another wave of Phaelix rush through the waterfall.

They're either brave or very fucking stupid, because like their buddies, they're melted on the spot.

At this point, I'm observing everything with detached fascination. It feels too unreal, more like a movie than reality.

"Three strokes west of the sun," Kian says.

Aruan turns his gaze in that direction. As Kian predicted, the Phaelix attack from a different angle on the ground. And then, poof. They're all liquefied.

The enormity of Aruan's power hits me then. If it hadn't truly sunk in before, it's staring me straight in the eyes now—and it's terrifying. Kian uses his mind-reading ability to announce from which direction the enemy will be targeting while Gaia and her mother create portals to bring in more guards. Some of the guards must have powers of their own because I saw one hurling Phaelix through the air without laying a hand on them while another set them on fire by simply looking at them. I'm not sure what the king's role in all this is, as he's given up on the waterfall, but it's clear that the guards' main purpose is to keep the enemy at bay long enough for Aruan to vaporize them as they attack from all sides.

It's almost too easy.

The Phaelix don't stand a chance.

Finally, there's a slump in the constant charging. The king uses the opportunity to drag the queen from the Great Hall as she seems set on ignoring his order to retreat. Vitai rushes toward us, saying something about getting the wounded guards to safety.

Gaia stops opening portals and grabs my hand. Aruan is still holding my other hand. When the reassuring grip of his fingers loosens around mine, I cling to him, a part of me unwilling and inexplicably incapable of letting him go.

"No," I say as he releases me with a soft, reassuring smile.

I don't want to leave him.

Of all the things I've never wanted to do in my life, including dying, abandoning him now is at the top of that list.

I can't explain it.

There's no logical reason.

All I know is that it's as if my soul is being torn in two when Gaia drags me away and pulls me through the purple lights.

I stumble, yanking my hand from hers, when we land in front of Aruan's quarters. "Wait, Aruan—"

"My brother can handle himself," she says in a stern manner. "You saw it yourself."

Everything inside me protests. "We can't just leave him there on his own." What if they get a jump on him? What if his power runs out? Can it run out? I have no idea what his limitations are, if any.

"Kian and Vitai are with him as well as the guards. You should go inside like the other royals. They're all in their quarters where it's safe."

"So that you can go back and make more portals while I sit here and twiddle my thumbs?" I ask with a snort.

A few tuataras scurry by, their sharp nails clacking on the flagstones as they run deeper into the palace. I duck as an anurognathus dives low through the air and whizzes past my head, following the pets to the farthest rooms, as far away from the danger as possible.

Pip.

They know. The animals know instinctively.

Aruan is fighting for his life—for all our lives. Kian and Vitai are helping as best they can. So is Gaia. The queen did what she could. The king, well, I don't know what he's doing, but I can't just hide in the palace with the rest of the royals.

Suno rounds the corner, running in the same direction as Pip and the tuataras. He stops in his tracks when he spots us.

"Dragons, Gaia. What are you doing here? The queen has collapsed. She's too sick to create more portals. I'm on my way to guard her so your father can return to the fight. You should be with your brothers. At least you'll be able to pull them to a safe location in the palace if necessary."

"I want to help," I say, looking between them. "What can I do?"

Suno's green eyes narrow as he regards me with

disdain. "You don't have a power, Elsie." He must see the surprise on my face because he continues with an unfriendly smile, "Yes, news travels fast in Lona and even faster in the palace. Aruan may claim that you're an Alit, but everyone knows you're not like us. You're useless. Stay here. You'll just get in the way."

Ouch. Okay, that may be true, but that was kind of tactless. What a dickhead. And to think I liked him.

"And what's your superpower? Ignorance?" I prop my hands on my hips and walk right up to him. "I may not have a power, but I'm not fucking useless."

He scoffs. "I can make any non-living matter invisible. My task is to ensure the enemy doesn't find our queen if—the dragons forbid—they breach the walls."

"Suno," Gaia says in a chastising tone. "This isn't the time for pettiness." She softens her voice before addressing me. "If you really want to help Aruan, the best thing you can do is not distract him. If he thinks you're in danger, he won't be able to focus on anything or anyone else."

I swallow hard. She's probably right. Not because he cares about me, but because I'm his "mate." Someone he believes belongs to him. His property.

And the potential loss of that property could make him lose control of his power, seeing as it seems to be tied to his emotions.

Is it like that for the other Alit? I still don't really understand how their powers work, or why they're all different. What the hell is this planet, and why is it so similar to and yet so different from Earth? What's the story with the dinosaurs? I know now's not the time to think about any of this stuff, but the questions are driving me mad.

Taking my silence for consent, Gaia pats my shoulder. "Don't worry. It's not the first time we've fought off a horde of Phaelix." She motions at the open archway behind me. "Will you go inside?"

"If you promise not to lock me in."

"Fine," she says, already raising her arm and flexing her fingers. "I won't seal the archway if you promise you'll stay put."

I cross my fingers behind my back. "Okay."

A small circle of lights appears in front of her. It slowly gains size until it's wide enough for her to step through.

"I'm going back," she says. "Stay in the room until Aruan comes for you."

The circle closes on her last word, and then she's gone.

A long line of guards runs down the hallway in the direction Suno was heading, toward the queen's quarters, I presume.

My fear morphs into frustration and then annoyance. "Why do the Phaelix keep on attacking if they can clearly see what happens to their comrades?"

"Because they're dumb." Suno steps aside to let a guard pass. "They have the intelligence of a sand snake. They'll keep on coming until their leader tells them to stop."

When the guards are gone, Suno gives me a long look. He opens his mouth, but seemingly thinking better of what he was going to say, closes it again before following hot on the guards' heels.

I hate to admit that he's right. What do I have to offer? I can't open portals, heal people, make walls invisible, or read minds. I don't even know how to defend myself with a knife. I'd most likely end up being in the way. And if Aruan is distracted, there's a good chance we'll all either end up dead or as slaves on a Phaelix barge.

The sounds of the continued fighting outside reach me through the window archways in the hallway. I run to the nearest one and peer outside. From here, I have a good view of the Sky Bridge, which is still swamped with Phaelix. The Alit are vastly outnumbered, but against Aruan, the Phaelix are doomed. That doesn't mean my insides aren't all twisted up. I watch with dread, growing sicker by the minute as I think about Aruan, Kian, Vitai, and Gaia alone out there.

It takes another few hundred storming Phaelix to be turned to goo before their leader shouts something in their language, and they finally fall back.

As soon as the bridge is clear, the waterfall parts. Aruan and Kian step through it onto the bridge.

Kian cups his hands around his mouth. "They're climbing up the back! They're making for the banquet hall windows."

Aruan's voice booms through the open space. "I'll seal off the windows."

Aruan abandons the fight in the front, leaving it up to his brothers and the palace guards to keep the fort there while he runs inside to prevent an invasion in the banquet hall.

Unable to stop myself, I run down the stairs to the hall where we had dinner. When I enter, Aruan is standing in the middle of the floor, surrounded by green puddles and ashes. Benches and tables have been turned over and strewn across the room. Tarix stands in the entryway that connects to the kitchen, a sword firmly gripped in both hands.

What the heck? How the hell did those lizards get in? Gaia said it was safe in the palace.

Aruan's chest rises and falls with heavy breaths. Voicing my thoughts, he asks angrily, "How the dragons did they get in? None of them could get past the main entrance, and the guards sealed all the exits."

"I don't know," Tarix says. "The bastards are like insects. They crawl out of the wood like termites."

My relief is so great I can't help myself from exclaiming, "Aruan, thank goodness you're okay." I don't examine that relief too deeply.

He turns his face my way, and what I see in his expression stills me. Sure, there's that murderous intent, that killing vibe from earlier, but there's also unexpected tenderness and stark relief that reflects my own.

"Elsie." He frowns, his eyes crinkling in the corners with concern. "Why aren't you in my quarters?"

Something passes between us, a knowledge that one

of us could've lost the other, and it sparks a deep and disturbing discord inside me, an ill feeling that makes me want to howl and tear my clothes in a dramatic act. And that says a lot because I hate drama. I've never been the dramatic type.

Awareness sizzles between us, crackling in the air. His focus changes from killing to something else, something that heats me like a red-hot rod dunked in a cup of water to boil it. My skin starts to tingle, and the tops of my ears begin to burn. Static noise drowns out all other sound. He watches me with undivided attention, his scrutiny so intense that it scares me.

Tarix and the rest of the world vanish. Nothing exists but Aruan. I don't know what's happening, but it's as if everything has been condensed into a narrow tunnel, and I already know I'm going to barrel down it no matter where it leads.

Aruan makes it to me in a few long strides, carelessly dropping his sword in the midst of crossing the floor. He aims for me like a missile locked onto a target, and I welcome the explosion with open arms.

His lips are on mine before I have time to suck in a breath. My heartbeat is all over the place, a crazy, wild rhythm that gallops in my chest.

"Elsie," he breathes against my lips.

I pull away to look at him, a desperate need compelling me to study his handsome face. Just as I do so, something moves in my peripheral vision. I turn my head toward it, and then horror turns me to stone.

A Phaelix has jumped out from behind one of the

side archways, his sickle raised in the air, and he's charging straight at Aruan.

"Aruan!" I scream, but it's too late.

The tip of the halfmoon blade catches Aruan's shoulder. Aruan must've caught on just before the Phaelix dealt the blow because the Phaelix is already disintegrating. But the blade has done enough damage. Blood pools from the cut in Aruan's shirt, blooming red over the white fabric.

"Aruan," I cry out again. "Your shoulder! You're bleeding."

He bends his arm and touches the gash at the back of his shoulder. Then he wipes his other hand over the wound and brings both hands to his face. Surprise transforms his features as he stares at the blood coating his palms. He didn't even feel that cut, but that fact doesn't put me at ease. The disconcerting thought that hits me is that Aruan isn't entirely invincible. Despite his strength and power, he's capable of dying. Very much so.

I'm trembling from my head to my toes. I've never felt fear so acutely, and it isn't for myself. The fear is for Aruan.

Aruan turns to me frantically, cupping my cheeks with his bloodstained hands. "Are you all right?"

I manage a terse nod.

He pulls me roughly against him, sheltering me against the hard wall of his chest. For once, I'm glad that I can lean against him and borrow some of his strength.

"Dragons," Tarix says. "I tried to get to him, but he had too much distance on me. It's a good thing you vaporized the vermin before he could get his blade deeper into you."

Despite the blood running down Aruan's arm, his stance remains vigilant. He doesn't show any signs of weakness or pain. "We'd better check if there's more of that scum hiding somewhere in the palace."

"There are none," Kian says from the double doors, entering the hall with long, easy strides. "The palace is empty of any signs of their pea-sized brains." He stops short of us. "We've cleared the grounds. The Phaelix have retreated. The village is safe too."

"Thank the dragons," Tarix says, wiping a hand over his brow.

Kian nods at Aruan's wound. "You'd better have that looked at before you bleed out. I'll tell Vitai to come."

Aruan glances down. "It's just a scratch. I can take care of it myself."

I stand rooted to the spot, following the conversation as if it's happening in a different place and to someone else.

"I'll get Vitai for you anyway," Kian says.

He nods in my direction and leaves promptly.

Tarix stares at the green puddle on the floor. "I'll get the guards to clean this up."

Aruan isn't listening anymore. He lifts me into his arms and carries me swiftly to his room. Once we're safely inside, he lowers me to my feet. I open my mouth to tell him we need to disinfect the cut while we wait for Vitai, because who knows what else the Phaelix chopped with that blade, but his mouth is on mine before I can utter a word. His bloodied hands are all over my body, touching and stroking as if he has to reassure himself that I'm here and alive.

The protest that had formed at the back of my mind dies prematurely as the fire running through me incinerates any inhibitions or objections. All that remains is the fear, the horrible fear that Aruan could've died, and with that thought, the strange accompanying sentiment that my soul is being shredded.

I barely register the hands that tug at the laces of my dress. His kiss is too all-consuming, my feelings too strange and overwhelming, almost as if they're not my own. He growls impatiently into the kiss, his urgency matching mine as it reaches a feverish pitch. The reason for his impatience becomes clear when he gives up on blindly undoing the laces, and I hear the tearing of fabric as he rips them free. The tight bodice gives, allowing me to breathe more easily. I drag the welcome air into my lungs just as I'm inhaling Aruan's very essence—that enticing male smell.

He groans his approval when I reciprocate by pulling at his shirt. As if my reaction somehow gives him the permission he needs, he quickly pushes the sleeves of my dress over my arms. The garment pools around my feet, leaving me naked except for my shoes. I have no idea how Aruan's shirt has come off, if I tore it from his body or if he did it himself, but when his chest is finally bare, I press myself against him and tangle my arms around his neck like vines.

He's tall enough that the action raises me onto my toes…and then higher as he fastens his hands on my ass and lifts me until my shoes dangle from my feet before finally dropping to the floor. The unyielding planes of his hairless chest are smooth and warm. Deep grooves define the hard-cut muscles. I can't stop rubbing against him, needing to get closer, needing more, so much more.

"Dragons, Elsie," he says through gritted teeth, practicing steely self-restraint.

I can't explain how I know that. I just instinctively understand what he feels—the fast-dwindling control, the building tide, and the terrible need.

I'm burning up inside, flames consuming me alive. I don't even care that we're covered in his blood and that his handprints are leaving red stains on my skin. I'm beyond thinking, especially when he bends down and kisses a sensitive spot on my neck.

I tilt my head, giving him better access. He plants a trail of burning kisses down to my collarbone and over the curve of my breast. When he takes my hardened nipple into his mouth, I nearly come on the spot. The way he flicks his tongue over the tip before teasing it with his teeth is wicked. I've never felt anything like it. Something contracts in my core, my pleasure building instantly.

"Yes," he says with a note of victory, releasing my

breast and letting me down to shed his boots and pants.

I drag my gaze over him, taking in the magnificent male body in front of me, the broad chest and flat stomach, the abdomen that's drawn in rock-hard squares like a slab of carved concrete, the deep V that cuts to his groin, and—

Oh, shit.

He's enormous. Huge. His cock is thick and long, ribbed with veins and adorned with a smooth, wide crest.

I drop my gaze lower, taking in his powerful legs. Aruan lets me watch, lets me get my fill, and a part of me mourns the fact that he has ruined me for other men. The unfairness makes me want to weep, but I don't know if it's with joy or sadness.

He's looking too, studying my body. Somehow, this is different from the other times I've been naked in front of him. His intentions aren't the same. But I'm too far gone to care, especially when he closes the distance between us and pulls me flush against him so that his hardness is nestled against my stomach.

When he bends his knees and slides that hardness through my thighs, I cry out in ecstasy. At the sound that escapes my lips, he becomes like a beast, holding my face in the vise of his hands while plundering my mouth and stroking my tongue with his, all the while gliding that thick cock over my folds, in and out of the narrow space between my pressed-together legs.

The act is a foretaste of what's to come, a

simulation of where we'll end up if I don't put an end to this, but I'm unable to formulate a single word.

He straightens without letting me go. I moan at the loss as he pulls his cock over my folds one last time before lifting me into his arms.

I wrap my legs around his hips for purchase.

Yes.

This feels even better.

He walks while still kissing me senseless, but not to the bed as I expected. As I want him to. Instead, he enters the cleansing room. The pool is already filled with water. He must've done that with his mind even as we were making out.

Understanding dawns when he ends the kiss and carries me into the water. He wants to wash the blood away. The color isn't clear as when I take a bath but cloudy, and that distinct scent of milk and honey hangs in the air again.

The water is warm and inviting, soothing me in a relaxing way without making me sleepy like the first time.

"Why am I not falling asleep?" I ask. "The water smells and looks the same as it did the day you brought me here, yet I'm not lethargic."

"The smell and color are due to the healing salts that are added," he says in a rough voice. "Last time, Gaia also mixed in a salt that induces deep sleep. It was necessary in order to heal you. I didn't want you to suffer through that."

The consideration makes me feel warm and fuzzy

inside, which is a huge contrast to how petrified I was when I thought he was going to drown me.

He sits on the built-in bench and arranges me on his lap so that I'm straddling him. His cock is trapped between us, a hot, velvety, iron-hard pressure against my belly. The crest is visible in the milky water where it's resting against his stomach, reaching his navel. I have a sudden urge to taste him, to slide to my knees and take him in my mouth.

Before I can act on the impulse, he claims my lips in another brutal kiss. Weaving my hands through the thick, soft strands of his hair, I hold on tightly as I seek the friction I need by grinding myself on the hard length of his cock. He grips my short hair in a fist in turn, tearing his mouth from mine to tilt back my head and stare into my eyes.

"Mate," he says, the single word infused with possession, desire, and an unmistakable warning.

My mind catalogues all those nuances, but they're just information I store away. They don't affect me one way or another. Their meaning doesn't come through. I can only focus on soothing this ache, this growing need.

"You're killing me," he says with a clenched jaw as I move up and down, working toward a reward I need more than air.

Tears sting my eyes as he pulls hard on the roots of my hair, trying to get across some message.

"You're not coming like this." His voice is hoarse.

Rough. "You'll come with my cock inside you, so if that's not what you want, you'd better stop now."

That sounds so right. What I need. What I want. I lift higher onto my knees until the broad head nudges my opening.

"Dragons," he bites out, staring at me as if he's in pain.

I move down, letting that thick crown part my folds.

Oh, how deliriously delicious.

A voice at the back of my head warns me to go slowly—no, to stop—but it's like background noise. Inconsequential.

I see his intention in his eyes, in the way the silver darkens to molten pools of charcoal and in the calculation that settles in their depths. A huge pull fills my entire being, compelling me to rush to the end, to a necessary completion.

Just as I'm about to take that plunge, Aruan tenses. The killing rage from earlier replaces the lust-crazed, predatory look in his eyes. It sobers me somewhat, pulling me from a deep, almost drug-induced state.

I gasp as I take in our positions, how vulnerable I am. It will only take a single tilt of his hips to spear his cock into me. I'm not even sure I can take him.

I hold perfectly still, my V-card, my life, and everything else hanging in the balance. What the fuck is wrong with me? What was I about to do?

That look that warned me we're not alone has pulled me back to the present and not a minute too soon. Not to mention that for all I know, there's a freaking Phaelix creeping up on us. Our lives could've been in danger while I wasn't thinking straight.

Aruan yanks me down into the water. My ass lands on his thighs, my legs dangling over his.

"Bad timing?" a man asks with a teasing laugh.

As Aruan's reaction already warned me that we have company, I don't give a start, but it's still an unpleasant sensation.

I twist my neck to look over my shoulder.

Vitai enters the room, an amused grin splitting his face. "If I'd known you were busy, I would've waited, but Kian said it was urgent." He stops at the side of the pool and stretches his neck to peer at the wound on Aruan's shoulder. "That's a nasty cut. I'm afraid it's too deep to wait. I'd better close it up. You'll have to finish what you've started later."

"By dragon, brother," Aruan says, his fingers digging into my sides. "I have a good mind to kill you. I told Kian I didn't need help."

Vitai straightens with a chuckle. "You have a strange way of showing your gratitude for my services."

"Get out," Aruan says in a deep, dark voice. "If you see my mate in any state of undress—"

"You'll have to kill me," Vitai says in a bored tone. "Yes, I know." Turning his back on us, he says, "Well, make sure your mate is decent so I can heal your wound and get to our soldiers. They need me too."

A muscle ticks in Aruan's jaw, but the mention of the soldiers seems to bring him to his senses.

"Don't move," he barks out, the command aimed at Vitai.

He lifts me gently out of the pool and onto the floor before rising from the water like a Greek Adonis in all his naked glory. If my mind had been too lust-befuddled and drunk on passion to fully appreciate and memorize his tantalizing form and features earlier, that's not the case now. The sight of him makes my mouth go dry. But fear and shame also pour back into my consciousness when I think about how I behaved and what I was about to do.

Aruan takes a big white folded sheet from a bench, shakes it out, and drapes it over my shoulders. He does so tenderly, treating me as if I'm made of rice paper that risks tearing.

"It won't take long," Vitai says. "I'll be quick."

I'm not sure if he's addressing me or Aruan, but his implied meaning sends heat to my cheeks.

To make matters worse, Aruan commands in that very male, very raspy timbre of his, "Go wait in my bed, Elsie. I don't want you to catch a cold."

I shake my head vehemently, trying to come up with an appropriate reply, but words refuse to form on my tongue.

He narrows his eyes. His comment is mocking, but there's a bite to it. "Lost your nerve, mate?"

The heat rising in my neck intensifies. I can't believe he's discussing this—that we almost had sex—

so callously in front of Vitai, as if it's perfectly normal to talk about what we did, *and* that I'm chickening out, in front of his brother.

Whatever mortification was keeping me silent evaporates in a burst of anger. "Have you never heard of discretion?" I snap, and clutching the sheet between my breasts, I spin on my heel and march away.

Or more like *run* away from what could've happened.

Aruan's laugh follows me. It's a dark, sardonic sound, saying what we both know. That at some point, if I stay here, I'm going to give in. No matter what I do, I've already lost. Like the Phaelix, I don't stand a chance against Aruan. Only, in this battle, the risk isn't being dissolved into a puddle.

It's losing my life as I've known it and never returning to Earth.

CHAPTER 13
ARUAN

My mate's rejection stings. We were a heartbeat away from fucking, from sealing our physical bond. One more breath, and she would've taken what can only be hers for eternity. I was a whisper away from impaling her on my cock and filling her with my seed, my mark. And then she changed her mind like the capricious western wind. That I can forgive her for. That I can understand. But not the shame that painted her face red. Anything but the horror that transformed her doll-like features.

Vitai says nothing, but the smirk remains plastered on his face while he heals me. I don't need Kian's power to know my youngest brother's thoughts. He thinks I've finally met my match, and it amuses him.

Well, he can go jump off the bridge. This situation isn't funny in the least.

When he's done, he leaves without a word, knowing it's dangerous to provoke me when I'm in a dark mood. That mood is also the reason I don't approach Elsie where she stands in front of the window with her back turned to me, pretending she hasn't heard me enter the bedroom. The stiffening of her narrow shoulders tells me she's aware of my footsteps on the floor.

She's changed into a pale-pink dress and clean slippers. The ones she wore this morning must be muddy. They're not very practical for walking outside. Boots are for men, but she would've been better equipped for our stroll with a pair.

In the afternoon light that streams through the window, her hair shines like ruddy moonbeams. Her smell drifts to me on the breeze, the faint womanly scent of her arousal still teasing my nostrils. They flare as I inhale deeply.

Dragons.

It's best that I don't hang around her when her body is ripe but her mind and heart are unwilling. Especially not when the killing rage in my veins hasn't completely abated. I'd never harm my mate, but I'm too explosive to face her, too close to ripping that dress off her body and finishing what we started.

Choosing wisdom in lieu of desire, I only linger long enough to grab a clean set of clothes from the trunk. I don't look at Elsie as I shove my legs into the pants, pull the tunic over my head, and fasten my boots.

As I walk from the room, an uncomfortable ache settles in my chest, almost like a persistent hiccup under my breastbone. I rub a fist over the spot in a futile attempt to ease the pain.

My father waits in my mother's quarters. He hovers next to the daybed on which she's reclined, poised like a big, brooding shadow over her. Suno is there, pressing a cool cloth to her forehead.

Concern eradicates most of the volatile anger and bitter disappointment that, together with frustration, war inside me. My mother isn't faking her weakness. She's truly ill, and despite what she may have done, what I *know* she did, I hate to see her like this.

"How is she?" I ask my father, taking in her half-mast eyelids and laborious breathing.

"Exhausted," he replies tightly. "She should've been focusing on healing, not on waging a war."

"Without the queen, it would've been a hopeless situation," Suno says.

"Never hopeless." I take my mother's limp, clammy hand. "I had it under control."

My father's voice is grim. "Tarix told me what happened." He dips his head and holds my gaze. "You know what that means."

My jaw tightens. "We have a traitor in our midst."

"The attack was too well timed." My father lifts a cup of water from the side table. "The Phaelix knew when our guards would be away and our defenses weakened, which means someone told them." He dips a finger in the water and drags it over my mother's cracked lips. "I personally sealed the window archways giving access to the exterior, yet one was open, and it just so happened to be in the kitchen, well away from where we were occupied in the fight."

My father looks between Suno and me, leaving the rest unsaid, namely that someone opened the archway deliberately.

Someone on the inside of the palace is working with the Phaelix, but why the dragon would anyone do that? The only thing I can think of is that they must be power hungry, enough so to risk everything in order to overthrow our reign.

"Let's hope Kian finds the traitor," Suno says with a sigh, pushing to his feet. His smile is condescending. "I'd like to know what reward the Phaelix offered for such an act of treachery. It must've been of very high value. Why else would anyone betray their own people?"

"You'd be surprised what motivations and ambitions drive some individuals," my father says, his face twisted into a wry expression.

I study my mother's washed-out features. "Will she be all right?"

"Vitai thinks so," my father replies.

I carefully lay her hand back on the covers. "How long does he think her recovery will take?"

"It's difficult to tell." My father inhales deeply. "Depleting what little energy she had left in the battle didn't help."

"What matters is that she rests," Suno says, fixing us with a pointed look.

My father puts the cup aside and tells Suno, "Stay

with her and don't let anyone in the room. I'm going to see if Kian has managed to track down any information that will lead us to the traitor."

I still want my answers as to how Elsie ended up on Earth, and I'll get them, but now I also have other questions. Too many questions.

After what Elsie told me about her illnesses, I want to know how and why that happened to her. I want to know everything she's been through and everything she's felt. I want to understand all of it, not only because she's my mate and it's natural that I want to live every beat of her life as if it were my own, but also because I want to prevent it from ever happening again.

Yet for now, I follow my father into the hallway, accepting that getting my answers will have to wait.

"First the poison and then an attack," the king says, walking briskly down the hallway and taking the stairs that lead to the inner court.

I easily keep up with his quick, urgent stride. "Do you think they're related?"

"I doubt it." His expression darkens. "But I won't eliminate the possibility, not yet."

"What a treacherous place Lona has become," I say with loathing.

"No more treacherous than it's always been," he replies. "The only thing that changes are the enemies."

We exit on the inner courtyard level where Kian as well as my uncles and aunts are gathered. They're sitting on stone benches arranged in a circle in the middle of the lush garden. Blue bell flower creepers twist around the trunks of old yellow bark trees, their sweet, subtle perfume faint in the air.

My father stops a distance away from the others and nods at my shoulder. "How's your mobility?"

"Fine." I swing my arm to loosen the muscles. "It was only a flesh wound."

"The Phaelix had a good shot at chopping off your head." His eyes narrow with calculation. "That has never happened before."

"He crept up on me."

He watches me with a perceptive gaze. "You were distracted."

By my mate. As always, the unsaid rings much louder than what's been said.

I gnash my teeth. "I felt him the minute he moved. Him ending up in a puddle on the floor is proof of that."

"You were lucky."

I take a wide stance. "What are you saying, Father?"

"You've never been wounded before."

"There's always a first time."

"Yes," he drawls. "And every time teaches us a lesson. I think it's safe to assume the presence of your mate diminished your vigilance in the attack."

"On the contrary, it heightened it."

"But it changed your priorities."

I don't reply because that may be true. Every one of my senses was tuned into the fight. I smelled that filthy Phaelix just as strongly as I felt him when he jumped through the air. But with Elsie there, I could only think about getting her to safety. The notion of anything happening to her made me volatile, triggering a protectiveness unrivaled by any other battle-hardened instinct.

As if to prove the point, a tremor shakes the floor at my recollection of that dangerous situation.

My father glances at the gathering of royals, who all have their eyes trained on us, and says in a lowered voice, "Don't let word of it get out. There's no point in broadcasting a weakness. Just be careful with your mate. Next time, lock her up in a safe place so she can't distract you in a fight."

I curl my fingers into a fist. "It's not Elsie's fault."

"In a way, it is," he declares with a truthful solemnness I rarely see on his face. "If you're not careful, she'll be your downfall."

"Don't start with that too," I bite out.

"I'm only telling the truth as a man who can speak with experience."

I take a moment to digest that. My father has lived almost a century of moon cycles with his mate, enough to have learned the advantages as well as the pitfalls of that union. He's had the benefit of time to master the art of successfully navigating said pitfalls. For Elsie and me, it's only just starting. Because she was stolen from me and condemned to a cruel fate.

"Elsie almost died on Earth." My words are measured. "The person who did that to her—to us— *will* pay."

My father watches me with an unfaltering gaze. "The issue at hand is the immediate threat. Your mate is clouding your thinking. Our duty is to protect our people."

My smile is cold. "Our duty is always first to our mates. That's the rule of our kind. Don't tell me you wouldn't protect Mother with your life."

The smile he offers in return is challenging. "I'll protect both your mother and our people."

"But you'll protect her first. Isn't that what you're trying to tell me?"

He doesn't answer, but he knows what I mean. He knows I believe the queen sent my mate to Earth. My own mother. Who else was powerful enough at that time to create a portal that could bridge the parallel worlds? Yes, that's what he's thinking too. I can see it in his eyes. He can't hide it from me.

It's also true that, since then, somebody has been very busy practicing the art of creating portals. How else would the humans have ended up here? Which brings me to a matter I wanted to discuss once I'd claimed and secured my mate. As it looks now, the claiming isn't going to be easy or quick, seeing how hard-headed Elsie is.

Keeping my voice down, I say, "There was a barge with human slaves on it when I rescued Elsie from the Phaelix."

My father grows still. "The rumors are true then."

"I'm afraid so."

He exhales, suddenly looking older than his age. "So

someone is bringing humans in from Earth. That makes for a lot of puzzles to solve—the poison, the traitor amongst us, and now the irrefutable proof that someone other than your mother can create portals to Earth."

"Correct," I say grimly.

By implication, it's an Alit, one of our own. We're the only race that possesses powers. The royals have the strongest powers, and I don't know any royals as skilled as my mother in creating portals—not in any of the five kingdoms. But there must be someone.

The question is, who?

My father drops his head, hiding his face from the people watching us with scrutinizing attention, and rubs his brow. "Keep this to yourself for now. We don't need a national pandemonium. Once we've solved our own problems on the inside, we'll return to the portal mystery."

He leaves me with that order and heads over to the group who waits in pregnant silence.

"Lorak," my uncle Incus—Suno's father—exclaims. "What in Zerra's name? Who dared to let the Phaelix in?"

My father turns to Kian, who gives an imperceptible shake of his head. He hasn't been able to find the guilty party, which may mean the culprit isn't inside the palace walls.

Only, everyone is accounted for. Everyone who lives in the palace has been screened by Kian. It had to have been someone on our side. Someone opened that archway from the inside. Then why isn't Kian picking up anything? It doesn't make sense.

Frustration mounts inside me.

My aunts shift to the far ends of their benches when I enter their circle. My uncles clear their throats.

Yes, they're still petrified of me, even more so now.

Giving them a sardonic grin that makes them cower, I sit down.

My father listens to everyone's complaints about the rising unrest in the kingdom. The people feel unsafe. The villagers don't want to make the journey to the borders to trade their grain and other harvested crops for precious opals and metals from the mines in the south. It's grown too dangerous. Too frequently, they're intercepted by Phaelix who steal their goods. It's impossible to go unarmed. We need to reestablish order.

Vitai arrives while the griping is in session. We move to the border of the courtyard where we can have a private conversation. I tell him about Elsie's sicknesses, everything she suffered on Earth. When I'm done, he looks at me curiously.

"Well?" I say, impatient. "Do you have any theories?"

He scratches his jaw. "I'll have to think about it."

"What about now?" My heart goes into a gallop with the speed of a rabid dragon on the loose. "She's not dying, is she?"

He replies calmly, "If she were, you'd know."

Yes, I'd feel it.

I probe the connection carefully, already feeling the

sharp sting of her resistant withdrawal at my unwelcome intrusion. As before, there's only vitality.

Vitai pats my back sympathetically. "I'll do some research and see what I can come up with."

I clench my jaw. "We need to speak to Mother."

Vitai knows why. If she sent Elsie to Earth, she may be the only one who knows why Elsie's body ended up malfunctioning so badly. The Alit are notoriously healthy and strong. We don't suffer from diseases. And Elsie is an Alit. Of that, there's no doubt.

Healthy or sick, she's my mate. She will be until the end of time, and nothing can change that. The knowledge is simultaneously soothing and frightening. To lose her a second time would kill me. She's the only cure against the lethal numbness that was slowly swallowing me whole. Now that she's here, I can be who I was born to be—a ruler. And when my father passes on the title, a king.

The fruitless discussion between the royals takes another hour to dwindle down to murmured complaints. Every person has said what they wanted to and repeated it to their hearts' content, until they've worn it out like a threadbare rug. They carry on expressing their fears and injustices, not looking for solutions but for a soundboard for their grievances. What matters is action.

At long last, it's agreed that we'll send the Phaelix a message. No more plundering. No more stealing. No more harassing. No more attacking.

My father shares a private look with me.

No more slave trading either. They will put an end to bringing in humans, however they're doing so.

Negotiators will deliver our ultimatums, everything but the embargo on the slaves. That part will be my responsibility. The situation is far too sensitive to let it leak out. Contact between Zerra and Earth is not only forbidden but also punishable. I understand my father's unspoken message only too well. I'm to stop the slave trade at all costs, which means finding the person or persons responsible for creating the portals and executing those who won't be swayed to give up their lucrative talents.

When the drinks that normally mark the end of a meeting are served, I excuse myself at last. I'm not tired, but I'm weary. The friction with Elsie is weighing on me.

Back in my quarters, Elsie sits in a chair facing the window, her elbow on her knee and her chin resting in her hand, staring unhappily—no, longingly—at the blue sky beyond.

She jumps when I touch her shoulder. This time, she genuinely didn't hear me enter.

"Are you hungry?" I ask by way of a peace offering.

It seems she doesn't like me or what I have to offer much, but food is the one thing I can give without getting it wrong.

"No." She shakes her head without moving her gaze away from the sky. "I ate a lot at breakfast. I'm not hungry."

I bend down to peer through the window. "What

are you searching for out there with such utter concentration?"

"I'm trying to spot a dinosaur again," she replies in a listless tone.

"A dinosaur? What's that?"

She sighs. "A dragon."

I think I get it. "Are you bored?"

"Terribly," she says, perking up a little as she faces me. "With the very few exceptions when you took me out of my cage, you've been keeping me locked up in here since you brought me to this palace."

"It's for your safety," I say in my most reasonable tone.

She scoffs and looks out the window again.

I pull up a chair and sit down where I have a clear view of her lovely face. "You could engage in plenty of pleasant activities to keep you occupied."

"Such as?" she asks in a monotonous tone.

"Painting and tapestry. You could play games."

She rolls her eyes. "I'd rather die of boredom, thank you very much."

"Mastering the art of leisure is as important as perfecting the art of war."

"Speak for yourself. And I don't do leisure, which is just a synonym for boredom."

"All right." I choose my words carefully, asking good-naturedly, "Have you never been *bored* before?"

"Ha." She turns her face back to me. "Not even for a second."

"No?" Intrigued, I smile. "What kept you so busy?"

"For starters, trying not to die." Shrugging, she continues, "I've always had a full life. Mom and Dad tried to make up for all the things I missed out on while I was in the hospital by taking me on trips and arranging enough fun activities to crowd every minute of my agenda." She shrugs again. "They meant well."

"Tell me about them, your parents."

Her face lights up. "I couldn't ask for a better mom or dad. Like all parents, they can be a bit overbearing, but that's understandable."

"They're not your biological parents," I state carefully.

Who knows what they told her? Maybe she doesn't know that. In that case, it will be even harder for her to come to terms with the truth.

"Like I told Gaia, that doesn't mean anything."

So she does know. Her parents didn't keep that information from her. "How did you end up with them?"

She looks away. "They adopted me." Shading her face with one hand, she points with the other at the window. "What's that point in the distance? Could that be a dragon?"

I see through her attempt to change the subject. She doesn't want to draw attention to the facts that so clearly argue in favor of her being an Alit, but she won't throw me off track so easily. "What do you know about the circumstances surrounding your adoption?"

She turns her face back to me, watching me with a wary light in her turquoise eyes. "Why do you ask?"

"Because I'm interested," I admit. "I'd really like to know."

She drops her hands in her lap and sighs. "Someone found an abandoned baby in a park. That baby was me. I was brought to a hospital and entered the foster care system, where I was swiftly put up for adoption. My parents couldn't have children, so there you have it."

Abandoned in a park.

I want to draw blood. To kill someone. Suppressing the explosive rage, I keep my voice level. "Did anyone try to locate your biological parents?"

"Of course. The authorities put out notices and checked hospital records for deliveries that had taken place during my estimated birth year."

I'm trying hard to follow, the concepts she's mentioning being strange to me.

"However—" She cuts herself off, clearly not wanting to say that they always came up empty-handed because it's another point in favor of the fact she's still denying.

"I did wonder about that often," she finally admits. "But I figured it must've been a home birth or some such. Either way, if my biological parents didn't want me, I didn't want to find them." She continues with a wry laugh, "Not that I had the energy to search for them."

Everything she's saying is proving me right and her wrong about her true identity. Her biological parents didn't abandon her. She was stolen from them. Yet that fact doesn't help to soothe her. On the contrary, talking about it upsets her.

Wanting to calm her, I point out the positive parts of the history she shared with me. "From what you told me, your adoptive parents were good to you. They did everything in their power to make you happy."

Her expression brightens a little. "That's true."

Since talking about her origins upsets her, I change the subject. "When your parents didn't keep you busy, what did you do with your time?"

She sits up straighter. "There were my studies."

I'm intrigued. "Studies?"

"I'm in college."

That tells me nothing. I know a little about Earth's history, thanks to my mother's lessons. Everything else, including the facets of modern-day life on that planet, is never discussed.

Still, I try to follow along. "And you do your studies in this college?"

"I take all kinds of classes, like *Greek Lit* and *anthropology*."

She's speaking her language instead of mine.

At my confused frown, she explains, "You know, to learn about ancient civilizations."

That's a bit clearer. "For what purpose?"

"It's always been my dream to become an archeologist or a paleontologist." Her smile is meant to be nonchalant, but it doesn't fool me. "Oh, don't get me wrong. I had no illusions about actually working in the field. I knew that would be impossible with all my health problems, but I wanted to get my degree at least."

I don't know what degree she's talking about, but I'm guessing it's important. And not easy to obtain. "What does an archeologist do?"

"They dig up the remains of bygone eras."

Odd. "For what reason?"

"To have an idea of how life was back then."

"Why?"

She makes an impatient sound. "Because it's interesting. Exciting. Because it teaches us how the world used to be, that it's so much older and bigger than just our self-centered little selves."

"I see." I'm charmed. My smile stretches. "What's your favorite Earth era?"

"Definitely the dinosaur periods," she says with enthusiasm. "Which is why I was hoping you could show me more, um, dragons."

"The dragons are dangerous. Going anywhere near them is strictly off-limits." I keep my tone amiable but make sure there's no doubt about how serious I am. "If I catch you anywhere near one, I'll lock you in here indefinitely."

Like a curtain falling, her eyes lose their spark and become shuttered.

A sudden rush of tenderness makes my question coaxing. "What's the matter?"

She looks away. "Here, I'm nothing but a prisoner."

I lean forward and take her hand. "No, Elsie. You're not my prisoner. You're not locked up in a cell in the dungeons. If you're in my quarters, it's because, one, I want to ensure your safety, and two, you're my mate."

She looks back at me, her eyes painfully bright. "Back home, I had dreams and a life. Yes, it might have been a short and mostly painful life, at least physically, but..." She bites her lip, unwilling to continue.

I stroke her knuckles with my thumb, enjoying the softness of her skin and the delicate bones of her tiny hand. Coaxing again. Willing her to continue, to open up to me like she did a heartbeat ago. "But what, my sweet?"

"But now that I'm no longer dying—which, by the way, I'm still trying to figure out—why can't you send me back to Earth?"

I stiffen. "Is that what you want?"

"Yes! More than anything. You have no idea how much I miss my parents. Oh, you'd make me so happy if you sent me back."

The sound of that is an acrid poison to swallow. Elsie doesn't feel the pull like I do. Our bond is nothing to her. Her happiness lies not in our connection but in our separation. Indeed, our bond is so insignificant to her she'd rather run away from it, back to the life of horrors and pain she led.

It's like a slap in the face. To be rejected by one's own mate is the worst humiliation a man can suffer.

The sweet softness she instilled in me mere moments ago grows hard and bitter. At the prospect of losing her, a tide of possessiveness surges inside me. It turns me into a monster, a beast that will slay anything standing between him and his mate.

The polished reflection stone explodes, twinkling stars of silver flying through the air.

Elsie jerks and gasps, but she sits as still as a good little house pet, no longer tempting the beast.

I let her hand go and pull mine away, feeling the frosty loss of that contact all the way to the solid wall coating my heart. My voice reflects that cold hardness, the steely resolve and sharp rejection that beats in my chest. "Your place is here, Elsie. This is where you'll stay. You've experienced the bond between us every time our clothes have come off. Lie to me about it if you're such a coward, but at least be woman enough to admit it to yourself." I stand, towering over her, over my mate who doesn't want me. "We've said our vows. I drank to the toast. You will drink too. Only one thing remains, and that's my possession of your body. I'll give you until the end of this moon cycle to get used to the idea." My hands curl involuntarily into fists. "But know this…When the moon is full, I *will* take you as my mate, with or without your consent."

She stares up at me with shock, her cheeks pale and her pink lips parted.

Unable to stand the clear message of revulsion that's written all over her face, I leave her with that promise.

In ten and four nights, I'll pin her beneath me, and before I'm done with her, she'll beg on her knees for me to fuck her like an animal in heat.

CHAPTER 14

ELSIE

Conflict is new to me. My parents never got angry with me. They were too busy feeling sorry for me and grieving my slow demise. So needless to say, Aruan's out-of-nowhere explosion has left me shaken.

A week passes during which we hardly speak, unless you count "good morning" and a stiff "good evening" as conversation. I sleep in his bed, but he doesn't join me there.

Thankfully.

I have no idea where he's sleeping and I have no intention of asking him.

He does try to keep me entertained. I can't fault him for that. He had paints made from colorful sands. Together with brushes and some kind of bleached hides to serve as canvasses, he had them delivered to his quarters.

The materials are stacked in the corner,

untouched. I've never been an artist. My talent in that domain is nonexistent. Not even boredom can drive me to paint stick men, even though the brushes are interesting. Fabricated with the tube-like stigmas of flowers, they move and wiggle, almost seeming to paint on their own. Judging by the size of them, those flowers must be enormous—at least the size of my head.

When coaxing me into painting didn't work, he tried to tempt me with a game played with colorful seeds that hop all by themselves over a patterned board. The aim is to flick the seeds into holes carved into the wood that trap them so they're unable to continue their hopping. Each seed color carries a certain value. The person who gets the most seeds of the highest value into the holes wins. I guess he summoned Gaia to play with me, who reported diligently for board game duty. She quickly gave up when she ended up playing the game by herself.

Aruan has even brought flowers and treats. At each mealtime, he delivers my favorite dishes, which he claims to make himself to protect me from further poisoning attempts.

For exercise, he takes me to an inner courtyard with a garden and a fountain in the center. Sparkly purple and red flowers turn their heads toward any movement, and trees with rubbery black trunks and white ropey vines draped over their branches give off a sweet, spicy smell that reminds me of aniseed. We stroll along the paths that cut through the exotic plants without saying a word to each other. Neither of us mentions our mating again.

Although it's hanging like a prison sentence over my head, we refrain from discussing that subject at all costs. We're both avoiding the inevitable fight and the uncomfortable strain that, as I've recently discovered, apparently goes hand-in-hand with conflict.

Sadly, that avoidance also prevents me from asking him questions about Zerra. I'm eager to solve the mystery of this world. Not knowing drives me nuts. But I can't bring myself to give in first and break our silent war. My pride and self-preservation are at stake.

When Aruan can't escort me to the interior garden himself, he sends Gaia or Vitai to do it. Sometimes, Kian accompanies me when neither Gaia nor Vitai are available.

Gaia and I have become friendly. I like her straightforwardness that never lacks tact or kindness. She takes me on a tour of the palace, showing me the majestic Great Hall and the Sky Bridge.

The Great Hall boasts life-size statues of all the Alit kings and queens that have ruled over Lona. They stand in circle upon circle around the hall, their stony faces stern and serious.

The Sky Bridge is the bridge I saw from Aruan's balcony, the one that connects to a platform in the center and a smaller cliff on the other end. The drop below is impressive enough to give me vertigo. From what I've seen, I thought there was only one set of stairs carved into the cliff, but as it turns out, there are two. On one side, the steps lead to the sea, and on the other, they go down to a hill.

Just as I get excited about going outside, she tells me that the waterfall can only be opened by authorized Alit, which is just another way of telling me how trapped I truly am.

I don't hesitate to pepper her with my questions, but she can only tell me the things I've worked out for myself already, namely that the Alit are a humanoid species who somehow ended up sharing their world with dinosaurs and other species, like the Phaelix. She seems clueless as to how their powers work from a scientific perspective, or how it is that she's able to open portals—though she does say that she's practiced portal work since she was a child.

Her power, like that of other Alit, seems to be something between an ability that she was born with and a skill that she's perfected.

Secretly, I like the brothers too. Kian is austerely quiet, but I've come to appreciate his silence. Only once have we chatted during a walk. As Aruan and I don't speak, he's never given me any information on how the investigations are progressing. So, one day, I posed my questions to Kian.

Have they found the person who let the Phaelix into the palace yet?

What about the person who tried to poison me?

He gave me a cryptic no, and then stopped abruptly to warn me in a serious tone to be careful.

What were his exact words? "Not everyone is happy

that you're here, Elsie. Be vigilant, trust no one, and always watch your back."

Yeah, that didn't help me feel at home.

Vitai, on the other hand, is the chatty one. I've learned more about Zerra from him than anyone else. I know, for example, that the Alit are spread across five kingdoms, and that their lifestyle is very much medieval-ish—exactly the vibe I got when I first arrived here. Nowhere on Zerra is there electricity or the modern inventions of Earth, yet the people possess these inexplicable powers. There are many types of "dragons," too many to count, not that I ever get a chance to see any. Aruan makes sure I can't get outside.

I've taken to snooping around, especially in the kitchen where most of the gossiping seems to happen. The cook, an elderly lady called Jina, has told me I'm not allowed to take anything from the pantry. It's not that she wouldn't like to feed me, but after the poisoning attempt, Aruan gave them strict orders that only he's allowed to prepare my meals. It's strangely sweet. Then again, he's only protecting his own interests. He can't let his possession perish, can he?

But Jina is content to let me hang around her working space where she shouts orders at a team of cooks and cleaners as long as I keep my fingers out of her cooking pots. Unfortunately, the gossip mostly involves personal matters, and I don't learn much from them.

I did discover that the king's quarters are on the opposite side of the palace from the queen's—a strange arrangement for a "mated" couple, if you ask me. More importantly, the doors are always guarded. There's no chance of getting in. The rest of the royals avoid me like the plague.

Deciding to resort to books for more information, I asked Gaia where the library was—because every respectable palace has a library, right?—and she shocked me by saying they don't have books on Zerra.

"But what about history and science?" I asked her once I'd explained the concept of books. "How do you teach that to your new generations?"

She just smiled and said, "It's in our heads. That's all we need. We tell it to our children, and they tell it to theirs in turn."

"But what about the scrolls?" I asked, at which she laughed and told me the scrolls weren't books.

I bombarded her with more questions. For starters, if the scrolls weren't books, then what were they? But she only waved a hand and changed the subject.

Which left me no closer to figuring out how this world came about or what it is. All I can do is speculate and come up with theories, gleaned mostly from my favorite books and movies. Such as the multiverse in Marvel comics—that's a real thing, right? Not Spider-Man and all the superheroes but the multiverse concept itself. Certainly, in *The Big Bang Theory*, the physicists seemed to think there could be multiple universes, each with its own unique Earth. So maybe that's what Zerra is—a parallel universe's Earth, one where history took a different turn, and the asteroid did not wipe out the dinosaurs.

That would explain why this place is so similar to Earth yet so very different. If this were truly an alien planet, I would've died within moments of setting foot on it. The atmosphere, the force of gravity, the surface temperature—everything would be drastically different and likely not compatible with human life. Case in point: Jupiter, Mars, or any other planet known to our scientists. But Zerra is not like that. Venomous critters and giant bugs aside, it's quite welcoming to humans... or at least to humanoid Alit. Which is yet another point in favor of my theory.

If Zerra were not a parallel Earth, there's simply no way there would be a humanoid species on it, not even one with crazy powers.

Yeah, I'm all out of theories on that one.

Mulling all this over takes up some of my mental space, but not any of my free time. So, with nothing better to do, I try to escape.

It's futile. Each time, I find the doors tightly sealed and heavily guarded. Unless I sprout wings and fly from the window, I'm not going anywhere soon, not unless Aruan allows it.

So, when he walks into his quarters with a brand-new pair of soft, suede-like boots and asks if I'd like to go for a walk on the grounds, I'm not too proud to jump on the opportunity.

A short while later, he escorts me down the cliff steps with my arm tucked through his. This time, I'm not wearing one of those long, impractical dresses. I nicked a pair of Aruan's pants, which I've rolled up several times and tied with laces around my waist. One of his white shirts that I've knotted in the front completes my outfit.

People working the fields next to the palace stare with open mouths as he leads me regally down the path, going in the opposite direction from the lake. They're obviously not used to seeing women in men's clothes. Or perhaps it's the formidable and intimidating sight of Aruan. Or maybe it's just me—Aruan's "terrifying" mate.

Aruan grins as he drags his gaze over me. "Did you miss me so much that you had to steal my clothes just to feel a little nearer to me, my sweet?" He continues with his wicked teasing, "You don't have to be ashamed to admit it."

Ah. It seems our quiet spell is broken.

"Ha." I turn up my nose. "No one can trudge through the mud in those long skirts." I lift a foot to admire the comfortable, perfectly fitting boot. "These are much better than those princess shoes."

"I'll have to rectify the situation." Laughter sounds in his voice. "I'll order you some men's clothes in your size."

Suspicious, I glance at him sideways. "You're in a good mood."

He looks down at me with a smoldering smile. "That's because the moon is almost full."

My heart gives a funny little jerk.

No.

I refuse to admit just how handsome he is when he smiles like that, both with arrogance and a soft warmth that reaches his eyes.

Regretting broaching the subject, I scoff. "Well, only one of us is looking forward to that. But don't think for one moment I won't fight you."

"Oh, I know you will." His eyes gleam. "I'm bargaining on it."

Fuck. My belly heats before bottoming out in a very anticipatory way. He knows how to get to me, and by *me*, I specifically mean my dormant lady bits.

I turn away to hide my flush. "Where are we going?"

"The sacred site," he answers, and it's all I can do to hide my excitement as he continues, "I've been very busy with politics these past few days, so I haven't had the time to take you there as I promised."

My ears prick up. "What do these politics involve?" Maybe I'll finally learn something.

He sighs and says cryptically, "Diplomatic issues."

Right. He's not going to divulge anything. So much for picking his brain.

"Is it far?" When he frowns, I add, "The sacred site."

He points toward a cluster of palm trees in the distance. "It's a short walk."

I pick up my pace as excitement courses through me. Soon, I'm the one leading, dragging Aruan faster down the path.

He laughs. "Slow down, my sweet. Don't you want to enjoy the fresh air, make it last?"

"I want to see the site," I say honestly, barely able to contain myself.

His voice is deep and gruff, sending goosebumps over my skin. "In that case, I won't make you wait. I'd loathe to disappoint you."

I don't reply because something else has captured my attention.

A brown-gray moth flutters past us before settling on the pineapple-shaped cone of a cycad.

A kalligrammatid!

It's bigger and duller than the average butterfly back on Earth, but like butterflies, eyespots mark their wings. On Earth, they lived from the middle of the Jurassic to the late Cretaceous period before becoming extinct.

I stop to admire it. Butterflies and moths evolved more than two hundred million years ago and co-existed with dinosaurs. So did bees, give or take one hundred million years. I noticed that Aruan uses a lot of honey in the food and drinks he prepares for me. There must be hives somewhere. Everything on Zerra confirms the theories scientists have developed about these animals and insects that once also populated Earth.

I watch with fascination as the big moth-like insect unfurls its proboscis and begins to suck up pollination drops from the gymnosperm.

"Come." Aruan tugs on my arm. "The sun is climbing, and I want to get there before it ruins your pretty skin by burning it red."

Reluctant to leave the kalligrammatid, of which I'd only seen pictures of fossils before now, I fall into step next to Aruan again.

It's much quieter on this side of the palace. The roar of the water that laps at the cliffs is absent. Even the distant cries of the pterosaurs are silent. There's only a faint buzzing sound, like the humming of bees.

A short way from the trees, I spot the hives that are nestled into cave-like hollows in the rockface.

Aruan points in that direction. "That's where our honey comes from. The stingers prefer the non-meat-eating flowers on this side of the palace."

"Stingers?" I wrinkle my nose. "Oh, you mean bees."

"Bees?"

"We have them on Earth too. They're very old, you know, millions of years. And sadly, they've become endangered."

I want to question him more, but a big body of water that appears in the distance as we reach the top of a hill draws my gaze.

Like the lake on the other side, the surface of the water is flat, but the sand is blueish instead of gray, and the water shines pink, not black, in the sun.

Huge trees with drooping branches that touch the water grow on the shore. The red, pointy leaves are big, creating a thick foliage that throws dark patches of shade on the ground. A few fallen leaves drift lazily on the water, floating close to a stretch of small white flowers shaped like blossoms that push up from yellow-green, round, fatty leaves.

I shade my eyes with a hand against the brightness of the pale, white sun. "What are those flowers growing on the water?"

"Those are pond lilies. The petals and the leaves are used to cook *yaryia*, the dish you like so much. It's a dangerous job to harvest them because the water is infested with finned and four-legged snakes, and the biggest and most aggressive of all the dragons lay their eggs beneath the branches of the blood trees on the shore."

A rainbow stretches from one end of the lake to the other, drawing a spectrum of red, purple, blue, and green across the sky.

"This is so pretty," I say, drinking in the sight.

Aruan sounds both pleased and proud. "There are many beautiful places on Zerra, Elsie."

What he's really saying is that, in time, I'll come to love my new "home." Or that's what he hopes.

Agreed, Zerra is an amazing world. Because… *dinosaurs*! I'm not saying I want to settle here, but damn. *Dinosaurs*.

I turn to face him. "How old are the dragons?"

"The dragons have always been here."

"And the Alit?"

"Not as long as the dragons."

"How do you know?"

"The scrolls," he answers. "That's what they say."

The mysterious scrolls. I can't wait to get my hands on them.

We continue toward a rocky outcrop at the foot of

the hill. When we get closer, I realize that the gunmetal-gray shapes protruding from the soil aren't random rocks. They're megaliths. A dolmen is built into a hill that stands in the middle of the menhirs dotting the landscape like loaf-shaped lumps of granite.

A guard sits on a slab of stone next to the entrance of the dolmen, dozing in the humid heat. All the Alit I've met so far are ridiculously handsome and well-built. This man is no exception, except that his chin protrudes a little, and he has slightly bulging eyes.

He jumps to his feet and stands at attention when he notices us. He looks frightened and ill at ease.

"This site is off limits to the public," Aruan says as he stops in front of a huge rock that's rolled in front of the porthole. "These artifacts are precious. We've lost too many of them through plundering and wars. Hence, people can visit the inside only once a year, on a special day, and permission must be obtained in the form of a permit well in advance."

And he's brought me here, just like that. I suppose when you're the future king, you have special privileges.

Aruan focuses on the entrance. The rock parts, forming a huge gap to let us through.

The guard looks on with round eyes, his pointed chin trembling. Although I'm just as awed, I try hard not to show it. Aruan's power to open stone walls never grows old or less intimidating. I wish I knew how it worked, how it is that he's able to break the molecular bonds with his mind.

We're still standing arm in arm. I thought Aruan was holding on to me so firmly because he thinks I'll take flight the minute he gives me freedom. But I'm proven wrong when he detangles our arms and stands patiently at a small distance. Apparently, he's not worried that I'll get away. I don't want to analyze what that says about him keeping our arms interlinked. I don't want to think that he could simply like to touch me.

"After you," he says, motioning at the opening in the rock.

Too curious to decline the invitation, I step inside the cave-like room. It's much cooler inside but not less humid. The air smells of wet soil and fungus.

A torch in a holder against the wall catches fire. I give a start, but Aruan only smiles and shrugs, saying without words that this is just another one of his incredible powers.

Turning my attention to the room, I look around in the light of the torch. The ceiling is low. I can stand up straight, but Aruan has to bend his tall body to prevent his head from bumping on the stone ceiling. He ushers me toward the back that, to my surprise, opens up into a narrow tunnel.

A distant hum reaches my ears, almost like chanting.

Aruan goes ahead through the tunnel, taking my hand to help me through. On the other side, more torches light up, illuminating a few steep steps.

We follow them down into another room. On

closer inspection, I realize it's a cist, a stone enclosure buried beneath the ground.

At the far end stands a stone altar with various items arranged on top of it. Men wearing white tunics and pants are kneeling in front of the altar in what seems to be some kind of prayer, which explains the chanting.

"What is this place?" I whisper, more to myself than to Aruan.

"We don't know," he says behind me, his breath fanning the hair on my nape and sending a tingle down my spine. "All we know is that we need to preserve the scrolls. They're fragile. Many of them have already been destroyed."

I expected actual rolls of paper or leather with writing captured on it, but the translucent pyramids in different sizes displayed on the altar don't look anything like scrolls. They seem to glow from within, transmitting light that projects on the dark, polished surface of the stone walls. The light fragments, like in a kaleidoscope, and then reassembles to form short flashes of a video that run across the walls. The colors are faint and the pictures distorted, making it difficult to decipher what it's showing. Then the light breaks down and reshapes again, and a different video clip plays in a staccato pulsing of RGB colors.

Spellbound, I stare at the images flashing on the walls. "These are the scrolls?"

"The priests believe they contain messages," Aruan says. "Various prophecies left behind for us. The guardians of the scrolls devote their lives to preserving them and to interpreting the messages they contain."

The kneeling men show no awareness of our presence. They continue to chant in their trance-like state, their eyes fixed on the walls and their faces lit in the colors of the strange projections.

"Do they live here, these priests?" I ask, watching them in fascination.

"Pretty much. Villagers bring them water, food, and other necessities. People believe they will be blessed if they take care of the priests and therefore of the scrolls the priests are tasked with preserving."

I wrinkle my nose. "What about bathing and toilet breaks?"

Aruan smiles. "The priests have a separate exit through the roof of the temple that's hidden from sight. No one knows exactly where it is or where it comes out. There are many tunnels hidden behind a secret opening. That's where they have their living quarters. The river that feeds into the lake sends bathing water into the temple via a vein that runs underground."

"What about removing their garbage?" At Aruan's frown, I explain, "Their waste products."

"They leave it at the entrance. The people who bring them food take it away."

"But that means they live like moles," I exclaim.

One of the men glares at me from over his shoulder.

"Sorry," I say, making a face. I've clearly interrupted his concentration.

Aruan seems amused. "Moles?"

"They're blind animals that live underground."

"Indeed." He cracks his neck, which must be aching from being bent into such an uncomfortable position. "Some of them go blind from reading the scrolls and living underground their whole life."

I want to say that's terrible, but I keep my judgement to myself.

Aruan motions me closer to the altar with a hand. "Have a look."

I step gingerly over some roots that break through the soil and stop short of the men to peer at the pyramids. At first glance, I thought they were made of a clear acrylic material or glass, but upon a closer look, they appear soft instead of hard, as if made of silicone.

This is beyond amazing. Whatever these small pyramids are, I'm staring at very advanced technology. Or magic. But my bet is on technology—a technology that seems far beyond what the Alit possess.

Where did it come from? Aliens? An advanced civilization that existed on Zerra in the past? If it's the latter, what happened to it?

"Does the light ever go out?" I ask.

"The light is eternal."

"How does it work?"

"We don't know."

I turn in a circle, studying the images that run along the walls. We're underground, so the scrolls can't be solar-powered. Some kind of super-long-lasting batteries? Maybe even fusion technology? "How old do you think the scrolls are?"

"It's difficult to say. Their origins are a mystery. As far as we know, they've always been here."

I look back at him. "And what do they say?"

His smile is wry. "Many things. Most of them incomprehensible. Some are interpreted as prophecies, though—one of which is about a ruler more powerful than Zerra has ever seen and his mate."

"Is that the one where you're supposed to destroy your world?" I study his face, the strong lines and handsome features, the undeniable masculinity. The striking perfection. "How can they be so sure that the prophesied ruler is you? Who says someone else more powerful won't be born?"

His smile disappears, and a shutter drops in front of his eyes.

"Aruan?" He's hiding something again. "What aren't you telling me?" When he remains quiet, I resort to outright manipulation. "If you want me to live here and be your mate, shouldn't I know what I'm getting myself into?"

He lets out a long breath before taking my arm and pulling me a short distance away where we're out of earshot before saying in a strained voice, "There was an incident when I was young. I was playing in the jungle when a sand snake bit me. I didn't mean to, but in my anguish, I set off an explosion that killed every living thing in a moon cycle's radius, except for me." I suppress a horrified gasp as he continues, "For many cycles later, nothing could live there. Every animal that crossed that circle died a short while later." His eyes darken. "People too. My father forbade anyone to go near that place and tried to keep it quiet, but the rumors spread like embers carried on the wind."

My heart thumps dully in my chest. It can't be what I'm thinking... can it? My voice shakes a bit. "How did the explosion look when it happened?"

"There was a big cloud, round like a venomous fungus, growing up and up while rippling the air. People saw it from a great distance. The noise was deafening."

I stare at him with a slack jaw.

No. That can't be.

That sounds like a nuclear explosion. Radiation would explain why the animals and people who became exposed died.

Fuck. Is that Aruan's superpower? He can set off a nuclear explosion... that he himself is able to survive?

Without meaning to, I take a step away from him. As I try to process everything I know about his power, my mind spins. He can manipulate matter by dissolving bonds between molecules and vaporize living things with just a thought. Can he dissolve *atomic* bonds with a mere thought too?

His gaze darkens further as he watches my retreat, so I force myself to stop. But I can't completely hide the tremor in my voice as I ask, "Have you ever used your power like that since?"

His lips flatten. "I've been diligent in practicing caution. I don't want to inflict that kind of damage ever again."

But he can.

If he wants to.

Or if he loses control.

This is terrible.

He's a literal timebomb. A living, breathing, walking nuclear weapon.

The magnitude of his power nearly makes my knees buckle. No wonder people believe he's the prince mentioned in the scrolls.

No wonder they're terrified of him.

And by extension, of me.

My stomach churns as I stare at the powerful man in front of me, even as uninvited sympathy invades my chest. How lonely he must be. Everyone must be too frightened to interact with him on any level deeper than a superficial one, including his own family. It's obvious that they care about him, but they're not as close as I'd expect siblings and parents to be.

I want to say something, but no words come as he takes my hand and pulls me back upstairs, through the dolmen, and into the sunshine. Feeling frozen to my bones, I welcome the tropical heat.

The rock closes behind us. The guard still stands at attention next to it, sweat dripping down his face. I can't say if it's from fear or from the weather. His shoulders sag in relief when Aruan leads me back up the path.

I understand his fear now more than ever. What exactly *is* the extent of Aruan's power? Can he truly destroy this world? A single nuclear explosion is unlikely to do that, but maybe a series of them?

Then again, maybe his power can manifest in some other, even more destructive way. In a way that's connected to his mate… which he's convinced is *me*.

Fuck. I need to leave this place, now. How do I do that? Somehow, the Phaelix can travel between worlds. That's how they bring the humans here. And if they brought me here, they must be able to take me back.

That is, if they don't enslave me first.

A few kalligrammatids flap up from the undergrowth, fluttering toward the lake. Undoubtedly cognizant of my internal turmoil, Aruan veers off the path to follow them.

"Look," he says, showing me a patch of alien flowers with black petals and pink, elongated cones in the center. "Night flowers. They've earned the name because they only give off their scent after sunset." He bends down and neatly breaks off a thick stalk on the ground. "Let's pick you some. You can put them in a vase and discover their perfume when night falls."

I watch, lost in thought, as he continues to gather a bouquet. I suppose what he's doing is romantic. No man has ever given me flowers, and I *am* curious about their smell. But it's not enough to make me forget about what I've learned.

A nuclear explosion.

What if something sets him off again?

I swallow and edge away from Aruan, closer to the blueish shore of the lake. I need time to think, to gather my thoughts and put everything in perspective. Or maybe just a private moment to come to terms with it all.

I dig the toe of my boot into the blue sand. It shimmers like sea sand in the sun, like the particles of broken mother-of-pearl and abalone. Does that mean there are shellfish in the water? I'd give anything to scuba dive to the bottom of this lake.

A rustling sounds near the overhanging branches of the blood tree. I turn to face it, and then my heart slams to a stop.

A long beak peeks through the strings of dense leaves. The pointed toes of a claw follow next. The whole tree appears to shake, the music of the leaves like the gentle jingling of a tambourine, and then a quetzalcoatlus steps out, its giraffe-like body throwing a long shadow that swallows me.

"Elsie!" Aruan yells just as the magnificent animal spreads its enormous wings and charges straight at me.

I know what Aruan is going to do without having to look at him. The strange connection that I always feel to him warns me of his intention.

I spin around, shouting, "No!" as I sprint toward Aruan. My heart beats with unfamiliar strength in my chest, fueling me to run faster. "No, Aruan! Don't hurt her!" Skidding to a halt in the mud, I fall at Aruan's feet and throw my arms around his legs. "Please don't kill her. She's not going to harm us. Look—she's stopped!"

A quick glance over my shoulder confirms that the

quetzalcoatlus has slowed down to a penguin-like waggle.

"It's Betty," I cry out when his jaw hardens at the quetzalcoatlus's approach. "Look," I say again. "She has a tear in her left wing at the tip."

He doesn't take his eyes off the quetzalcoatlus as he replies in a grim tone, "It'll eat you for a snack."

"She won't," I insist. "I know her."

Proving the point, the pterosaur stops and tilts her head before lifting her beak as if smelling the air.

I hug his legs tighter. "Please, Aruan. Please. If you care even one iota about me, please don't harm her."

An internal battle rages in his eyes.

Sensing the shift in him, I stare up at him with my best pleading look. "She knows me. See?"

"How the dragon would it know you?" he asks through gritted teeth, breaking his stare at the perceived danger to glance at me.

Yes. My begging has the desired effect. His expression softens a fraction.

"She flew past your window," I say. "She *knows* me."

"You're dreaming. It'll gobble you down whole."

"Give her a chance." I climb to my feet, holding Aruan's gaze. "She's not going to hurt us."

He doesn't seem convinced. Staring down the pterosaur again, he says, "I've seen what these dragons are capable of with my own eyes."

"Aruan," I say in a no-nonsense manner.

He glances at me again.

I cross my arms. "If you hurt her, you hurt me."

He works his jaw from side to side, but the killing rage inside him diminishes. It hovers there, just in case, but apparently, he does care enough to listen to my plea.

When I sense his power retracting, I blow out a sigh of relief.

"Not so fast, mate," he says with narrowed eyes. "If it shows any signs of aggression, it's dead."

"Yes, I know. It'll take you a millisecond to vaporize her. So just relax for now, okay?"

Despite my flippant tone, I'm worried for Betty, even though she won't be aggressive toward me. I can't explain how I know it, but I do.

Betty comes closer.

And closer still.

Aruan tenses behind me, and I sense his power welling up again.

"She won't hurt me," I reiterate, my gaze glued to the prehistoric creature that's now standing over me, staring into my eyes. "Please, just give her a chance."

Aruan's power crackles in the air around us, potent and deadly, but to my relief, he doesn't unleash it. Maybe it's because he knows he can kill Betty faster than she can do me harm, or maybe it's because she's not showing any signs of wanting to rip me to pieces with her claws or to grasp me in her beak and fling me through the air.

I hold my breath as she lowers her head and sniffs me.

Aruan stands like a lethal weapon behind me, ready

to vaporize the five-hundred-pound pterosaur if she dares to step out of line, but all she does is tilt her head and… rub against me.

Aruan goes still. It's more than the mere quiet that defines an absence of sound. His whole being freezes in the way that follows in the wake of disbelief and miracles.

The creature closes her eyes as if in ecstasy and rubs her fine-haired head against my neck. The tuft of feathers on her crown tickles my nose.

A giggle bubbles over my lips.

Aruan clenches my shoulders in his big hands, his grip like an iron vise. But Betty continues to rub herself against me, dragging her chin over my hair. She nudges me softly and gently runs her barbed, prehensile tongue over my hand before returning to caressing my face.

"Dragons," Aruan says, his voice not sounding like his own.

Carefully, he pulls me away from the pterosaur, walking us backward toward the path, the black flowers forgotten where he dropped them on the ground.

Betty is undeterred. She follows us, her long neck swaying as she trudges after me like a tame goose with her huge claws sinking into the wet soil. It's not until we reach the border of the farming fields that she pauses.

This must be her cut-off point, the closest to the Alit she's prepared to go on foot.

As Aruan and I climb to the top of the hill, her cry pierces the sky—a lonely, hauntingly sad sound.

The villagers look up with fright, then drop their forks and spades, getting ready to run for their lives.

With a last stretch of her neck in our direction, Betty unfolds her wings and bounces off her powerful legs to leap eight feet into the air. Screams from people running for the nearest shelter echo through the valley as she dives low, swirling over Aruan and me, before flapping her wings with strong strokes and heading back toward the lake with the speed of a car on a highway.

"Wow." I stare at her fast-disappearing shape in wonder. "Wasn't that amazing?"

When I turn back to Aruan, he's staring at me with astonishment and confusion.

CHAPTER 15
ARUAN

Leading Elsie by the hand, I pull her into Kian's quarters.

My brother frowns. His private rooms are his sanctuary, and he doesn't appreciate visitors or interruptions.

He sets aside the small chisel he's been using to cut a priceless moon-colored opal and brushes away the residue powder with an annoyed flick of his hand.

"Aruan." His smile is flat. "What a pleasant disruption."

"Cut the sarcasm, Kian." I bring Elsie to stand next to me. "As much as it pains me, I need your opinion."

He doesn't have to ask about what. He shifts his expressionless gaze to Elsie. "What did she do? I got the impression that the idea of me sifting through your mate's thoughts didn't appeal to you."

"It doesn't." The idea alone sets my teeth on edge. "Do it anyway."

"Hey," Elsie says, more than a little irked. "It's *my* mind." She pulls her hand from mine. "Don't I get a say?"

My brother arranges his arms on the armrests of his chair with an eloquent motion. "What am I to be looking for, Aruan?"

"Apparently not," Elsie mumbles, rolling her eyes.

Turning her to me, I cup her delicate face between my palms. My words are soft, soothing. "Don't you want to understand what just happened?"

"Is it important?" she asks, not seeming fazed in the least.

I stare at my mate in disbelief. There's only one reason why that dragon would be at the lake. It must have a nest there with eggs. Flying dragons, especially ones that lay leathery, soft-shelled white eggs, are notoriously aggressive, and even more so when they have eggs to protect. Yet the beast licked Elsie's hand as if to caress her, and then it followed her like a trained spiked dragon pet.

"Yes," I say with finality. "It concerns your safety."

"Enough of the nest scraping." Kian examines us as if we were interesting rocks in his precious stone collection. "Get to the point, and tell me what's going on."

Elsie's brows snap together. "Nest scraping?"

"It's a metaphor for courting, meaning that mates are behaving in a loving and affectionate way." I shoot Kian a cutting look. "When a male dragon excavates a pseudo nest for a potential mate to prove his ability to provide for her, it's called nest scraping."

Kian's lips pull into a rare grin. "Which means that my brother here is going to be scraping for real very soon, and I'm going to enjoy every minute of watching him grovel."

I return his gesture with an unfriendly smile of my own. "Your turn will come."

The pleasure he was taking from the prospect of seeing me grovel is wiped off his face. At some point, all males grovel for our mates, especially when our mates' bellies grow big with our babies. There are no lengths an Alit male won't go to to please his female. And to Kian, there's no bigger punishment than being shackled to a lifelong companion. Whereas most Alit are proud to claim their mates, Kian would rather grow old alone, free of any emotional burdens.

Adopting his usual stoic mask, he says, "Well, ask me the question you've come here for or go do your nest scraping elsewhere. I have work to do."

Ignoring his antagonism because this is important to me, I quickly relay what happened at the lake.

When I come to the end of my story, Kian fixes unblinking eyes on Elsie.

"You weren't scared," he says, stating that as a fact instead of a question.

"Not for myself," she says. "Only for Betty when I thought Aruan might vaporize her."

"What do you think?" I ask my brother. "Why didn't the dragon devour her like a juicy piece of meat?" I hesitate before uttering the question that's at the forefront of my mind, something inside me stirring with hopeful excitement as well as caution. "Could this be Elsie's power?"

"What?" Elsie gapes at me. "I don't have a power. I'm not an Alit."

Another rare display of emotion crosses Kian's features, and the sympathy I see there doesn't set me at ease. He thinks I'm right, that Elsie has a mental hold over these powerful predators. And he knows if that's the case, I'll never sleep easily again.

Commanding dragons would be an immensely strong power. A useful power. A dangerous power. Those beasts are unpredictable at best.

"What do you pick up?" I ask, meaning in Elsie's mind.

Kian turns his gaze toward a water dragon that has just landed on the windowsill. The insect flutters its lacey wings, performing a dainty dance before finding a comfortable position in which to settle.

"I want you to try something, Elsie," Kian says. "Look at that water dragon and will it to come to you."

Does Kian truly think Elsie's power extends beyond the predators? Could her power be a mental command of *all* non-Alit living forms? Taming a dragon is one thing—a very difficult thing, I admit—but it has a mass of mind matter to tap into. An insect is a lot more delicate. Wielding power over it will be intricately complicated.

Elsie seems both incredulous and intrigued. "Are you serious?"

"Try," I urge. "Let's see what happens."

She blows a puff of air through her lips, but she's curious enough to fix her attention on the water dragon.

She holds out her hand. The insect lifts its wings, crisscrossing them like the sharpening of blades, and takes off into the air. It flies to the ceiling where it flits for a few beats, and then it descends swiftly and lands neatly on Elsie's palm.

For the first time in my life, I'm at a loss for words. Kian seems to suffer from the same speechless condition. Elsie is the only one who's unperturbed.

She utters a delightful laugh. "Aww, how sweet."

And then her laugh dies as she directs round, startled eyes at me.

The water dragon takes off again. Elsie stands frozen with her arm outstretched. Kian and I stare at her as the knowledge settles in the silence that follows.

Elsie never lost her power.

It's always been there—dormant, waiting.

And by dragon, what a power it is.

The shock on her face can easily be mistaken for devastation. Instead of being glad that her power wasn't destroyed when she was sent to Earth, she's dealing with a truth she doesn't want to admit, a truth she's bitterly denied.

She's one of us.

There's no arguing that fact anymore.

This is her home.

This is where she belongs.

Her manner turns stilted. Like a sleepwalker, she drops her arm at her side.

The reason for Kian's sympathy becomes clear. He wasn't pitying me, knowing that I'd never know peace again as long as my mate commands dragons. He was pitying Elsie, his mind-reading power having warned him of how the truth would affect her.

"I—" She wets her lips with the tip of her tongue. "It's not what you think."

"The pixie dragon that knocked that poisoned drink from Aruan's hand..." Kian starts in an uncharacteristically gentle way. "It wasn't an accident."

"It was protecting you," I say in wonder. "It *knew*."

She shakes her head hard enough to bring on a dizzy spell. "You don't know that."

Kian pushes to his feet and makes his way to the door. "Come with me."

I take Elsie's hand, offering her comfort.

This is hard for both of us, albeit for different reasons.

She doesn't object when I lead her into the hallway. We follow Kian to the banquet hall, where spiked pet dragons that hunt for scraps of food are always present.

"Call them to you," Kian says, a spark of excitement breaking through the boredom normally reflected in his eyes.

She doesn't ask what or who. It only takes a turn of

Elsie's head before the spiked dragons scurry out from under the tables and clack their way over the flagstones to line up in front of her.

The cooking and cleaning staff, who've come out of the kitchen to see what all the commotion is about, stare at the scene with transfixed faces. Unless there's food, the pets shy away from us. They're used to being shooed away by the brooms of the cleaners who are irritated with them for always getting under their feet.

Turning away from the curious and openly petrified stares, Elsie walks to the exit as stiffly as a wooden plank. The spiked dragons follow in a long queue behind her. Now that her power has been unleashed, it appears impossible to rein in.

Whispers break out among the servants. There's no point in admonishing them. The rumors will spread. They can't be contained.

Kian stares after Elsie as she crosses the threshold. We exchange a look before I go after her.

Spiked dragons pour from every crevice of the palace, the little scavengers forming a dark river down the hallway as they're drawn to my mate. Pixie dragons burst through the archways and dive through the air. There are so many of them that their flapping wings stir a breeze inside the walls. One nearly gets tangled in my hair.

"Elsie." I grip her shoulders and make her face me. "Let it go. That's enough."

She blinks once, twice, and sags beneath my palms.

The animals linger, but their hordes don't descend on us any longer.

The royals have peeled out of rooms and courtyards to gawk at the spectacle with a mixture of shocked awe and fright. Their urgent whispers are full of concern and more than a hint of terror.

When I take Elsie's hand and quickly lead her to my quarters, away from the fearful scrutiny, the winged and four-legged pets follow.

I leave the creatures outside and seal us in my room.

For a moment, we simply stand there facing each other. Words are redundant. She needs time to come to terms with her discovery.

Dragons, so do I.

"Elsie." I will her to look at me, to let me soothe the unease that has crawled into the hollowness that has settled in her chest. "You'll learn to control it, my sweet."

It's a futile attempt at easing her disappointment.

She slides a look of contempt my way. She knows what I feel. My elation and pride at the strength of my mate's power must be like a blade of betrayal through her stomach.

Her words are bitter. "Everything you told me is true. I'm not Elsie Barnikoff, am I?"

I soften my tone to make up for the blow I'm about to deal. "You *are* Elsie. But you were Laliss first."

Just saying it brings back the old, incurable pain of losing her. I learned to live with it. It became a part of my very essence. But now my joy is my mate's pain.

She'll grow used to it, like I did. In time, she'll embrace it, and then it will be our shared joy in the way it's meant to be for mates.

She lifts a wary, absent gaze to me. "I can feel it—the power."

I nod my understanding, helplessness engulfing me for my inability to take away her suffering. "It'll get better."

Her eyes turn hard, the blue-green glittering like brilliant river stones. "Who did this to me, Aruan? Who destroyed my life?"

"It's not destroyed," I say, taking her hand, although I understand why she'd feel that way.

"Who?" she asks, watching me with that steadfast, unforgiving gaze.

"My mother," I admit with no small amount of anger. "And it's time to find out why."

CHAPTER 16
ELSIE

"Everything is a lie."

My voice sounds strange to my own ears, as if it belongs to a different person, which it does. Because I'm not Elsie. I've never been. I'm someone else, and I have no idea who that woman is, except that she's a stranger. An alien from a different world.

And that scares the living daylights out of me.

Already, I feel her, this stranger, creeping into my mind with her weird notion of power and slowly taking over my body. Even that's not my own anymore. The scars and weakness that have defined me for so long have made space for this being, this female with a strong, healthy body. She's molding it to her needs, growing stronger inside me by the minute.

I slam my hands over my ears, not to block out sound but to keep the madness at bay.

I'm going fucking crazy.

Aruan reaches for me. "Elsie."

I step away from him.

A big, fat lie.

My existence is nothing but a farce.

Do I know what's real? It sure as hell doesn't feel like it.

Actually, it does. Even now, the power is vibrating beneath the surface of my skin like a parasite that's invaded the body of a host.

"Elsie," he says again, this time sterner.

Shaking my head, I bite out, "I'm *not* Elsie." And I'm so fucking angry about that.

"Do you prefer that I call you Laliss?" he asks in a gentler tone.

No, I definitely don't want him to call me that.

He doesn't lower his arm. He holds out his hand, offering it to me like an olive branch. "It'll get better."

That same empty promise again.

It won't.

I can never get back the life that was stolen from me here or the life I had on Earth. I'll never know my biological parents. Neither will I see my adoptive parents again, not if it depends on Aruan. My life here was finished before it began, and it looks as if my life as Elsie Barnikoff is dead for good.

So what now? Am I supposed to simply pick up the pieces and move on from where I left off when my name was Laliss? Except, I'm not Laliss. The only name I know is Elsie, but I don't feel like her either.

A hollow laugh tears from my chest.

"Elsie." Aruan closes the distance between us and catches my wrists to pull my hands from my ears. He holds them at my sides in the vise of his fingers, not allowing me space or a chance to flee. "This isn't the end of the world. It's just the beginning."

"The beginning of what?" Another hysterical laugh bubbles over my lips. "Of our happy ending?" I wrestle to free myself from his hold, but he doesn't let up an inch. "If that's what you think, you're fucking naïve." I lift my chin. "Do you know what this is? This isn't you and me galloping off together into the sunset." Thinking about that prophecy again, I continue, "This is the beginning of the mother of all clusterfucks."

"Calm down," he says, a muscle ticking in his jaw. "There's no point in upsetting yourself. This situation doesn't have to be bad for you."

"Not bad for me? I'm your prisoner, Aruan. I don't want to be here, do you hear me?" I get into his face. "I don't want to be Laliss, and I don't want to be your fucking mate!"

A deadly quiet comes over him. He stares at me with narrowed eyes, something disturbing gleaming in their silver depths. "You're mine, Elsie. *Mine*. That's how fate designed it. That's your destiny. You can either do this the hard way by fighting it, or you can accept it." His eyes narrow further, all the way into slits. "Whatever you choose, the fact that you're mine isn't going to change."

The unjustness wells up inside me until it's about to blow.

"Get your hands off me," I say through gritted teeth, fighting him anew.

Instead, he wraps me up in his arms, trapping me even more effectively.

"Let go!" I scream, kicking for all I'm worth, but my efforts have no effect on him.

He easily lifts me off my feet. It's difficult to breathe. I think he may crush my ribcage in the unyielding squeeze of those muscled arms.

"Are you done?" he asks in a tight voice.

I'm beyond thinking or acting rationally. All I want is to get out of here, to escape from this prison and frightening reality.

I twist and kick, fighting like never before.

"Stop it, Elsie, or you'll leave me no choice but to restrain you before you hurt yourself."

I don't stop. I can't. I'm like a wild animal trapped in a cage, clawing my way to freedom.

In the back of my mind, I'm aware that we're going down to the floor. The ceiling tilts. Aruan breaks my fall with one hand beneath my head and the other on my back. He absorbs the shock of the hard flagstones, shifting his hold to pin both my wrists above my head in one hand while holding himself up on his arm.

I go quiet.

His weight is anchoring without crushing me. We stare at each other in a frozen moment of shock, one of us in anger and the other with calculation. My chest heaves with laborious breaths. With Aruan's torso like a slab of granite merely an inch from mine, there's scarcely space to breathe. Every inhale makes my breasts brush against those hard muscles. The layers of our clothing are not nearly enough of a barrier. My nipples harden. His closeness sparks an unwelcome but undeniable awareness of him deep inside me.

That scent.

He smells so fucking good.

The way he fits against me *feels* so good. He's hard in all the right places, especially where his cock presses against my stomach.

The quickening of my breathing is no longer from the physical exertion of fighting. The urge to wrap my arms around him and hold him to me is strong. I almost act on it, remembering too late that he's pinning my arms to the floor.

Dangerous.

My position is vulnerable.

Yet I can't stop myself from spreading my legs to make space for him between my thighs.

"Elsie," he says with an animalistic growl.

A warning.

But I'm helpless against the pull of my body. My mind is useless. It's no match for the strange instinct that has taken over and is now dictating my actions. I can fight it as little as I can fight Aruan and win in physical strength. I know I've lost even before I've had a chance to fight. Despite the excruciating heat that grows in my belly, my imminent defeat fills me with helpless anger.

As if sensing my surrender, he loosens his hold on

my wrists. Something almost tender shifts into his eyes. When he presses our mouths together, it's not with the clashing, violent urgency from our first kiss as I expected. The way he molds his lips around mine is tender and probing yet assertive enough to make me part my lips for him without being prompted.

His kiss is like a drug, overwhelming my senses and confusing my thoughts. My inner muscles clench in response, a strong need building in my core.

I want.

God, do I ever want.

When he lets my wrists go, I thread my fingers through the thick strands of his soft hair. I cling to him even as I push him away, my mind and body battling even though there's no question about the outcome of that fight.

I kiss him back as he explores my mouth. I tangle my tongue with his and hungrily learn the shape of his lips in turn. The moans echoing in the space can't be coming from my mouth. Yet every time that sound fills the room, Aruan groans, tying me a little tighter to him with his intoxicating kiss and the delicious way he rotates his hips. He frames my face between his palms, holding me in place and keeping my mouth accessible for his plundering.

Shifting slightly, he tilts his hips, hitting a soft spot between my legs that makes my toes curl with pleasure.

Ah.

I rub myself against him and wrap my legs around his ass to get even closer.

"Elsie," he says, tearing his mouth from mine.

We look at each other, our chests rising and falling rapidly. The way he said my name was another warning. He's telling me we're getting to the point of no return.

The implication of being tied to a mate hits me like a sack of potatoes on the head. There's no escaping this destiny. That's what he meant when he said I couldn't fight it. My body has already made the decision for me. Despite its newfound health and vitality, I can't help but hate it for betraying me as I give in to the mindlessness, almost angrily chasing after the release my body needs by moving harder against the thick cock that's nestled between my legs.

"Slow down," Aruan says in a choked voice. "You don't want me to take you right here on the floor."

My reply is born from spitefulness and vexation. "Just do it already."

One thick, black brow raises in a perfectly arched, mocking curve. "Like this?"

"Does it matter where or how we do it?" I move my hand between our bodies to lock my fingers around the thick length tenting his pants. A part of me doesn't want to enjoy it. Maybe if I don't, I won't want to do this again. I won't have to fight battle after battle only to lose each one. "Just get it over with."

He hisses. "Carry on touching me like that, and we'll both regret the consequences. I'll fuck you like a beast on the stones instead of in my bed like my mate deserves."

"I'm not your mate," I taunt. "Not yet."

He catches my hand, squeezing it around his cock to still my movements. "You're playing dangerous games."

Throwing back his own words at him, I ask, "Lost your nerve?"

"If this is what you want," he replies with finality that, despite my bravado, scares me.

He lets me go and lifts off of me. I watch his frame grow taller until he towers over me. Perversely, I feel colder without his touch. Emptier.

He holds my gaze as he strips, drinking me in like a man who adores the sight in front of him so much that he can't help but hate it. Yes, indeed, he's hating himself for needing me, hating that his determination to "claim" me is taking away his control. I feel it in that place in my chest where his thoughts and sentiments echo.

I don't know if it's a blessing or a curse that he can never lie to me. He can't tell me sweet nothings or that he cares. He can't tell me that this is even just a little about me. No, this is all about him, about the mate *he* wants. For selfish reasons.

"Maybe it's better like this," he says as he sheds his final piece of clothing. "We won't be wild with lust on the potion and therefore blind to pain or injuries. There's less chance of me hurting you if I remain in control."

The words "pain" and "injuries" drift into one ear and out the other, not hooking into my brain like they should. I'm too busy studying the perfect male specimen standing over me. He's built like a fighting machine with unrelenting muscles and powerful arms and legs. His cock juts out, thick and long, the smooth crest already glistening with a drop of pre-cum.

I swallow, realizing that my mouth has gone dry. Because he's beautiful. And because, once again, I realize how big he is. *Really* big.

If I hadn't been so sick all my life, I might've experimented more, perhaps tried a vibrator or two, but I could never scrape together enough energy—or arousal—to make an effort.

I regret that terribly now, not knowing what's in store for me.

With a wicked grin, he widens his stance slightly, letting me watch even as he offers me a hand. I look at his proffered hand, so huge and manly with that dusting of dark hair.

It's a clever move. Taking it will mean I give him my consent. He's making sure that *I'm* making the choice, that I won't be able to accuse him later of forcing me.

And if I don't take his hand, he may call me a coward again.

He wouldn't be wrong. That's what I feel like. A coward. And I've been many things throughout my life, but never a coward.

Slowly, I reach out and place my hand in his, even as the same duality I sense in him—wanting something so badly it aches, and hating it for that reason—wars inside me.

Approval flashes in his eyes, but it doesn't warm me like the appreciation of someone who loves me. He's merely praising me for doing something he wants me to do.

I cling to that thought, reminding myself that we're not doing this because we actually give a damn about one another. It's vital that I protect myself if I'm to make it out of this mess with my mind and heart intact.

He pulls me close enough for our bodies to touch. The heat of his skin scorches me through the layers of my clothes. No matter how hard I focus on the negative aspects of what we're about to do, all those notions are incinerated once there's no longer any distance between us.

I can feel his power. It buzzes in a low hum, stoking mine to life. It's like the soft purr of a big cat. Of an alpha lion. On the one hand, it's soothing, and on the other, it's making me so jittery with dormant but explosive energy that it feels as if a shot of espresso has been injected straight into my bloodstream.

The hum penetrates my breastbone. For some reason, he's persistent, using this trick on me until we're buzzing in tandem. It's like being tipsy without the alcohol.

When I give over to that feeling, he undresses me, starting with the boots. The pants follow next. Then the shirt. And then I'm naked, because they don't bother with underwear here.

He cups my head and tilts back my face, swooping down to press a kiss on my neck. He follows it up with a gentle bite that makes me gasp with pleasure. The kisses he plants on the column of my neck cause shiver after shiver to trickle down my spine. Goosebumps run over my arm when he sucks my earlobe into his mouth and whispers something about a promise in my ear.

A promise to make it good. Like a bandage on a cut before the blade has nicked the skin.

But I can hardly concentrate on his words or their meaning while he's palming my breasts in his gigantic hands, kneading them until they feel swollen and heavy.

The world gives way from under my feet. He's scooped me up into his arms. The room passes in a blur. Somewhere in the middle of the floor, our discarded clothes lie in two heaps like wilted flowers. The harsh white light of day washes through the window, unlike the soft, forgiving beams of the moon. There's no evening breeze to cool the heat mounting under my skin, no darkness to hide the unwanted emotions on my face—the lust, the ecstasy, the defeat, and the bitterness. The ever-present, unfading anger. But his kisses are sweet, and that static hum of power that reaches out to the power inside me is calming.

My back hits a cool, silky surface—the sheets of his bed. I sink into the softness, the weight of Aruan's body pinning me down. Like before, it's a comfortable weight. He keeps himself up on his elbows while he goes back to kissing me. His movements are tender and seductive, coaxing me into opening not only my lips for him but also my legs.

He lifts my arms above my head and secures them firmly on the mattress by shackling my wrists in the strong grip of his hands. Once I'm securely bound, he moves down my body and sucks a nipple into his mouth. I arch my back, begging for more. The tip hardens on his tongue. He does something with his teeth that has me crying out. The sound invites his praise. I'm not cognizant of what he's saying. I'm too focused on the sensations he provokes as he teases me so wickedly with his tongue and his teeth.

He transfers both my wrists into one large hand and slides the other between my legs. I jerk when he touches my folds. I'm so wet my arousal is slick on my thighs. This earns me more praise and a louder purr of power that emanates from his chest.

"So ready for me," he says, looking up at me with molten silver eyes.

I'm panting by now, chasing after the friction of his finger as he gently—too gently—teases my throbbing clit.

"Is this what you want, my sweet?" he asks in a gravelly voice.

We haven't even started yet, and I'm already burning up. I manage a nod, doing my best to stay lucid.

"Don't worry, my beautiful, feisty mate. I'm going to take care of your pleasure." Making good on his promise, he lets go of my arms and plants one hand over a breast, tweaking the nipple while teasing my folds with the fingers of his free hand. "Do you want to come on my hand or my face?"

Blood rushes to my cheeks. I'm not exactly practiced in sex talk, and he makes it sound both crude and hot. I stutter something incomprehensible at which he chuckles.

"How about I choose?" he says, already moving down my body.

I close my legs involuntarily as my courage fails me, but he grips my knees and pries them open before lowering his head between my thighs.

Oh, fuck.

I think I've died and gone to heaven for real this time.

The things he's doing with his tongue… they should be illegal.

He traces my slit, waking nerve endings I didn't know existed. When he parts me with his thumbs, stretching me wide open before sucking my clit deep into his mouth, my whole body lifts off the mattress. It's like being zapped with lethal volts of electricity. The pleasure doesn't coil slowly through my lower body like when he touched me in the hallway after the episode with the poison. The strong suction of his lips and the sharp little nips of his teeth detonates it from the center of my core like a shooting star expanding into space.

I dig my fingers into the covers, scrunching silky sheets in my fists.

One more lick and flick of his tongue, and an

orgasm tears through my body with the destructive force of a hurricane.

"Such a good girl," he murmurs. "You take your pleasure so beautifully for me." He lifts his head, fixing me with that eerie, metallic-gray gaze. "You're going to do it again, my sweet mate, and this time, you're coming on my cock."

I didn't know pleasure like this existed. I'm still coming down from the explosive release, endorphins fogging my brain, when something velvety smooth yet hard nudges my entrance.

"Take a deep breath, Elsie," Aruan says, pressing a soft kiss on my lips.

He's gone back to trapping my arms above my head, but it feels more intimate because he's intertwined our fingers and is pushing the backs of my palms against the mattress.

I close my eyes and allow myself to drift in the afterglow of my orgasm. The aftershocks are so powerful that purple-and-white stars dot my vision behind my eyelids.

My eyes fly wide open when that solid pressure between my legs increases steadily to part my folds. An intrusion slips between them, its presence exhilarating and foreign. Frightening.

"Relax," he says, planting a kiss on my jaw. "It'll be easier. You'll enjoy it more."

Relaxing is out of the question when he rotates his hips and lodges that thick, hot hardness a little deeper inside me.

There's not enough space for him. He's too big. The stretch of my body isn't enough to accommodate his size.

I close my fingers around his with bruising force and arch my hips, trying to throw him off like a wild horse ditching the rider who breaks it in.

"Shh," he says, kissing me on the mouth again. "Don't fret, my sweet."

The euphoria of earlier lifts a little, letting in a fresh bout of reality—and with it, fear.

"Look at me, Elsie," he commands even as he slides another inch deeper.

I cry out, battling to breathe through the discomfort. I'm wet, but it doesn't ease his way. I think he may tear me in two.

"You're a virgin," he says with no small amount of male pride and satisfaction but also surprise.

"No shit," I bite out, digging my nails into the back of his hands as he moves yet another inch.

"You should've told me," he says roughly. "I would've prepared you with my hand."

I suck in a breath, clenching hard against the pressure. "This… isn't going to work."

"Hush, my sweet. Do your best to relax." He holds still, mercifully giving me time to adjust and try to do as he says. "It's going to hurt, but I'll take care of you, my beautiful little mate."

Like he promised, it hurts. It hurts with a burn that flares as he pushes all the way in. A scream tears from my chest that he catches in a smothering kiss. I'm about to regret my body's unbending will to take this all the way when he starts to move.

At first, the pain intensifies. I want to fight, but I don't. I just lie there, vanquished, praying that it will soon be over.

Aruan's face comes into focus as he pulls away to look at me. His jaw is bunched, and sweat beads on his forehead. The look in his eyes is one of utter concentration.

He's holding back. For my sake.

"Do it," I say, grinding my teeth together against the pain. "Finish this already."

"No." The word is harsh, but his expression is tender. "I won't let you rush me. I'm going to take my time with you."

I moan in despair. "Aruan, please." Tears I can't hold back run from the corners of my eyes. "I beg you, please end this."

He kisses away the tears and whispers in my ear those sweet nothings I don't want to hear, encouraging words and praise for how well I'm taking him.

Him.

This is all about him.

And just when I'm about to hurl the accusation at him, the pain turns into something different, a pleasure much more carnal and intense than I experienced when he used his mouth.

"Ah." I shift my hips, seeking stimulation despite the rawness inside. "More."

"Slowly," he says with a chuckle. "Or you'll be too sore to walk tomorrow."

Why can't he just do what I ask? When I want him to stop, he moves, and when I want him to go faster, he goes slowly.

"You're insufferable," I choke out.

"If I'm insufferable, it's because I don't want you to be tender afterward."

But even as he says it, he starts to thrust with a lazy pace that soon has me delirious with need again. I wrap my legs around his ass and lift myself higher.

"Dragons," he mutters, gripping my fingers so hard they ache.

"Aruan, please…" I clench around him, needing this like nothing before.

The expression on his face is equal parts agonized pleasure and victory. "Are you begging me to fuck you, mate?"

He told me I'd beg, he warned me, but I can't even bring myself to care. "Do you want me to?" I manage to ask with a bite. "Will it make you feel more wanted? More desirable?"

"So dramatic." He clucks his tongue even as more beads of sweat appear on his forehead. "You don't have to beg for what already belongs to you."

There's something wrong with that statement, but I don't stop to examine it. Sensing that he's close to losing control, I don't slow down like I know I should. No, I test my power over him, tempting the beast by rubbing my nipples over his chest and moving my hips faster.

The breakdown comes quicker than I anticipated and long before I'm ready for it. Letting go of my hands, he locks his fingers in a bruising grip on my hips and holds me fast to the bed as he pounds into me with a crazed rhythm, pummeling my body into a speedy submission of fluttering spasms as another orgasm explodes through me, contracting my inner muscles around his cock.

"Elsie," he growls.

The power of his thrusts would shift me over the mattress if he weren't pinning my hips onto the bed. The loss of his control is both petrifying and beautiful. But I no longer feel the fear or the pain. All I'm conscious of is the earth-shattering—or rather, Zerra-shattering—pleasure that overwhelms me physically and mentally. I'm like jelly, incapable of moving or thinking. I can only lie there beneath him, shivering with brutal aftershocks of unending ecstasy.

He slams into me one last time before his whole body goes taut. His cock grows impossibly thick, and then a flush of warmth bathes me inside. A ripple of pleasure runs through me, goosebumps covering my skin. Locked inside me, he rides out his pleasure with a clenched jaw, his features set as if he's in pain.

When it's over, he rests his forehead against mine to catch his breath. Finally, he releases my hands to wrap me up in his arms and cradle me against the welcome heat and safety of his chest. My arms go around him instinctively, needing something to hold on to. He buries his face in my neck and kisses a tender spot before nuzzling the curve of my shoulder.

It's done.

We've mated.

If I expected something to happen—some feelings to change or a bond to appear magically—I'm sorely disappointed. Stripped of physical pleasure, all that remains is the same old anger and confusion.

He pushes onto his elbows, studying my face. "How are you doing?"

I frown. "Aside from feeling as if I've been ripped in two?" Everything crashes down on me, all the accumulated irritation and built-up rage. The unjustness. Tears gather at the back of my eyes, but I refuse to shed them. I bite hard on my lip to prevent myself from giving him that weakness. Instead, I lash out, fighting with the only weapon I have. "I hate you."

"I know," he says with easy acceptance that irks me more than I'd like to admit. His tone is sober. "I can tell by the mere fact that our mating isn't complete."

"What do you mean our mating isn't complete? You came inside me."

Possessiveness sparks in his eyes, but his expression is veiled, his voice almost toneless. "Yes, I did a good job of filling you with my seed. I stuffed you to overflowing. Even now as we're connected, I can feel what you can't hold inside spilling from your pussy."

Fuck.

Birth control.

How could something so crucial have slipped my mind? It's this damn mating urge. It clouded my reason and drugged my brain.

"I don't want to have children," I say in a hoarse voice.

At least, not now. Not like this.

He wipes every trace of emotion from his face so efficiently that he'd give Kian a good run for his money. "Then we'd better hope you didn't conceive." Then, just as quickly, he gives me a cold, wry smile. "But don't worry. Alit women don't conceive easily. It rarely happens on the first try."

Not reassured, I ask, "Why didn't you use protection?"

"Because it's assumed that a mated couple would welcome a child. Couples don't only welcome the idea; they wish for it desperately."

"Well, we're not a mated couple. You said so yourself."

"Yes," he replies like a robot, not allowing me to get a read on him.

"If you did such a good job, how come it's not complete?" I ask with a good dose of sarcasm.

I'm physically sated, but I'm far from satisfied. A part of me wants to hurt him like I'm hurting. I want to punish him for keeping me here against my will and for making it impossible for me to fight our attraction. I want to punish him for making me submit to him.

Finding myself on the losing end is a humiliating experience. Pleasurable but humiliating. I don't have a choice but to bend under this incontrollable need. He can only win, time and again, and it's not fair.

He adopts a stony look as he lets me go, lifts off of me, and gets to his feet. Like earlier, the loss of his touch leaves me oddly bereft. I have no idea why I'm so disappointed. I only know that he's disappointed too.

Was the sex not what he expected? Did it not please him? Was I too inexperienced?

Was that what I saw in his expression before he hid it so well? *Disappointment?*

For some reason, the thought floors me. It hurts me much more than it should. His opinion of my skills in bed shouldn't affect me. I shouldn't care. I don't. Then why do I feel like crying as he walks away without as much as a backward glance?

The unwelcome tears I can't hold back anymore run over my cheeks. Wiping impatiently at my face, I push up onto my elbows. As he walks to the other room, I watch his chiseled ass and the muscles of his back that seem to be sculpted from marble.

Whatever. He can go fuck himself.

I didn't expect pillow talk, but I don't appreciate being left cold when he's just claimed my V-card.

I swallow my tears as he returns with one of those big, folded bath sheets in his hand.

"Here," he says in that same emotionless tone, holding it open for me.

So much for post-sex intimacy. If anything, we're

more like strangers than ever. The atmosphere is so uncomfortable I wish I were anywhere but here. The sex must've been truly awful if this is how he's behaving. He's shown me more warmth in our non-sexual interactions than he has after the act.

He wraps me up in the sheet, telling me he doesn't want me to be cold, and then he holds out his hand. When I take it on autopilot, he leads me to the cleansing room.

He gets into the water and waits for me to drop the sheet before helping me in too. I settle on the bench facing him, and he doesn't invite me to join him on his side or to sit on his lap as he did before. Instead, he seems caught up in his thoughts, far away from me and what we just did.

As if it doesn't matter.

Because it doesn't.

Why should it?

He got what he wanted, and he liked it less than he hoped. I should be relieved. Then why does a heaviness settle in my heart and more of those cursed tears burn at the backs of my eyes? Why does it hurt with enough force to reduce me to sobbing?

He rinses his face and brushes back his hair with his big hands. Drops cling to his long, dark lashes.

"Do you need a pomade or a drink to dull the pain?" he asks casually, factually, as if he doesn't really care but is asking because he feels compelled by some weird sense of duty to take care of me.

Yes, that's it. He's not asking as if he gives a damn

but as if he *has* to, as if it's nothing but a pesky responsibility.

I'm raw inside, but I'm not going to tell him that.

"I thought the water had healing powers," I say with a snideness designed to hide my hurt and humiliation.

"It does," he replies patiently. "But seeing that you were a virgin and that I didn't prepare you, you may feel some discomfort for a day or two."

"What do you care?"

"Your wellbeing concerns me. It's my duty to take care of you."

And there it is, the confirmation that he's only doing his damn duty.

My already-volatile anger explodes. "Don't worry. I can take care of myself."

The line of his jaw hardens. "I know my responsibilities, and I've never shied away from them."

I bat my eyelashes and give him a sugary smile. "I wouldn't want to put you out."

"It's no trouble." Sparks dance in his silver eyes, but he does a good job of keeping his anger in check. "I'll have something sent over."

Then again, maybe he doesn't have to force calmness. Maybe he's simply uninterested.

He stands, drops of water rolling off his powerful torso and flat stomach. His cock hangs heavy and thick below the dark nest of curls between his thighs. Despite the delectable portrait he makes, I want to slap him. I *am* hurting, but the physical pain is nothing compared to the ache in my heart. His rejection is humiliating. I've never regretted anything more than I'm regretting having sex with him.

His tone is icy. "You could at least try not to show your regret so openly."

I bite my tongue to prevent myself from saying something truly insulting.

He gets out of the water like the Adonis he is and takes a sheet from the bench that he uses to dry himself with.

"I'm going to talk to my mother," he says, not looking at me. "I'll put a female servant at your disposal. If you need anything, she'll get it for you."

With that, he walks out in all his naked glory.

I shrink into myself, making myself small in the water, wishing I could curl up into a ball and hide somewhere... anywhere... as long as it's far away from here.

At the first opportunity I get, I'm out of here. I'll figure out a way of getting off this planet. After what has happened, there's not a chance I'm staying. I'm not going to sit here and wait for Aruan to give me the cold shoulder. And I sure as hell won't hang around to have more sex that's clearly unsatisfying and to be humiliated again just because the way we're wired makes it impossible to resist.

No way. Not me.

Goodbye, Aruan.

A tear runs down my cheek even as I mentally punch the asshole in the gut.

Have a nice fucking life.

I get out of the water, dry myself, and walk to the bedroom.

It's empty.

He left.

Ignoring the coldness that settles in my stomach, I quickly dress in another pair of Aruan's pants and a shirt that smells too much like him for my liking. My actions are mechanical, yet the power inside me pulses stronger still, an undeniable force that won't be ignored.

In a distant corner of that awareness, I become conscious of Betty. She's out there, closer now, her presence a balm on my trampled emotions.

I'm not cognizant of opening the window and stepping onto the balcony. It's automatic. Instinctive. I reach for her, searching for comfort, and she doesn't disappoint. She answers the call, her gigantic wings turning visible in the distant sky.

I watch her grow bigger as she comes nearer. How beautiful and majestic she is. I already know she's going to land on the balcony before her claws hit the rail because that's what I want. That's what I will her to do.

The balcony shakes under the onslaught of her weight as she hops to the floor. I grab a pillar for purchase.

Aruan's voice comes from somewhere far-off. "Elsie!"

Betty locks her wings at her sides and tilts her head to study me with her beady eyes.

"Betty," I whisper, stroking her soft, rubbery neck. "You came."

"Elsie!"

Aruan's voice cuts me like shards of glass, but if I stay here, it will only get worse. Wiping at the wetness on my cheeks, I ignore the sharp pain that tears into my chest as I carefully climb onto the rail, holding on to the pillar with both hands. The abyss gapes beneath me, but I'm not scared, not with Betty there to catch me.

And then white-hot fear flares in my chest as Aruan's intention manifests in my mind.

He's going to vaporize Betty.

Already, his presence grows stronger as he prepares to portal himself here.

To stop me.

I act fast, leaping from the rail onto Betty's back. Aruan won't kill her if my safety is at stake. He's not going to risk my life. That's one thing he's made clear.

"Go," I urge, wrapping my arms around her neck and holding on for dear life.

Betty doesn't hesitate. She pushes off the balcony, using her strong legs to propel us into the air. My stomach dips as she dives before righting herself, and then we're flying.

A mixture of fury and dread rides on the echo of my name that chases us through the valley, but I don't listen. I refuse to. However, it's impossible to ignore the distress that bleeds into that place in my chest where Aruan's feelings live.

I can't help but feel what's reflected inside me, how everything in that soft, warm place turns to cold, hard stone.

WHAT TO READ NEXT?

Thank you for following Elsie and Aruan's journey! Their story continues in *Dark Prince's Mate*.

To be notified about our upcoming books, sign up for our newsletters at www.annazaires.com and www.charmainepauls.com. All of our titles are available in print and audio as well.

Craving more edgy, suspenseful romance? Check out *Devil's Lair* by Anna Zaires and *Coerced Kiss* by Charmaine Pauls. And don't miss our action-packed mafia romance collaboration, *White Nights*!

Turn the page for sneak peeks and to learn more about our books.

EXCERPT FROM WHITE NIGHTS BY ANNA ZAIRES AND CHARMAINE PAULS

Power. That's what I think of when I spot him across the ER. Power and danger.

One of the wealthiest Russian oligarchs, Alex Volkov is as ruthless as he is magnetic. He always gets what he wants, and what he wants is me, in his bed.

He's the kind of trouble every woman should run from. The bullet his bodyguard took for him proves that.

I should stay far away, but for one night, I give in to temptation. Before I know it, he's pulling me deeper into his world of excess and violence, invading not only my life but my heart.

How much trust can I place in a man so dangerous? How much do I dare risk for his love?

~

Turning away from the sink, I look back at the wounded man, making sure everything is okay with him before I go check on my other patients.

At that moment, I catch a pair of steely blue eyes looking at me.

It's one of the men standing near the victim, likely one of his relatives. Visitors are generally not allowed in the hospital at night, but the ER is an exception.

Instead of looking away, as most people will when caught staring, the man continues to study me.

Both intrigued and slightly annoyed, I study him back.

He's tall, well over six feet in height, and broad-shouldered. He's not handsome in the traditional sense. That's too weak of a word to describe him. Instead, he's magnetic.

Power. That's what comes to mind when I look at him. It's there in the arrogant tilt of his head, in the way he looks at me so calmly, utterly sure of himself and his ability to control all around him. I don't know who he is or what he does, but I doubt he's a pencil pusher in some office. This is a man used to issuing orders and having them obeyed.

His clothes fit him well and look expensive. Maybe even custom made. He's wearing a gray trench coat, dark gray pants with a subtle pinstripe, and a pair of black Italian leather shoes. His brown hair is cut short, almost military style. The simple haircut suits his face, revealing hard, symmetric features. He has high cheekbones and a blade of a nose with a slight bump, as though it had been broken once.

I have no idea how old he is. His face is unlined, but there's no boyishness to it. No softness whatsoever, not even in the curve of his mouth. I guess his age to be early thirties, but he can just as easily be twenty-five or forty.

He doesn't fidget or look uncomfortable as our staring contest continues. He simply stands there quietly, completely still, his blue gaze trained on me.

To my shock, my heart rate picks up as a tingle of heat runs down my spine. It's as though the temperature in the room has jumped ten degrees. All of a sudden, the atmosphere becomes intensely sexual, making me aware of myself as a woman in a way I've never experienced. I can feel the silky material of my matching underwear set brushing between my legs and against my breasts. My entire body seems flushed and sensitized, my nipples pebbling underneath my layers of clothing.

Holy shit.

So that's what it feels like to be attracted to someone. It's not rational and logical. There's no meeting of minds and hearts involved. No, the urge is basic and primitive. My body has sensed his on some animal level, and it wants to mate.

He feels it too. It shows in the way his blue eyes darken, lids partially lowering, and in the way his nostrils flare as though trying to catch my scent. His fingers twitch, curl into fists, and I somehow know he's trying to control himself, to avoid reaching for me right then and there.

If we were alone, I have no doubt he'd be on me already.

Still staring at the stranger, I back away. The strength of my response to him is frightening, unsettling. We're in the middle of the ER, surrounded by people, and all I can think about is hot, sheet-twisting sex. I have no idea who he is, whether he's married or single. For all I know, he's a criminal or an asshole. *Or a cheating scumbag like Tony.* If anyone has taught me to think twice before trusting a man, it's my ex-boyfriend. I don't want to get involved with anyone so soon after my last, disastrous relationship. I don't want that kind of complication in my life again.

The tall stranger clearly has other ideas.

At my cautious retreat, he narrows his eyes, his gaze becoming sharper, more focused. Then he comes toward me, his stride graceful for such a large man. There's something panther-like in his leisurely movements, and for a second, I feel like a mouse getting stalked by a big cat. Instinctively, I take another step back, and his hard mouth tightens with displeasure.

Dammit, I'm acting like a coward.

I stop backing away and stand my ground instead, straightening to my full five-foot-seven height. I'm always the calm and capable one, handling high-stress situations with ease, yet I'm behaving like a schoolgirl confronted with her first crush. Yes, the man makes me uncomfortable, but there's nothing to be afraid of. What's the worst he can do? Ask me out on a date?

Nevertheless, my hands shake slightly as he approaches, stopping less than two feet away. This close, he's even taller than I thought, a few inches over six feet. I'm not a short woman, but I feel tiny standing in front of him. It's not a feeling I enjoy.

"You're very good at your job." His voice is deep and a little rough, tinged with some Eastern European accent. Just hearing it makes my insides shiver in a strangely pleasurable way.

"Thank you," I say, a bit uncertainly. I *am* good at my job, but I didn't expect a compliment from this stranger.

"You took care of Igor well. Thank you for that."

Igor must be the gunshot patient. It's a foreign-sounding name. Russian, perhaps? That would explain the stranger's accent. Although he speaks English fluently, he's not a native speaker.

"Of course." I'm proud of the steadiness of my tone. Hopefully, the man won't realize how he affects me. "I hope he recovers quickly. Is he a relative?"

"My bodyguard."

Wow. I was right. This man is a big fish. Does that mean—

"Was he shot in the course of duty?" I ask, holding my breath.

"He took a bullet meant for me, yes." His tone is

matter-of-fact, but I get a sense of suppressed rage underneath those words.

I swallow hard. "Did you already speak to the police?"

"I gave them a brief statement. I will talk to them in more detail once Igor is stabilized and regains consciousness."

I nod, not knowing what to say to that. The man standing in front of me was nearly assassinated today. What is he? Some mafia boss? A political figure?

If I had any doubts about the wisdom of exploring this strange attraction between us, they're gone. This stranger is bad news, and I need to stay as far away from him as possible.

"I wish your bodyguard a speedy recovery," I say in a falsely cheerful tone. "Barring any complications, he should be fine."

"Thanks to you."

I give him a half-smile and take a step to the side, hoping to walk around the man and go to my next patient.

He shifts his stance, blocking my way. "I'm Alex Volkov," he says quietly. "And you are?"

My pulse picks up. The male intent in his question makes me nervous. Hoping he'll get the hint, I say, "Just a nurse working here."

He doesn't catch on, or he pretends not to. "What's your name?"

He's certainly persistent. I take a deep breath. "I'm Katherine Morrell. If you'll excuse me—"

"Katherine," he repeats, his accent lending the familiar syllables an exotic edge. His hard mouth softens a bit. "Katerina. It's a beautiful name."

"Thank you. I really have to go."

I'm increasingly anxious to get away. He's too large, too potently male. I need space and some room to breathe. His nearness is overpowering, making me edgy and restless, leaving me craving something that I know will be bad for me.

"You have your job to do. I understand," he says, looking vaguely amused.

Still, he doesn't move out of my way. Instead, as I watch in shock, he raises one large hand and brushes his knuckles over my cheek.

I freeze as a wave of heat zaps through my body. His touch is light, but I feel branded by it, shaken to the core.

"I would like to see you again, Katerina," he says softly, dropping his hand. "When does your shift end tonight?"

I stare at him, feeling like I'm losing control of the situation. "I don't think that's a good idea."

"Why not?" His blue eyes narrow. "Are you married?"

I'm tempted to lie, but honesty wins out. "No, but I'm not interested in dating right now."

"Who said anything about dating?"

I blink. I assumed—

He lifts his hand again, stopping me mid-thought.

This time, he picks up a strand of my hair, rubbing it between his fingers.

"I don't date, Katerina," he murmurs, his accented voice oddly mesmerizing. "But I would like to take you to bed. And I think you'd like that too."

~

Order your copy of *White Nights* today at
<u>www.annazaires.com</u>!

EXCERPT FROM DEVIL'S LAIR BY ANNA ZAIRES

Live-in tutor wanted for four-year-old. Must be willing to relocate to a remote mountain estate. $3K/week cash.

On the run from ruthless killers, I'm down to ten bucks in my wallet and a half-tank of gas in my ancient car when I spot the ad. The job sounds like the answer to my prayers, but there's a catch.

The child's father is the most beautiful, most dangerous man I've ever met.

Darkly seductive and filthy rich, Nikolai Molotov is a tantalizing mystery, a lethally alluring contradiction. Bruised knuckles and tailored suits, tender endearments and dirty promises—my new employer draws me in like a magnet, even as my instincts scream for me to run.

I should've heeded them… because I'm not the only one with secrets.

My safe haven just might be the devil's lair, and once he's claimed me, it will be too late to run.

There's no reason to freak out.

Nothing happened.

Nikolai caught me when I would've fallen, that's all.

Except… something could've happened if Alina hadn't interrupted. I'm ninety percent sure Nikolai had been about to kiss me. And I definitely didn't imagine the hard bulge pressed against me.

He does want me.

There's no longer any doubt about that.

I take another deep breath, but my heart continues to pound, my palms sweating like crazy. Wiping them on my jeans, I walk around the side of the house, taking in mountain views in an effort to calm my racing thoughts.

It's fine. Everything's fine. Just because Nikolai is attracted to me doesn't mean anything is going to happen between us. I'm sure he realizes how inappropriate the whole thing is. No matter what Alina said, it was an accident, us bumping into each other. I don't know why she would imply otherwise. Maybe she thinks I was coming on to him? But no. It seemed almost as if she was warning me away from him, as if—

The sound of voices catches my attention, and as I round the corner, I see Pavel and Slava. They're standing by a tree stump some fifty feet away, with the big fish laid on top of it. As I approach, I see the man-bear slice it open halfway, then hand the sharp-looking knife to Slava.

What the hell? Is he expecting the child to finish the job?

He is. And Slava does. By the time I get there, the boy is scooping out fish innards with his little hands and throwing them into a plastic bag Pavel is helpfully holding open for him.

Okay then. I guess they know what they're doing. I've cleaned fish a few times myself—my freshman-year roommate, a fishing-and-hunting enthusiast, taught me how—so I'm not grossed out, but it is unsettling to see a four-year-old doing it.

They're really not worried about him with knives.

Stopping in front of the stump, I put on my brightest smile. "Good morning. Mind if I join you?"

The boy grins up at me and rattles off something in Russian. Pavel, however, looks less than pleased to see me. "We're almost done," he growls in his thickly accented voice. "You can wait in the house if you want."

"Oh, no, I'm fine out here. Do you need any help with that?" I gesture toward the fish.

Pavel glowers at me. "You know how to remove scales?"

"I do." I'd actually rather not do it, lest I get my only clean clothes dirty, but I want to continue teaching

Slava, and the best way to do that is to spend time with him, engaged in whatever activities he's doing.

In my experience, children learn best outside of a classroom—and so do most adults.

"Here then." Pavel thrusts a descaling knife at me. "Show the kid how to do it."

Judging by the smirk on his brick-like face, he thinks I'm bluffing—which is why it gives me great pleasure to take the knife from him and say sweetly, "Okay."

Taking care not to get any splatters on my shirt, I get to work, explaining to the boy the entire time what I'm doing and how. I tell him what every part of the fish is called and make him repeat the words, then let him try the descaling himself. He's as good at it as he was at the slicing, and I realize he's done it before.

When Pavel told me to show him, he was just testing me.

Hiding my annoyance, I let Slava finish the job and put the cleaned fish back into the bucket. Pavel carries it into the house, and Slava and I follow. The man-bear goes straight for the kitchen—probably to prepare the fish for lunch—and I tell him I'm taking Slava upstairs to get changed. Unlike me, the boy has fishy splatters all over his shirt.

Pavel grunts something affirmative before disappearing into the kitchen, and I shepherd Slava into the nearest bathroom. We both thoroughly wash our hands, and then I lead Slava up to his room.

To my surprise, Lyudmila is there when we walk in,

presciently laying out a clean shirt and jeans for Slava on the bed.

"Thank you," I say with a smile. "He's in dire need of a change."

She smiles back and says something to Slava in Russian. He walks over to her, and she helps him out of the dirty clothes. I tactfully turn my back—the boy is old enough to be shy in front of strangers. When it seems like they're done, I turn around and find Lyudmila helping him with the buckle of his belt.

"All good," she announces after a moment, stepping back. "You teach now."

I grin at her. "Thank you, I will." Seeing her gather Slava's dirty clothes, I ask, "Is there a washing machine somewhere in the house? I need to do laundry."

She frowns, not understanding.

"Laundry." I point at the pile of clothes in her hands. "You know, to wash clothes?" I rub my fists together, mimicking someone doing laundry by hand.

Her face clears. "Ah, yes. Come."

"I'll be right back," I tell Slava and follow Lyudmila downstairs. She takes me past the kitchen and down a hallway to a windowless room about the size of my bedroom. There are two fancy washers and dryers—I guess to run multiple loads at once—along with an ironing board, a drying rack, laundry baskets, and other conveniences.

"This, yes?" She points at the machines, and I nod, thanking her. Returning to my room, I gather all my clothes and bring them down. Lyudmila is gone by then, so I begin loading the washers. In a half hour, I'll come down again to move the clothes over to the dryers, and by dinnertime, everything will be clean.

Things really are looking up, the situation with my boss notwithstanding.

My heart rate speeds up at the thought, the butterflies in my stomach roaring back to life. Slava and Pavel provided a much-needed distraction, but now that I'm away from them, I can't help thinking about what happened. My mind cycles through everything, over and over, until the butterflies turn into wasps.

I felt Nikolai's erection against me.

He looked like he was about to kiss me.

He didn't let go of me when his sister was there.

It's that last part that freaks me out the most, because it means I was wrong. He does intend to act on this attraction. If Alina hadn't insisted he take the call, he would've kissed me, and maybe more. Maybe at this very moment, we'd be in bed together, with his powerful body driving into me as—

I stop the fantasy before it can progress any further. Already, I feel overly warm, my breasts full and tight, my sex pulsing with a coiling ache. It must be some weird aftermath of my impromptu masturbation session last night; that's the only explanation for why I've suddenly acquired the libido of a teenage boy.

Taking slow, deep breaths to calm myself, I finish loading the laundry. The situation is undoubtedly tricky. An affair with my employer would be unwise on many levels, yet I'm less than certain of my ability to resist him. If I go up in flames merely thinking about him, what would it be like if he touched me? Kissed me?

Would my self-control evaporate like water on a frying pan?

There's only one solution I can see, only one thing I can do to prevent this disaster.

I have to avoid him—or at least, being alone with him—for the next six days.

Thus resolved, I set the washers to run, and turn around—only to freeze in place.

Standing in the doorway, golden eyes gleaming and mouth curved in a devastating smile, is the very devil who occupies my thoughts.

"There you are," he says softly, and as I watch, paralyzed in shock, he steps deeper into the room and shuts the door.

~

Order your copy of *Devil's Lair* today at
www.annazaires.com!

EXCERPT FROM COERCED KISS BY CHARMAINE PAULS

I'm an alibi for a killer, but he demands so much more than my testimony.

I stumbled across something I wasn't supposed to discover. I saw something I wasn't meant to see, and now I'm an alibi for a killer.

He's the most feared and powerful man in the New York underworld. I don't have a choice but to do as he says.

But he commands so much more than just my testimony.

$\sim$

Come on, baby.
  Give it to me.

There's no point in playing hide and seek.

I'm going to find it.

You know I always do.

"You should go home," someone says, cutting into the one-sided conversation I'm having with my computer in my head.

By the toneless inflection, I know who the owner of the voice is before I look up from my screen.

Mr. Lewis stands in the door frame with his briefcase in his hand. He's donned his double-breasted summer coat and black Fedora hat. His neck is so short it appears as if his head is attached to his shoulders. Coupled with his ramrod straight pose, he reminds me of those boxy nutcracker dolls that stand at attention. The fact that his face never betrays a hint of emotion adds to the illusion. So does the beard, except that his isn't white but brown. He doesn't sport a single gray hair despite being close to sixty. Does he dye the whole works, eyebrows included?

"I'm clocking out." He checks his watch with a brisk and precise lift of his arm, the movement almost mechanical. "It's late."

A glance at the hour on my menu bar confirms it's close to midnight. The open-plan office I share with three other junior accountants is long since dark and deserted. The only light in the room comes from the bluish glow of the desktop computer.

"You should go," Mr. Lewis repeats in his impassive manner.

I've been so absorbed in my work I didn't keep

track of time. Frowning, I turn my attention back to the spreadsheet on my screen. The credits and debits don't balance, and I hate leaving a problem unsolved. I never let the numbers win.

"I'll just be another minute," I mutter as I do a quick mental calculation.

His reply is neutral, but it's more distracted than disinterested. "Remember to switch off the lights when you go."

"'Kay."

I lift my head when he turns to leave. He carries his average height and thin frame with his habitual air of solemn dignity, but just before the dark hallway swallows his shape, his shoulders curl inward. The cardboard-like outline of his body stoops. The forlorn look is so foreign on him that it gives me pause.

He hasn't been himself lately. Ever since the two men in their fancy suits walked unannounced into his office a couple of weeks ago, he's been preoccupied and jittery.

"Mr. Lewis?"

He stops and looks back at me.

"Is everything all right?" I ask carefully, not wanting to overstep my boundaries.

Mr. Lewis is my boss, and he discourages familiarity at the office. He doesn't share his personal life at work, let alone his problems. His dispassionate bearing makes him unpopular with both the staff and the managers, but I respect him for building this firm from the ground up. He'll always have my gratitude for giving me an opportunity when no one else would. Fine, he only gave me the job because he owed Livy a favor, but he still took a chance on me.

"Sir?" I probe when he doesn't answer.

His laugh sounds forced. "Of course."

I get the message. He doesn't want to talk about whatever is eating him. That doesn't stop me from worrying. Besides, if the business is in trouble, it affects me too. I like this job. I need the money, now more than ever.

"If there's anything I can help with—" I start, but he cuts me short.

"Just doing your job will do. That means nine to five, Ms. Brennan. I don't pay overtime."

I open my mouth to tell him I don't mind, but he doesn't give me the chance.

"You look tired," he says.

Only, he's not looking at me. He's peering through the window behind me with a nervous twitch of his eyes.

What does he see that makes him so jumpy? I follow his gaze. The Meatpacking District of New York City stretches behind us under a blanket of lights. The top floor of the red-brick building that houses Frank Lewis's accounting firm looks out over the High Line and the Hudson River in the distance. The prime location alone is proof of his hard-earned success.

His voice reaches me from farther away. "Don't forget to check that the guard sets the alarm when you leave."

When I face forward again, he's crossing the reception area in the dim light of the desk lamp. The click of the door announces his exit.

I chew my nail as I contemplate his uncharacteristic behavior. Judging by the big clients on his books, the firm is thriving. Then again, anything can look good on paper. I know that better than anyone. I hope the business is secure. Without a diploma, I won't find a similar job anywhere in the city, and I can't live in Livy's building without paying rent forever. My position in the firm is nothing but charity. That's why I'm working three times harder than everyone else. I want to show Mr. Lewis how grateful I am for his faith in me as much as I want to prove that I'm capable. Plus, there's my professional pride. I don't like failing. Until my probation period is over, nothing is certain. Once Mr. Lewis has signed my permanent contract, I'll breathe easier. I'll make sure he never regrets employing me. I'm not afraid of long hours and hard work.

Guilt needles my conscience when I think about the fact I omitted in my application. I must make myself indispensable before my secret becomes known. I hate lying. I just didn't see another way. I can only hope Mr. Lewis will forgive me.

Rubbing my eyes that burn from tiredness, I push away the troubling thoughts and focus on the number puzzle in front of me. It's not going to solve itself.

"Come on," I coax. "Don't be so stubborn. Give it to me. You know you want to."

I do a few more subtractions, and then the erroneous formula jumps out at me.

"Gotcha," I say with a victorious grin aimed at the screen.

I save the balance statement and email it to Mr. Lewis so that he can look it over first thing in the morning. He'd want to send it to the client as soon as possible.

My back is sore from being bent over my computer for hours. I stand and stretch to relieve the ache in my muscles. I should take better care of myself. The salad I gobbled down at my desk more than four hours ago wasn't enough to sustain me. I'm already hungry again.

I grab my bag and do a quick tour of the floor to switch off the hallway lights. Mr. Lewis is a stickler for saving costs, and rightly so. We're in the middle of a worldwide energy crisis.

The lock on the door is electronic. It opens with a code typed into a keypad. Locking up requires nothing more than shutting the door behind me. After flicking off the light switch on the landing, I take the elevator to the lobby where the night guard sits behind the reception desk.

"Hey, Zack." I smile. "What are you reading tonight?"

He lifts his book to show me the cover.

"Another horror novel?" I bend sideways to read the title. "Is it good?"

He grins. "It certainly keeps me awake."

"Well, that's positive then," I tease. "We can't have you sleeping on the job, can we?"

"You'll be sleeping on the job if you keep up the late hours."

"Don't exaggerate," I tease. "It's the first time I worked *this* late."

"You should've left with Mr. Lewis." Zack earmarks the page and closes the book. "He could've walked you home. It's not safe for a woman out alone at this hour. You just missed him with a couple of seconds. If you hurry, you can catch up with him. He's heading toward the subway on Fourteenth Street and Eighth Avenue."

"I don't live far," I say thoughtfully, stuck on what Zack said about Mr. Lewis leaving shortly before. "Wait. I thought Mr. Lewis left twenty minutes ago."

"He came downstairs but went to the archive room."

"The archive room?"

"He said he needed to do some filing."

That's odd. We have dedicated staff for filing, and Mr. Lewis never sets foot in the dusty underground vault. Whenever he needs a document, he calls down and asks that it's brought to his office.

"Best get going now," Zack says. "Don't let Mr. Lewis get too far ahead."

"I'll be fine," I say on my way to the door, still puzzled about the information Zack shared.

"You have my number if you run into trouble," he calls after me before adding with a hint of humor, "And don't worry, I won't forget to set the alarm upstairs."

It's no doubt an order Mr. Lewis repeats daily.

"Thanks," I shoot over my shoulder as I open the door.

I can't shake the feeling that something is wrong. I make a mental note to ask Livy if she noticed anything strange about Mr. Lewis's behavior.

The early fall breeze is cool on my cheeks when I walk outside. Pulling my cardigan tighter around myself, I make my way down the quiet cobblestone street. Most of the buildings in the vicinity are offices, and the workers are long gone. My apartment building is only two blocks north. It's a short walk, but a shiver crawls down my spine as I pass in front of the deserted premises with their blackened windows. The sidewalks that are always bustling with pedestrians when I walk home are now eerily empty. I often work overtime, but staying until after midnight is a first for me.

I take my phone from my bag and clutch it in my hand. Having all the emergency numbers as well as Zack's programmed in my quick dials makes me feel better. The rubber soles of my ballerina flats fall soundlessly on the concrete as I quicken my pace. A bar up ahead stays open late. Light spills from the windows. At least there's life around.

I'm at the corner of the building when a grunt comes from the alley. I jerk my face toward the sound, and then I freeze. Two men stand under the pale light that streams from an upstairs window, pushing a third against the wall. When the tallest of the two lifts his hand, I open my mouth to shout a warning, to demand what they're doing, but the scream dies on my lips when the shiny edge of a blade catches the light.

He brings his arm down in one fluent swoop, drawing a line across the throat of the man in his grip. In the grim light, the line runs black, the color spilling like a fountain of ink down the man's neck and into his collar.

I stand frozen in horror, unable to process the sight even as my brain catalogues the briefcase and the hat that lie on the ground. My mind takes stock of the familiar features of my employer as Mr. Lewis utters a gurgling sound. The man with the knife holds him up when his knees buckle. In a warped way, it looks like a gentle act, almost as if the killer is giving him comfort as my boss's gargling goes quiet and his body slumps.

I register everything about the man with the knife all at once—the well-tailored suit and the lean, broad body that fills it so well, the hard lines of the handsome square face, the modern cut of the midnight-black hair, and the chilling blue of his eyes. It's a face I saw only once but would recognize anywhere. A face like that is too beautiful to forget. They're the men who paid Mr. Lewis a surprise visit at the office. They make a formidable, terrifying pair. The tall man's partner is bulkier, but he leaves less of an impression. The energy emanating from him isn't as dark and deviant.

A clang echoes through the alley. My heart jolts in my chest. My phone. It lies at my feet. The screen is dark. Cracked.

Aghast, I look from the cause of the noise to the

men in the alley. The man loosened his hold on Mr. Lewis. My boss lies on his side next to his briefcase, staring at me with wide, glassy eyes.

"Fuck," the bulky man says, snarling as he trains his gaze on me.

Heatwaves of shock run through my body, propelling me back into action even as I lock eyes with the killer. Something passes between us—the knowledge that I'm done for. The way in which he tilts his head holds a strange kind of apology.

I don't think. If I do, I'm dead. I spin on my heel and run.

The stocky man's words follow me like a demon's promise down the dark street.

"Get her and finish her."

∾

Get your copy of *Coerced Kiss* today at
<u>www.charmainepauls.com</u>!

ABOUT THE AUTHORS

Anna Zaires is a *New York Times, USA Today,* and #1 international bestselling author of sci-fi romance and contemporary dark erotic romance. She fell in love with books at the age of five, when her grandmother taught her to read. Since then, she has always lived partially in a fantasy world where the only limits were those of her imagination. Currently residing in Florida, Anna is happily married to Dima Zales (a science fiction and fantasy author) and closely collaborates with him on all their works. To learn more, please visit www.annazaires.com.

Charmaine Pauls loves to write dark and edgy romance that will melt both your e-reader and your heart. She's a mom of two teenagers, an adorable dog, and a dominant cat. Her country of birth is South Africa where many of her stories play off. Her French husband kidnapped her to the south of France where she currently lives with her family. When she's not writing, you'll find her in the kitchen baking cakes or in the gym lifting weights (because ... all those cakes!).

Made in the USA
Monee, IL
09 August 2025